GALAXY'S EDGE
CREATED BY MIKE RESNICK

ISSUE 49: March 2021

Lezli Robyn, Editor
Martin L. Shoemaker, Assistant Editor
Taylor Morris, Copyeditor
Shahid Mahmud, Publisher

Published by Arc Manor/Phoenix Pick
P.O. Box 10339
Rockville, MD 20849-0339

Galaxy's Edge is published in January, March, May, July, September, and November.

ISBN: 978-1-64973-084-8

SUBSCRIPTION INFORMATION:
Paper and digital subscriptions are available (including via Amazon.com) . Please visit our home page: www.GalaxysEdge.com

ADVERTISING:
Advertising is available in all editions of the magazine. Please contact advert@GalaxysEdge.com.

FOREIGN LANGUAGE RIGHTS:
Please refer all inquiries pertaining to foreign language rights to Shahid Mahmud, Arc Manor, P.O. Box 10339, Rockville, MD 20849-0339. Tel: 1-240-645-2214. Fax 1-310-388-8440. Email admin@ArcManor.com.

CONTENTS

EDITOR'S NOTE

by Lezli Robyn

While I sit here looking out at a gorgeous vista of majestic trees and lush ferns on Hilton Head Island in South Carolina, writing this editorial, most of the United States is being buried under a deluge of snow and ice and record sub-zero temperatures. Millions are left without power when they need it the most, and thousands of turtles in Texas are being rescued and brought to warming centers due to suffering severe shock at the acute temperature plunge.

This new year had been advertised to us as being an improvement on the previous one—I mean, what could be worse than a pandemic being declared?—but so far it looks like 2021 turned around and looked back at 2020's carnage and said "I can do better."

Well, I, for one, am not impressed.

But I also have a solution…

Lets bury ourselves in fiction, instead. Remember those good old days where we would lose ourselves in a book and shut out the realities of the world?

Yes, I know that is quite hard to do at the moment. COVID-19 cases are on the rise, there is still significant political unrest in this country, and so many people are suffering from the financial losses incurred in 2020.

But fiction makes for great escapism, and we have put together a wonderful issue of *Galaxy's Edge* to help you forget about your troubles. Why not take advantage of being able to travel again—if only in your imagination.

In this issue, our lone female fiction writer is the wonderful M. O. Muriel, gifting us a delightful steampunk tale, "A Matter of time," the first of her pieces to ever appear in our magazine. The Atomic Clock—power generator for Lagoon City—has sped up by one micro-unit, throwing all of its citizens into a tizzy. Can Mada, Ace, and Gebrielle solve this matter of time before all of industry comes to a screeching halt?

It is also a pleasure to welcome David Farland to our magazine. In 1898, Martians attacked Earth, according to H. G. Wells in his classic *War of the Worlds*. Wells told the story of what happened in England, but what about the rest of the world? In "After a Lean Winter," David reimagines the invasion from the point of view of international bestseller Jack London—with dark and fascinating results.

Finnish author, Ville Meriläinen, is also new to our pages with "The Language of Leaves," about the witch, the wolf and the Huntsman's burial. A wolf and a girl share a curious kindship…

You will have to read more to find out what that connection entails.

If you are looking for a less magical and more science-fictional change of pace, flip to "Ping" by J. Scott Coatsworth, a humorous story about a Seattle man who discovers aliens in the Museum of Popular Culture. Their need to get off this planet and return to their own world makes for an entertaining ride for our readers

Along with our regular columnists gifting us more insight into the Science Fiction and Fantasy field, we continue our new tradition of publishing a Mike Resnick piece in every issue of the magazine going forward—this particular story being a coda to Mike's Doc Holliday novel series. We also welcome another favorite back into the fold: Todd McCaffrey. We're thrilled to be able to publish "Golden," which tells the trials and tribulations of a dragon princess.

And last but not least, we also have new fiction by Andrew Dykstal and the first half of an absolutely fascinating novella by Walter Jon Williams, "Incarnation Day." In the outer solar system, children are raised as computer simulations and then incarnated into physical bodies when they come of age. If that captivating premise isn't sufficient enough to distract you from the harsh realities of our world and remind you there are better discoveries on our horizon, real or imagined, then I don't know what will.

Ville Meriläinen writes fiction like the Finnish winter: Long, dark, and someone probably gets hurt. Find his short story collection and novels 30 Rounds of Silver *and* Ghost Notes *on Amazon.com.*

THE LANGUAGE OF LEAVES

by Ville Meriläinen

In the light of a cold summer dawn, condensing mist dripped off pine needles to make a sound like rain, and a wolf caught a fawn by the lakeshore.

The fawn stumbled on rocks when it burst out of the thicket, and the wolf crushed its neck with a single bite. He had grown enormous the past winter, on grief, some said; he hunted alone, without a pack or his mate, and wasted half his kills due to an appetite too small for his size. The tall men had taken his cubs, tried to take him too, but the woods cared for him and warned him when they approached.

The wolf dragged his kill into hiding, away from the path the tall men used to bring their nets to the lake. Violets sang their laments for the fawn, but blueberries congratulated his success. The language of leaves was a symphony of whispers spanning the forest, one voice for every shared soul. Somewhere within the swelling choir his pack howled on an ethereal hunt, their voice gone from his throat and given to the trees on the night he betrayed them with a lie.

The tall men had lost the language like he had, but amidst them dwelled those who still remembered it. The wolf raised his blood-tinged muzzle from the fawn to sniff at the air, picking up a scent amidst the late summer blooms. Pulse quickening, he left his meal to the foolhardy fox spying on him from behind a stump, and loped toward the path from where the scent came.

In the mist he saw a splash of scarlet, trailing down the shoulders of the one who'd first shown the color to him. The girl was one of the tall men, yet as much of the woods as he: She sang with two tongues, one for the wilds, one for warding beasts, and the irony therein was their harmony had entranced the wolf.

The wolf had never stepped before her, for fear that she would run or cry like others of her kin, but had listened to her singing for so long her melodies had encircled his heart like wisterias and captured it. Her songs weren't meant for him to hear, but were private confessions to the forest. Eavesdropping kindled shame in his chest, but the wolf sympathized with her feelings of being surrounded by those who feared her.

Whether there was magic or wisdom in her singing, she had taught him to feel as she did, to perceive as she did, until he had found the color of fresh blood in the throats of his prey, on the wet, shiny cowberries around him, and in the hair of the young witch on the path. He moved with her as a shadow in the murk of pines, following her precious voice, and the leaves helped hide the rustling of his step. They knew he'd visit no harm upon her.

When the girl came to the lake, she paused by the bloodied rocks to inspect them with a frown. She looked around with caution, straight at the wolf for a while, but his black fur blended into the shroud the trees cast. The girl continued, circling the lake toward a house hidden in the distance.

She shivered in the chill of the lake, and the wolf wished he could curl up around her and warm her, as he'd once done to his mate. The wolf didn't know whether the leaves told her she was there, if they told her not to fear him, or if they told her anything at all. He heard their voices, but could not ask, and so was privy only to what they chose to share. He knew the house she came to visit belonged to her mother's mother, that both were witches, and that the woods were fond of them—mostly. He had come across the grandmother once, when she was harvesting lavenders and her lingering scent of rabbit stew had enticed him to follow. A gangly old birch nearby had forbidden him from attacking, and though it stood alone on the mountain slopes, its voice chorused with all its kind down the foothills. The crone had watched him warily, asked if he would eat her, and gone back to harvesting herbs when he'd merely sat staring.

The pines later told him she'd killed an eagle for its beak and feathers and that ash trees wanted her dead for it. He had ignored their plight, and the birches thanked him every day.

The girl ceased singing and vanished inside the house. The wolf returned to the fawn, growled at the fox who'd come for scraps to scare it away, and brooded over the longing she had unwittingly taught him.

That afternoon, when the mist receded and the tall men arrived with their nets, a huntsman came with them to the lake. The wolf had not learned anger from the girl, who—he was certain—was too sweet to know the vile feeling anyhow. He had learned it from this man, who did not speak the language of leaves, but made the woods cry with only his presence. Now and again the wolf did the same when he ate a creature to which one plant or another had taken a liking, but they knew he only killed to survive and forgave him in time.

The bitterness toward this man was different. It was sown deep in the soil and the grass and the roots, where the leaves who remembered his crimes had rotted. Sometimes he would fire his pistol at a squirrel or robin and laugh when his victim fell from its branch. He would set traps for rabbits and badgers, but never check them. Once, the wolf had shared his title as the crownless king of the woods with an old bear, but the huntsman had shot it dead because he thought its fur would look fine around his shoulders.

Tall men loved him for killing the beasts they feared, as did scavengers. The forest had pleaded the wolf to hunt the man in turn, and he had answered.

A thousand voices had screamed in the tender dark of spring, when the huntsman murdered three princes and a queen and left them bleeding on melting snows. The wolf had taken his arm in revenge, and both of them still bore the scars of that encounter; one beast in his heart and hide, one underneath a sleeve stapled shut.

The wolf realized too late a growl seeped out of his throat while he watched the fishers and the huntsman, and the latter turned toward him with his pistol in hand. The wolf was gone before he approached, a swoosh the man mistook for wind hiding his leaving.

The wolf slept until the scent of beef aroused him, but fairy slippers warned him it was a trap, and told him instead of a rabbit who'd hurt herself and cried for rescue. The wolf padded away from the lake, until he found the rabbit at the edge of a wild field and gave her peace. When he lay down to feed, he caught an odd scent and noticed the tall grass moving.

From the grass emerged a she-wolf unfamiliar to him. Though he was mere steps away, the she-wolf did not notice him—until she faced him and jolted, as though she relied only on her eyes instead of her nose. Curiously, it was the copse of birches that first called out to him, telling him not to attack. Why should he have? She was the first of his kin he'd met in months, after loneliness had gnawed at him for so long he'd come to love one of the tall men.

And yet, she feared him. It was clear in her posture, even her eyes, peculiar as they were. He could not smell it from beneath her thick odor, and that disturbed him more than the lone ash on the far side of the field ordering him to tear open her throat. The trees fell into an argument when the wind picked up a whorl of leaves full of vitriol, and the wolf surmised there was something more wrong about the she-wolf than the miasma masking other scents.

She took off in a loping run and the wolf followed, unsurprised that she veered toward the direction of the crone's house. He knew painfully well the tall men wore the furs of beasts, but not that they could *become* beasts. Yet his suspicion only grew back in the deep woods, where the she-wolf lay crouched amidst the shrubs and listened to shouts coming from the house.

The shouts caught the wolf's attention as well, and elation and sympathy bristled through him at once when the girl came out. He'd been wrong earlier—she appeared intimately familiar with anger, face flushed as red as her hair when she sent the huntsman running out of her grandmother's house. He understood nothing of what she said, nor was there anything sweet about the sharp pitch and vicious tone of her voice. The language of leaves was absent from her tongue, as it was from around the wolf, as though the whole wood listened fearfully to their exchange.

The man responded in kind, pointing his pistol at her in a way that made the wolf want to charge him—the way he'd pointed it at his mate—but the girl retreated indoors and slammed the door shut so hard the windows rattled. The man shouted at her once more, then stormed off toward the path to the village. The fishermen had left for the day, and when the shore was deserted, the she-wolf arose and rushed for the house. She still hadn't noticed the wolf looming behind her.

She scraped the door of the house and the girl reappeared to let her in. The trees stayed silent, and more than ever, the wolf wanted to ask them what had happened, with the girl and the she-wolf and the hunter. Perhaps the pines heard the anguished pace of his heartbeat, for their voice laden with age and wisdom told him to run now, very fast and very far. They cared for him the deepest, and as it always was with favored sons, the wolf ignored their advice. He had made a vow to his dying mate not to give up the hunt before the huntsman was dead, and he had already failed her once.

When the girl left that night, the wolf followed her bobbing lantern all the way to the village. There remained a simmering fury underneath the sweetness of her song, and it burned the wolf's thoughts like cinders. Never had he felt more kinship toward the girl, for he knew the hate was for the huntsman and it echoed within him. If only he could have told the leaves to beg for her to stay, to come find him in their shroud.

But he could not speak, and the girl could not hear, and so his yearning went unrequited as she climbed over the walls and her light disappeared behind them.

All the way back to his hunting grounds, the pines pleaded and pleaded for him to leave, and all the way the wolf ignored them in favor of brooding. When the huntsman returned under the cloak of night, the indignant pines did not warn him again.

The wolf awoke to a terrible silence. It was worse than when the witch and the huntsman had fought, as though all of the forest held its breath. He recognized the huntsman's presence from his smell of sweat and lamp oil and fermented grain, mixed with the primroses near the crone's house, but could not tell what caused the silence. It was only when he reached the house he understood.

The forest had gone mute with horror as it watched the one-handed huntsman hacking his axe into the crone outside her house.

What had prompted the attack, the wolf neither knew nor cared. In that moment, the opportunity of finding the huntsman alone in his domain seared the wolf's mind blank and he lunged out of the thicket.

Despite the smell in the man's breath, he dodged nimbly and swung his axe at the wolf. The forest roused as one, crying for the wolf to be careful—but so loud was their worry they disoriented him, and the huntsman buried his axe in the wolf's side. Fury redoubled, the wolf sunk his teeth in the flesh of the huntsman's thigh and tore with all his might, but the axe rose and fell even as the huntsman screamed, until the wolf's maw parted and released the man.

The huntsman dropped his axe as he stumbled away from the wolf, both maimed and bleeding. The wolf tried to rise, but his legs shook and would not carry. The axe had crushed more bone and parted more flesh than his fangs had, and though the wolf collapsed every time he pushed himself up, the huntsman managed to gain his feet. He gaped in turn at his side and the wolf, trouser torn and glistening in the moonlight like the surface of the lake. He studied the wolf's wounds, mouth hanging open, then fumbled for the pistol on his belt. His hand quivered as he aimed for the killing blow, but before he found the courage to pull the trigger, a voice spoke out from amidst the trees.

"Everyone will know of your crime," it said, startling both the man and the wolf. "Everyone will know what you've done."

To the wolf, the voice was hushed and small, like that of berry bushes—but there was a force behind it, the way there was in the witch girl's song. The man stepped back, searching for the speaker in the thicket, then dove for the axe on the ground, threw it into the lake and limped down the path as fast as he could.

Moonlight faded in the wolf's eyes. The blood pooling around the crone and creeping toward him grew redder, redder, as if it absorbed all the little light left in the night. A cold breeze chilled the warmth streaming out of his side, but as it carried leaves to float on the waters, it brought back the new voice.

"Feed on my flesh," it said, and now the wolf recognized the crone. She had spoken the language of leaves once before, in the mountains, when she had asked if he planned to eat her. "It is of no use to me now. I have no power to fulfil my threat to him, but at least I can heal you."

The wolf tried to rise again, but his hind legs had gone numb. He crawled to the body and took a feeble bite of its arm. There wasn't much of the tiny woman to eat, but then, he never ate much at all. After he had reduced the arm to bones, he felt strong enough to stand. His bleeding had stopped, and though he still felt drained, he knew he would not die abandoned like his pack had. He wished he could have thanked the woman, but it seemed his voice was beyond the crone's ability to heal, and now hers was gone too. It had weakened with each bite, until she had given her farewell to the woods.

He noticed crows gathering on the branches reaching over the house. They looked disappointed enough at the loss of one meal, and on the wind he heard the distant plea of birches begging him to deny them the other as well. The house's door was ajar, and the wolf dragged the crone's body inside for shelter. With some effort, he managed to lift her on her low bed and position her as though she were asleep, the way he'd seen the tall men do to their deceased out at the graveyard by the foothills. The room itself was a sepulchre of sorts: On the walls were mounted the head of a deer and a pike; on the table was an ornament of eagle talons, pinions and beak; and over the bed hung the skin the crone had used to transform herself, filling the room with its unnatural stench or absorbing it.

The wolf collapsed beside the corpse. His lids drooped shut, and though he feared the huntsman would return with allies, the forced mending of his flesh had left him terribly, terribly weary, so that he could not bring himself even to leave the house. Sleep came for the wolf and took him without invitation, to a place halfway from where Death resided. So deep was his slumber the sunlight starting to filter in through the leaves and dusty windows did not awaken him, nor the cawing of the crows, nor even the warning cry of pines. Only when the witch girl screamed did he bound to his feet.

How great was her fury, how enormous her wrath! The red-haired girl covered her mouth with her palms, her muted keening flooding the room, but in her eyes blazed a fire set to consume the wolf. When she lowered her hands, her teeth were bared in a grimace and she lashed out with a knife for his throat. The confines of the cottage were too small for a creature of his size to evade with any nimbleness, and so the wolf crashed against a shelf of tinctures.

Amidst the shower of falling vials and their shards, the girl cut into the muscles of his thigh. Her steel sent lightning through the wolf's bones, but he held against his instinct to bite the girl's outstretched arm, dashed past her to the open door, and broke for the thicket through morning mist.

The girl ran after him, shrieking with mad rage, ignoring or unable to hear the forest's pleas to stop and listen. The wolf fled over streams and under fallen trunks, but the reopened wound ensured he could not shake her. Every flower, every leaf, every blade of grass she ran over cried out that she'd been deceived, but her pursuit went on, down the slopes and mossy climbs toward the field.

The wolf hoped the tall grass would hide him, but as he laid still and watched the girl come out of the woods, his heart sank when they both noticed the trail of blood he'd left. His gambit had cost him distance, for the mist was too thin on the fields to give him shelter. The wound was wearing the wolf down, but he broke into a run again, intent upon losing her at the dry ravines farther from the forest.

Soon the grass underfoot gave way for loose rocks and the terrain turned steeper. The girl gained on him, and out in the barren foothills there were few places to hide. Farther up, the hills grew craggy, and in their maze he might shake her off.

As he ran up the hill, from behind came a rumble and a yelp. He stopped to see the huntress tumbling down a scree. Her foot, so much less sure than the wolf's, had slipped on the uneven ground, and she'd caused a rockslide when she fell.

She rolled down into a pit, and when the dust and rocks settled, the wolf saw her lying still, buried under a pile. For a spell, his heart stopped, but the girl's meek whimper from beneath her cairn made him spring into motion and slide down the steep face of the cliff.

The wolf shoved rocks aside until he found an arm stretching out, palm up to the sky. The girl was beaten and bruised, but alive. Both her legs were crushed under a boulder, and the darkening skin under her torn clothes spoke of cracked ribs. Her eyes, though open, were unfocused and searched the sun beyond the veil of mist.

The wolf's heart ached for her fleeting life, one nail driven through it for every emotion she had taught. The coating of dirt and dust did nothing to hide the redness of her scattered tresses, wetted with blood at the roots. The wolf leaned closer to lick the wounds at her temple, and she reached up, closed feeble fingers around his muzzle. He yearned to thank her for everything she'd given, but his voice remained stolen from his throat, cast out somewhere on the winds ever since he had told his cubs he would keep them safe.

Then, a thought struck him. He turned from the girl, leaving her with the sun and the silent forget-me-nots to send her away—though if he was fast, they might yet mourn too soon.

His limp grew more pronounced the further he exerted himself, and only when he was back at the house he realized the shift in coloration of his crusted fur. He did not eat more of the crone, for fear of the uncanny lethargy taking him over again, but yanked the wolfskin off the wall and threw it over his back, then bit off a pound of flesh from the crone's side. Though he did not swallow his morsel, some of the power it contained seeped onto his tongue and hastened his flight back to the ravine.

The witch girl had cleared away what rocks she could, but still lay where the wolf had left her. She did not cry for help, but stared vacantly toward the sky, arms stretched at her sides, legs pinned beneath the boulder she hadn't had the strength to move. She turned her head sideways when the wolf approached, then rolled away in disgust when he dropped the slab of saliva-coated meat beside her. He recognized the emptiness in her mien, the resignation to embrace the coming end. He had seen it in his mate when she watched their cubs slip away, one by one. When his promise had become a betrayal.

If he could have, he would've uttered those words again, earnestly, with certainty. The girl was inches away from salvation, yet when the wolf whined and prodded her, tried to get her to take the cloak, she pushed him away. Her face was ashen, breathing shallow, and unless she took the wolf's offering, her passing was but moments away.

He bowed his head, listened to the wind howling with beloved voices, sought from it the words long left unspoken, words he had forgotten. The howling grew louder in his ears, as though the pack spurred

him on. His prior yearning had been selfish; now he needed them to save a life.

And so, with effort, he extracted the right words from amidst the calls. When he opened his mouth, the girl faced him with astonishment.

"Witch girl," he said, with the deep voice of a king. "Wear the skin. Eat the flesh. You will be made whole again."

She stared at him now, as though trying to see past his fur and skin into his very soul. "Why would you help me?" she asked, stained brows furrowing. "Don't you understand I'm wounded? I couldn't run if I tried. Better you bite into my throat and release me from this pain."

"Given no choice, I would." He nudged the piece of meat closer. "But I owe you too much to do so. Wear the skin. Eat the flesh."

She continued to study him until her eyes welled with tears that flowed sideways down her cheek and over the dusty ridge of her nose when she asked, "Did you kill my grandmother?"

The wolf said, "No."

Finally, the girl accepted the skin and pulled it off his back. She wrapped it around herself, until it ceased being a cloak and knitted together to enclose her. The glass eyes came alive with the gray in her own, and the mouth parted to suck in a breath.

She remained trapped through the transformation, but as she chewed the meat, the wolf summoned all his strength, pressed his shoulder against stone and pushed the boulder off her. The girl said nothing when she ate, nor after, but fell asleep as soon as she swallowed the last piece. Hesitant of leaving, lest the huntsman was brave enough to come out of his hut today and stumbled upon her, the wolf curled around her and whispered, "I will keep you safe."

The girl slept through the day and into the evening. The wolf left her only to hunt, and when he returned with a grouse, she was awake. She did not know how to shed the second skin—her grandmother hadn't taught her to wear one yet, though it was only a matter of time until she would find a way on her own. The wolf was glad for the company, however brief it would be.

She told him the huntsman had come to her house last night and told her he'd been out laying a trap for the wolf, when he'd found its tracks near her grandmother's house. She had not believed—the huntsman feared the crone too much to go anywhere near her house, especially alone at night. It was why they'd fought the day before: He wanted desperately to marry her, save her before she left the village and became a slave to the devil in full, and she had thrown him out for slandering her family. Why would she stay amongst people who were frightened of who she was any longer than she had to? The woods had always been kind, and she was determined to leave as soon as she had learned enough to survive on her own.

But, seeing the wolf in the bed had driven her mad with grief, and in that moment the huntsman's words of seeing the wolf rip apart her grandmother and then attack him became an infallible truth. In turn, the wolf told her what he'd seen, and had it not been for the lupine guise, she would've wept bitterly. Come nightfall, her sorrow had solidified into hatred mirroring the wolf's, and together they hatched a plan of revenge.

They traveled to the village, first running together, then with the girl riding on the wolf's back, the skin draped over her shoulders, once she learned how to part it. The girl had healed his thigh with a touch, and he loped through the woods with newfound vigor owing both to the healing and the approaching retribution. The forest cheered them on, nettles urging them to torture the huntsman, spruces wishing them to be careful.

A wall of poles surrounded the village, but the girl scaled them with ease. They were made to keep wildlife out, and no one had minded when she had etched handholds on them for freedom of coming and going, given that it kept her away from their children until they were safely tucked in. She lifted the bar shutting the gates off its holder and let the wolf creep into the settlement.

The tall men slept soundly in their tall houses, every window dark, save for a hut past the sheep pen and the chapel. The girl guided the wolf there, told him to wait for her signal, and knocked on the door. The huntsman appeared shortly, leaning on a cane, and gasped with shock when he laid eyes on her.

"You were right," she said, tongue parting to speak both the language of leaves and of men. "I found the wolf and slew it."

The huntsman stammered a response, but the wolf did not understand. The girl shook her head and said, "I'm fine. I simply needed time to grieve." She paused, hummed with a mockery of careful thought. "I also considered your offer. I will need someone to look after me, now that my grandmother is gone. And, I suppose… I suppose I could consider staying in the village, if you would still take me. Maybe I won't be looked at strangely anymore if people know I won't leave them for the woods one day."

The huntsman answered with excitement, and the girl stepped inside. In his glee, the huntsman didn't notice she left the lock unlatched, and that a thin strand of his lantern's light still escaped outside.

They sat at his table, the girl facing the door, and the wolf peered through the opening. The huntsman animated everything he said with his hand, but the gestures were as arcane to the wolf as the rolling of his tongue. The girl wore a placid smile, but under the table, she drew her knife from its sheath.

"I accept," she said, when he finally stopped talking. "But I want you to do it properly. If you want me to be your wife, kneel before me."

He laughed, but rose from his seat and searched his drawer for a brass ring. He brimmed with pride showing it to the girl, set his cane against the table, and knelt with grunts and winces in front of her. He spoke a verse, a rising lilt, as the daisies did with their endless questions.

Through a smile, the girl's tongues twined into one and brought the susurrus of falling leaves into the hut. "Come, wolf."

She slashed her knife across the huntsman's throat, and as he fell, the wolf barged in and sunk his teeth into the huntsman's belly. A flush of blood, viscera, and gastric fluids glistened with firelight on the floor as the girl tossed the lantern on the table onto the carpet. Coaxed by the girl's magic, the fire caught the huntsman's shirt, the blanket hanging off the edge of the bed, and climbed up the tablecloth like it were oiled. It filled the ceiling with smoke as black as the wolf's fur, and before the blaze swallowed him, the huntsman watched the girl he'd coveted whisk the skin on her shoulders over herself and become one of the beasts he feared and hated.

✿

The witch and the wolf watched the huntsman's burial the morning after, hidden in the mist and the shadows of trees. The girl had donned the wolfskin, as much for warmth as for the comfort it offered. After the preacher had spoken and the villagers had interred the huntsman, the wolf asked how would they remember him. The girl said nothing; the birches told him it wasn't worth knowing, and that it said enough they hadn't buried the crone at all, but burned her bones together with her house.

The witch and the wolf ran far from the village and the woods and the lake, to another forest nesting between the mountains, where the pines welcomed their new king and queen with familiar voices. The girl never came to love the wolf the way he loved her, but grew to care for him, and their simple life was a happy one. With every season, the times she took off her cloak became fewer and fewer, until she enclosed it over her shoulders for the last time and forgot she was human at all, like her mother once had. On that night, when the snows were bright with starlight, the witch and the wolf climbed up to the jagged peaks and sang with the language of leaves. The forest answered, a thousand voices calling to the gentle night until it birthed aurorae in the shapes of a fallen queen and her princes. With their wild hunt over, the wolf gave his family to the great beyond, where they ran forever, free and avenged.

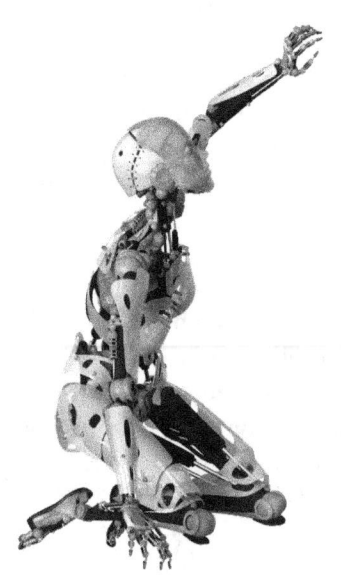

David Farland is an international and New York Times *bestselling author with over fifty published novels. He began his career writing under his name real name Dave Wolverton, when in 1986 he won L. Ron Hubbard's Writers of the Future Contest. In the mid-1990s he began to follow his love for writing Fantasy and Science Fiction under the pen name David Farland, where he became best known for his international bestselling Runelords series.*

AFTER A LEAN WINTER

by David Farland

There were no enemy ships on the horizon, so I watched as Pierre swept into Hidden Lodge on Titchen Creek late on a moonless night. His two sled dogs huffed and bunched their shoulders, then dug their back legs in with angry growls, hating the trail, as they crossed that last stubborn rise. The runners of his sled rang over the crusted snow with the sound of a sword being drawn from its scabbard, and the leather harnesses creaked.

The air that night had a feral bite to it. The sun had been down for days, sometimes hovering near the horizon, and the deadly winter chill was on. It would be a month before we'd see the sun again. For weeks we had felt that cold air gnawing us, chewing away at our vitality, like a wolf pup worrying a shard of caribou bone long after the marrow is depleted.

In the distance, billowing thunderclouds raced toward us under the glimmering stars, promising some insulating warmth. A storm was chasing Pierre's trail. By agreement, no one came to the lodge until just before a storm, and none stayed long after the storm began.

Pierre's two poor huskies caught the scent of camp and yipped softly. Pierre called "Gee," and the sled heeled over on a single runner. Carefully, he twisted the gee-poles, laid the sled on its side next to a dozen others. I noted a heavy bundle lashed to the sled, perhaps a moose haunch, and I licked my lips involuntarily. I'd pay well for some meat.

From out under the trees, the other pack dogs sniffed and approached, too tired to growl or threaten. One of Pierre's huskies yapped again, and Pierre leapt forward with a dog-whip, threatening the lean beast until it fell silent. We did not tolerate noise from dogs anymore. Many a man would have pulled a knife and gutted that dog where it stood, but Pierre—a very crafty and once-prosperous trapper—was down to only two dogs.

"S'okay," I said from my watch post, putting him at ease. "No Martians about." Indeed, the frozen tundra before me was barren for miles. In the distance was a meandering line of weazened spruce, black in the starlight, and a few scraggly willows poked through the snow along the banks of the winding frozen creek just below the lodge. The distant mountains were dark red with lush new growth of Martian foliage. But mostly the land was snow-covered tundra. No Martian ships floated cloudlike over the snowfields. Pierre glanced up toward me, squinting in the brittle light of the stars.

"Jacues? Jacues Lowndunn? Dat you?" he called, his voice muffled by the wolverine-fur trim of his parka. He pronounced my name, Jack London, in a thick accent, his lips frozen. "What news, my fren'? Eh?"

"No one's had sight of the bloody-minded Martians in two weeks," I said. "They cleared out of Juneau."

There had been a brutal raid on the town of Dawson some weeks before. The Martians captured the whole town, harvesting the unlucky inhabitants for their blood. We'd thought then that the Martians were working their way north, that they'd blaze a path to Titchen Creek. We could hardly go much farther north this time of year. Even if we could drag along enough to feed ourselves, the Martians would just follow our trail in the snow. So we dug in, holed up for the winter.

"Ah 'ave seen de Marshawns. Certayne!" Pierre said in his nasal voice, hunching his shoulders. He left the dogs in their harness but fed them each a handful of smoked salmon. I was eager to hear his news, but he made me wait. He grabbed his rifle from it scabbard, for no one would walk about unarmed, then forged up toward the lodge, plodding toward me through the crusted snow, floundering deeper and deeper into the drifts with every step, until he climbed up on the porch. There was no friendly light behind me to guide his steps. Such a light would have shown us up to the Martians.

"Where did you spot them?" I asked.

"Anchorawge," he grunted, stamping his feet and brushing snow out of his parka before entering the warmer lodge. "De citee ees gone, Jacues—dead. De Martians keel everybawdy, by gar!" He spat in the snow. "De Martians es dere!"

Only once had I ever had the misfortune of observing a Martian. It was when Bessie and I were on the steamer up from San Francisco. We'd sailed to Puget Sound, and in Seattle we almost put to port. But the Martians had landed, and we saw one of their warriors on the beach wearing a metal body that gleamed sullenly like polished brass. It stood watch, its curved protective armor stretching above its head like the chitinous shell of a crab, its lank, tripod metal legs letting it stand gracefully a hundred feet in the air. At first, one would have thought it an inanimate tower, but it twisted ever so insignificantly as we moved closer, regarding us as a jumping spider will a gnat, just before it pounces. We notified the captain, and he kept sailing north, leaving the Martian to hunt on its lonely stretch of beach, gleaming in the afternoon sun.

Bessie and I had thought then that we would be safe back in the Yukon. I cannot imagine any other place than the land near the Circle that is quite so relentlessly inhospitable to life, yet I am intimate with the petty moods of this land, which I have always viewed as something of a mean-spirited accountant which requires every beast upon it to pay his exact dues each year, or die. I had not thought the Martians would be able to survive here, so Bessie and I took our few possessions and struck out from the haven of San Francisco for the bitter wastes north of Juneau. We were so naive.

If the Martians were in Anchorage, then Pierre's tidings were mixed. It was good that they were hundreds of miles away, bad that they were still alive at all. In warmer climes, it was said, they died quickly from bacterial infections. But that was not true here by the Circle. The Martians were thriving in our frozen wastes. Their crops grew at a tremendous rate on any patch of frozen windswept ground—in spite of the fact that there was damned little light. Apparently, Mars is a world that is colder and darker than ours, and what is for us an intolerable frozen hell is to them a balmy paradise.

Pierre finished stamping off his shoes and lifted the latch to the door. Nearly everyone had already made it to our conclave. Simmons, Coldwell and Porter hadn't shown, and it was growing so late that I didn't anticipate that they would make it this time. They were busy with other affairs, or the Martians had harvested them.

I was eager to hear Pierre's full account, so I followed him into the lodge.

In more congenial days, we would have had the iron stove crackling merrily to warm the place. But we couldn't risk such a comforting blaze now. Only a meager lamp consigned to the floor furnished any light for the room. Around the lodge, bundled in bulky furs in their unceasing struggle to get warm, were two dozen stolid men and women of the north. Though the unending torments of the past months had left them bent and bleak, there was a cordial atmosphere now that we had all gathered. The rifles rested in corners of the room. A special batch of hootch warmed on a tripod above the lamp. Everyone rousted a bit when Pierre came through the door, edging away enough to make room for him near the lamp.

"What news?" One-Eyed Kate called before Pierre could even kneel by the lamp and pull off his mittens with his teeth. He put his hands down to toast by the glass of the lamp.

Pierre didn't speak. It must have been eighty below outside, and his jaw was leather-stiff from the cold. His lips were tinged with blue, and ice crystals lodged in his brows, eyelashes, and beard.

Still, we all hung on expectantly for a word of news. Then I saw his mood. He didn't like most of the people in this room, though he had a warm spot in his heart for me. Pierre had Indian blood on his mother's side, and he saw this as a chance to count coup on the others. He'd make them pay for every word he uttered. He grunted, nodded toward the kettle of hootch on the tripod.

One-Eyed Kate herself dipped in a battered tin mug, handed it to him. Still he didn't utter a word. He'd been nursing a grudge for these past two months. Pierre Jelenc was a trapper of almost legendary repute here in the north, a tough and cunning man. Some folks down at the Hudson Bay Company said he'd devoted a huge portion of his

grub stake to new traps last spring. The north had had two soft winters in a row, so the trapping promised to be exceptional—the best in forty years.

Then the Martians had come, making it impossible for a man to run his trap lines. So while the miners toiled in their shafts through the dark winter, getting wealthier by the minute, Pierre lost a year's grub stake, and now all of his traps were scattered in their line, hundreds of miles across the territory. Even Pierre, with his keen skills, wouldn't be able to find most of those traps next spring.

Two months ago, Pierre had made one desperate attempt to recoup his losses here at Titchen lodge. In a drunken frenzy he started fighting his sled dogs in the big pit out behind the lodge. But his dogs hadn't been eating well, so he couldn't milk any fight out of them. Five of his huskies got slaughtered in the pit that night. Afterward Pierre had left in a black rage and hadn't attended a conclave since.

Pierre downed the mug of hootch. It was a devil's concoction of brandy, whiskey, and hot peppers. He handed the cup back to One-Eyed Kate for a refill.

Evidently, Doctor Weatherby had been reading from an article in a newspaper—a paper nearly three months old out of southern Alberta.

"I say, right then," Doctor Weatherby said in a chipper tone. Apparently he thought that Pierre had no news, and I was of a mind to let Pierre speak when he desired. I listened intently, for it was the doctor I had come to see, hoping he would be able to help my Bessie. "As I reported, Doctor Silvena in Edmonton thinks that there may be more than the cold at work here to help keep the Martians alive. He notes that the 'thin and rarefied air here in the north is more beneficial to the lungs than air in the south, which is clogged with myriad pollens and unhealthy germs. Moreover,' he states, 'there seems to be some quality to the light here in the far north that causes it to destroy detrimental germs. We in the north are marvelously free of many plagues found in warmer lands—leprosy, elephantiasis, and such. Even typhoid and diphtheria are seldom seen here, and the terrible fevers which rampage warmer climes are almost unknown among our native Inuit.' He goes on to say that, 'Contrary to speculation that the Martians here will expire in the summer when germs are given to reproduce more fervently, it may be that the Martian will hold forth on our northern frontier indefinitely. Indeed, they may gradually acclimatize themselves to our air, and, like the Indians who have grown resistant to our European measles and chicken pox, in time they may once again venture into more temperate zones.'"

"Not a'fore bears grow wings," Klondike Pete Kandinsky hooted. "It's cold enough to freeze the balls off a pool table out thar this winter. Most like, we'll find them Martians all laid out next spring, thawing in some snowbank."

Klondike Pete was behind the times. Rumor said that he'd struck a rich vein in his gold mine, so he'd holed up in the shaft, working eighteen-hour days from August through Christmas, barely taking time to come out for supplies. He hadn't attended our previous conclaves.

"Gads," Doctor Weatherby said, "I say, where have you been? We believe that the Martians came here because their own world has been cooling for millennia. They're seeking our warmer climes. But just because they are looking for warmer weather, it doesn't mean they want to live on our equator! What seems monstrously cold to us—that biting winter that we've suffered through this past three months—is positively balmy on Mars! I'm sure they're much invigorated by it. Indeed, the reason we haven't seen more of the Martians here in the past weeks seems blatantly obvious: they're preparing to migrate north, to our polar cap!"

"Ah, Gods, I swear!" Klondike Pete shook his head mournfully, realizing our predicament for the first time. "Why don't the Army do somethin? Teddy Roosevelt or the Mounties ought to do somethin."

"They're playing at waiting," One-Eyed Kate grumbled. "You know what kinds of horrors they've been through down south. There's not much the armies of the world can do against the Martians. Even if they could send heavy artillery against the Martians in the winter, there's no sense in it—not when the varmints might die out this coming spring, anyhow."

"There's sense 'n it!" one old timer named Tom King said. "Folks is dyin' up here! The Martians squeeze us for blood, then toss our carcasses 'way like grape skins!"

"Yeah," One-Eyed Kate said, "and so long as it's the likes of you and me that are doing the dying, Tom King, no one will do more than yawn about it!"

The refugees in the room looked around gloomily at one another. Trappers, miners, Indians, crackpots who'd fled from the world. We were an unsavory lot, dressed in our hides, with sour bear grease rubbed in our skin to keep out the weather. One-Eyed Kate was right. No one would rescue us.

"I just whist we 'ad word on them Martians," old Tom King said, wiping his nose on the sleeve of his parka. He looked off into a corner with rheumy eyes. "No news is good news," he intoned, the hollow-sounding supplication of an atheist.

None of us believed the adage. The Martian vehicles that fell in the southern climes were filled only with a few armies and scouts. Thirty or forty troops per vehicle, if we judged right. But now we saw that these were only the advance troops who were meant, perhaps, to decimate our armies and harass the greater population of the world in preparation for the most massive vehicle, the one that fell two months later than the rest, just south of Juneau. The mother ship had carried two thousand Martians, some guessed, along with weird herds of humanoid bipeds whom the Martians harvested for blood. The enormous vehicle had hardly settled when thousands of their slaves swarmed from the ship and began planting crops, scattering otherworldly seeds that sprouted nearly overnight into grotesque forests of twisted growths that looked like coral or cactuses, but which Doctor Weatherby assured us were more likely some type of fungus. Certain of the plants grew two hundred yards high in the ensuing month, so that it was said that now, one could hardly travel south of Juneau in most places. The "Great Northern Martian Jungle" formed a virtually impenetrable barrier to the southlands, a barrier reputed to harbor Martian bipeds who hunted humans so that their masters might feast on our blood.

"If no news is good news, then let us toast good news," Klondike Pete said, hoisting his mug.

"Ah've seen dem Marshawns," Pierre said at last. "En Anchorawge. Dey burned de ceety, by Gar, and dey are building, building—making new ceety dat is strange and wondrous!"

There were cries of horror and astonishment, people crying out queries. "When, when did you see them?" Doctor Weatherby asked, shouting to be heard above the others.

"Twelve days now," Pierre said. "Dere is a jungle growing around Anchorawge now—very thick—and de Marshawns live dere, smelting de ore day and night to build dere machine ceety. Dere ceety—how shall I say?—is magnificent, by Gar! Eet stands five hundred feet tall, and can walk about on eets three legs like a walking stool. But is not a small stool—is huge, by Gar, a mile across!

"On de top of de table, is huge glass bowl, alive with shimmering work-lights, more bright and magnificent dan de lights of Paris! And under dis dome, de Marshawns building dere home."

Doctor Weatherby's eyes opened wide in astonishment. "A dome, you say? Fantastic! Are they sealing themselves in? Could it keep out bacteria?"

Pierre shrugged. "Ah 'uz too far away to see dis taim. Some taim, maybe, Ah go back—look more closer. Eh?"

"Horse feathers!" Klondike Pete said. "Them Martians couldn't raise such a huge city in two months. Frenchie, I don't like it when some pimple like you pulls my legs!"

There was an expectant hush around the room, and none dared intervene between the two men. I think that most of us at least half-believed Pierre. No one knew what the Martians were capable of. They flew between worlds and built killing death rays. They switched mechanical bodies as easily as we change clothes. We could not guess their limitations.

Only Klondike Pete here was ignorant enough to doubt the Frenchman. Pierre scowled up at Pete. The little Frenchman was not used to having someone call him a liar, and many honest men so accused would have pulled a knife to defend their honor. A fight was expected, but in any physical contest, Pierre would not equal Klondike Pete.

Pierre obviously had another plan in mind. A secretive smile stole across his face, and I imagined how he might be plotting to ambush the bigger man on some dark night, steal his gold. So many men had been taken by the Martians that in such a scenario we would likely never learn the truth of it.

But that was not Pierre's plan. He downed another mug of hootch, banged his empty mug on the lid of the cold iron stove at his side. Almost as if magically summoned, a blast of wind struck the lodge, whistling through the eaves of the log cabin. I'd been vaguely aware of the rising wind for the past few minutes, but only then did I recognize that the full storm had just hit.

By custom, when a storm hit we would set a roaring blaze and lavish upon ourselves one or two hours of warmth before trudging back to our own cabins or mine shafts. If we timed it properly, the last of the storm would blanket our trail, concealing our passage from any Martians that might fly over, hunting us.

Still, some of us were clumsy. Over the past three months, our numbers had been steadily diminishing, our people disappearing as the Martians harvested us.

My thoughts turned homeward, to my own wife, Bessie, who was huddled in our cabin, sick and weakened by the interminable cold.

"Storm's here, stoke up the fire!" someone shouted, and One-Eyed Kate opened the iron door to the old stove and struck a match. The tinder had already been set, perhaps for days, in anticipation of this moment.

Soon a roaring blaze crackled in the old iron stove. We huddled in a circle, each of us silent and grateful, grunting with satisfaction. During the storms, the Martian flying machines were forced to seek shelter in secluded valleys, it was said, and so we did not fear that the Martians would attack. The bipeds that the Martians used for food and as slaves might attack, I suspected, if they saw our smoke, but this was unlikely. We were far from the Martian Jungles, and it was rumored that the bipeds held forth only in their own familiar domain.

After the past two weeks of damnable cold, we needed some warmth, and as I basked in the roaring heat of the stove, the others began to sigh in contentment. I hoped that Bessie had lit our own little stove back in the old mining shack we called home.

Pierre put his gloves back on, and the little man was beginning to feel the effects of his drinks. He weaved a little as he stood, and growled, "By Gar, your dogs weel faht mah beast tonait!"

"You're down to only two dogs," I reminded Pierre. He wasn't a careless sort, unless he got drunk. I knew he wasn't thinking clearly. He couldn't afford to lose another dog in a senseless fight.

"Damn you, Jacques! Your dogs weel faht mah beast tonait!" He pounded the red-hot stove with a gloved fist, staggered toward me with a crazed gleam in his eyes.

I wanted to protect him from himself. "No one wants to fight your dogs tonight," I said.

Pierre staggered to me, grabbed my shoulder with both hands, and looked up. His face was seamed and scarred by the cold, and though he was drunk, there was a cunning glint in his eyes. "Your dogs, weel faht, my beast, tonait!"

The room went silent. "What beast are you talking about?" One-Eyed Kate said.

"You looking for Marshawns, no?" he turned to her and waved expansively. "You want see a Marshawn? Your dogs keeled mah dogs. Now your dogs weel faht mah Marshawn!"

My heart began pounding, and my thoughts raced. We had not seen Pierre in weeks, and it was said that he was one of the finest trappers in the Yukon. As my mind registered what he'd brought back from Anchorage, as I realized what he'd trapped there, I recalled the heavy bundle tied to his sled. Could he really have captured a live Martian?

Suddenly there was shouting in the room from a dozen voices. Several men grabbed lanterns and dashed out the front door, the dancing light throwing grotesque images on the wall. Klondike Pete was shouting, "How much? How much do you want to fight your beast?"

"I say, heaven forbid! Let's not have a fight!" Doctor Weatherby began saying. "I want to study the creature!"

But the sudden fury with which the others met the doctor's plea was overwhelming.

We were outraged at the Martians for our burnt cities, for the poisoned crops, for the soldiers who died under Martian heat beams or choked to death in the vile Black Fog that emanated from their guns. More than all of this, we raged against the Martians for our fair daughters and children who had gone to feed these vile beasts, these Martians who drank our blood just as we drink water.

So great was this primal rage, that someone struck the doctor—more in some mindless animal instinct, some basic need to see the Martian dead, than out of anger at the good man who had worked so hard to keep us alive through this hellish winter.

The doctor crumpled under the weight of the blow and knelt on the floor for a moment, staring down at the dirty wood planks, trying to regain his senses.

Meanwhile, others took up the shout, "There's a game for you!" "How much to fight it?" "What do you want?"

Pierre stood in a swirling, writhing, shouting maelstrom. I know logically that there could not have been two dozen people in the room, yet it seemed like vastly more. Indeed, it seemed to my mind that all of troubled humanity crowded the room at that moment, hurling fists in the air, cursing, threatening, mindlessly crying for blood.

I found myself screaming to be heard, "How much? How much?" And though I have never been one to engage in the savage sport of dog fighting, I thought of my own sled dogs out in front of the lodge, and I considered how much I'd be willing to pay to watch them tear apart a Martian.

The answer was simple: I'd pay everything I owned.

Pierre raised his hands in the air for silence, and named his price, and if you think it unfairly high, then remember this: we all secretly believed that we would die before spring. Money meant almost nothing to us. Most of us had been unable to get adequately outfitted for winter, and had hoped that a moose or a caribou would get us through the lean months. But Martians harvested the caribou and moose just as they harvested us. Many a man in that room knew that he'd be down to eating his sled dogs by spring. Money means nothing to those who wish only to survive.

Yet we knew that many would profit from the Martian invasion. In the south, insurance hucksters were selling policies against future invasions, the loggers and financiers were making fortunes, and every man who'd ever handled a hammer suddenly called himself a master carpenter and sought to hire himself out at inflated prices to rebuild burned cities.

We in this room did not resent Pierre's desire to recoup his losses after this most horrible of winters.

"De beast has sixteen tentacles," he said, "so Ah weel let you fight heem with eight dogs—at five t'ousand doughlars a dog: Two t'ousand doughlars for me, and de rest goes for de winner, or de winners, of de faht!"

The accounts we'd read about Martians suggested that without their metallic bodies, they moved ponderously slow here on Earth. Scientists said the increased gravity of our world, where everything is six times heavier than on Mars, weighed them down greatly. I'd never seen a bear pitted against more than eight dogs, so it seemed unlikely that the Martian could win. But with each contestant putting in two thousand dollars just for the right to fight, Pierre would go home with at least $16,000—five times what he'd make in a good year. All he had to do was let people pay for the right to kill a Martian.

Klondike Pete didn't even blink. "I'll put in two huskies!" he roared.

"Grip can take him!" One-Eyed Kate said. "You'll let a pit bull fight?"

Pierre nodded, and I began calculating. If you counted most of my supplies, I had barely enough for a stake in the fight, and I had a dog I thought could win—half husky, half wolfhound. He'd outweigh any of the other mutts in the pit, and he pulled the sled with great heart. He was a natural leader.

But I caught that sly gleam in Pierre's dark eyes. I knew that this fight would be more than any of us were bargaining for. I hesitated.

"By Gol', I'll put in my fighter," old Tom King offered with evident bloodlust, and in half a moment four other men signed their notes to Pierre. The fight was set.

✿

The storm raged. Snow pounded in unbounded avarice, skirling across the frozen crust of the winter's buildup. One-Eyed Kate held a pair of lanterns over the fighting pit. At the north end, a bear cage could be lowered into the pit by means of a winch. At the south end, a dog run led down.

Klondike Pete leapt in and flattened the snow, then climbed back up through the dog run. Everyone unhitched their dogs from the sleds, then herded them down the run. The dogs smelled the excitement, yapped and growled, stalking through the pit and sniffing uneasily.

Someone began winching the big cage up, and the dogs settled down. Some of the dogs had battled bears, and so knew the sound of the winch. One-Eyed Kate's pit bull emitted a coughing bark and began leaping in excitement, wanting to draw first blood from whatever we let loose into the pit.

It was a ghoulish mob that stood around that dark pit, pale faces lit dimly by the oily lanterns that flickered and guttered with every gust of wind.

Four men had already lugged Pierre's bundle around to the back of the lodge. The bundle was wrapped in heavy canvass and tied solidly with five or six hide ropes of Eskimo make. A couple of men worried at the knots, trying to untie the frozen leather, while two others stood nearby with rifles cocked, aimed at the bundle.

Pierre swore softly, drew his Bowie knife and sliced through the ropes, then rolled the canvas over several times. The canvas was wound tight around the Martian six turns, so that one moment I peered through the driving snow trying to make out the form that would emerge from the gray bundle, and the next moment the Martian fell on the ground before us.

It burst out from the tarpaulin. It backed away from Pierre and from the light, a creature frightened and alone, and for several moments it made a metallic hissing noise as it slithered over the snow, searching for escape. At first, the hissing sounded like a rattlesnake's warning, and several of us leapt back. But the creature before us was no snake.

For those who have never seen a Martian, it can be difficult to describe such a monstrosity. I have read descriptions, but none succeed. My recollections of this monster are imprinted as solidly as if they were etched on a lithographic plate, for this creature was both more than, and less than, the sum of all our nightmares.

Others have described the fungal green-gray hue of the creature's bulbous head, fully five times larger than a human head, and they have told of the wet leathery skin that encases the Martian's enormous brain. Others have described the peculiar slavering, sucking sounds that the creatures made as they gasped for breath, heaving convulsively as they groped about in our heavy atmosphere.

Others have described the two clumps of tentacles—eight in each clump, just below the lipless V-shaped beak, and they have told how the Gorgon tentacles coiled almost languidly as the creature slithered about.

The Martian invites comparison to the octopus or squid, for like these creatures, it seems little more than a head with tentacles. Yet it is so much more than that!

No one has described how the Martians were so exquisitely, so gloriously alive. The one Pierre had captured swayed back and forth, pulsing across the ice-crusted snow with an ease that suggested that it was acclimated to polar conditions. While others have said that the creature seemed to them to be ponderously slow, I wonder if their specimens were not somehow hampered by warmer conditions—for this beast wriggled viciously, and its tentacles slithered over the snow like living whips, writhing not in agony—but in desperation, in a curious hunger.

Others have tried to tell what they saw in the Martian's huge eyes: a marvelous intelligence, an intellect keen beyond measure, a sense of malevolence that some imagined to be pure evil.

Yet as I looked into that monster's eyes, I saw all of those and more. The monster slithered over the snow at a deceptively quick pace, circling and twisting this way and that. Then for a moment it stopped and candidly studied each of us. In its eyes was an undisguised hunger, a malevolent intent so monstrous that some hardened trappers cried out and turned away.

A dozen men pulled out weapons and hardly restrained themselves from opening fire. For a moment the Martian continued to hiss in that metallic grating sound, and I imagined it was some warning, till I realized that it was only the sound of the creature drawing crude breaths.

It sized up the situation, then sat gazing with evident maleficence at Pierre. The only sound was the gusting of wind over the tundra, the hiss of frozen snow stinging the ground, and my heart pounding.

Pierre laughed gleefully. "You see de situation, mah frien'," he addressed the Martian. "You wan' to drink from me, but we have de guns trained on you. But dere ees blood to drink—blood from dogs!"

The Martian gazed at Pierre with calculating hatred. I do not doubt it understood every word Pierre uttered, every nuance. I imagined the creature learning our tongue as Pierre talked to it and his dogs on the lonely trail. It knew what we required of it. "Keel dem if you can," Pierre admonished the creature. "Keel de dogs, drink from dem. If you ween, Ah weel set you free to fin' your own kind. Ees simple, no?"

The Martian expelled some air from its mouth in a gasp, an almost mechanical sound that cannot adequately be described as speech. Yet the timing of that gasp, the pitch and volume, identified the beast's intent as certain as any words uttered from human lips. "Yes," it said.

Haltingly, with many a backward glance at us, the Martian slithered over the ground on its tentacles, entered the bear cage. Klondike Pete went to the winch and lifted the cage from the ground, while Tom King swiveled the boom out over the floor of the pit, then they lowered the cage.

The dogs sniffed and yapped. Snarls and growls mingled into a continuous sound. One-Eyed Kate's pit bull, Grip, was a grayish creature the color of ash, and it leapt up at the cage as it lowered, growling and snapping once or twice, then caught the alien's scent and backed away.

Others were not so circumspect. Klondike Pete's dogs were veterans of the ring, used to fighting as a team, and their teeth snapped together with metallic clicks as we lowered the Martian into the pit. They jumped up, biting at the tentacles that recoiled from them.

When the cage hit the floor of the pit, Klondike Pete's huskies snarled and danced forward, thrusting their teeth between the pine-wood bars at each side of the bear cage, trying to tear some flesh from the Martian before we pulled the rope that would open the door, freeing the Martian into the ring.

The dogs attacked from two sides at once, and if it had been a bear in that cage, it would have backed away from one dog, only to have the other tear into it from behind. The Martian was not so easily abused.

It held calmly in the center of the cage for half a second, observing the dogs with those huge eyes, so full of malevolent wisdom.

Klondike Pete pulled the rope that would spring the door to the cage, releasing the Martian to the pack of dogs, and what happened next is almost too grisly to tell.

The Martian became, in an instant, a seething dynamo, a twisting, grisly mass of flesh bent on destruction. It hurled against one side of the cage, then another, and at first I believed it was trying to demolish the cage, break it asunder. Indeed, the Martian was roughly the size and weight of a small black bear, and I have seen bears tear cages apart in a fight. I heard timbers crack under the monster's onslaught, but it was not trying to break the bars of its cage.

It was not until after the Martian settled into the midst of its cage that I realized what had happened. Each of a Martian's tentacles is seven feet long, and about three inches wide near the end. With several tentacles whipping snake-like in the air, striking in precision, the Martian had snatched through the bars and grabbed one husky, then another, and pulled, pinning the dogs helplessly against the sides of the bear cage, where it held them firmly about their necks.

The huskies yelped and whined to find themselves in the Martian's grasp, and struggled to pull away, desperately scratching at the beast's tentacles with their forepaws, tugging backward with their considerable might. These were not your weak house dogs of New York or San Francisco. These were trained pack dogs that could drag a four-hundred-pound sled over the bitter tundra for sixteen hours a day, and I believed that they would easily break free of the Martian's grasp.

The door to the cage began to drop open, and with one tentacle, the Martian grasped it, twined the tentacle about the door, and held it closed as securely as if it were held by a steel lock, and in this manner it kept the other dogs somewhat at bay.

The other dogs barked and snarled. The pit bull lunged and experimentally nipped the tentacle that held the door closed, then danced back. One or two dogs howled, trotted around the pit, unsure how to proceed in their attacks. The pit bull struck again once—twice, and was joined quickly by the others, and in a moment three dogs were snarling, trying to rip that one tentacle free of the door. I saw flesh rip away, exposing tender white skin, almost bloodless.

The Martian seemed unconcerned. It was willing to sacrifice a limb in order to sate its appetite. Holding the two huskies firmly against the cage, the Martian began to feed.

It must be remembered that Pierre had held this Martian for nine days without food, and any human so ill-treated perhaps would also have sought refreshment before continuing the fight. It has also been reported that Martians drink blood, and that they used pipettes about a yard long to do so. From other accounts, one might suppose that such pipettes were metallic things that the Martians kept lying about near their vehicles, but this is not so.

Instead, from the Martian's beak, a three-foot long rod telescoped, a rod that might have been a long white bone, except that it was twisted, like the horn of a narwhal, and its tip was hollow.

The Martian expertly inserted this bone into the jugular vein of the nearest husky, who yelped and snarled ferociously, trying to escape.

A loud, orgasmic slurping issued from the Martian, as if it were drinking sarsaparilla with an enormous straw. The dog's death was amazingly swift. One moment it was kicking its hind legs convulsively, bloodying the snow at its feet in its struggles to escape, and in the next it succumbed totally, horribly, and it slumped and quivered.

The tiniest fleck of blood dribbled from the huskie's throat as it ceased its frantic attempts at flight.

In thirty seconds, the feeding over, the Martian twisted with a snapping motion, inserted its horn into the second husky, and drank its blood swiftly. The whole process was carried out with horrid rapidness and precision, with as little thought as you or I might give to the process of chewing and swallowing an apple.

By now, the other dogs had gotten a good portion of the flesh on the Martian's tentacle chewed away, and as the Martian fed upon the second of Klondike Pete's prize-fighting huskies, the Martian struck with several tentacles, pummeling the dogs on their snouts, frightening them back a pace, where they snarled and leapt left and right, seeking an opening.

The Martian stopped, regarded Klondike Pete balefully, and tossed the corpse of the second husky toward him. The look in the creature's eyes was chilling—a promise of what would happen to Klondike Pete if the Martian got free.

The Martian exhaled from its long white horn, and droplets of blood sprayed out over our faces. The sound that this exhalation made—this almost automatic cleaning of the horn—was most unsettling: it sounded as a trumpeting, ululating cry that rang through the night, slicing through the blizzard. It was a mournful sound, infinitely lonely in that dark setting.

At that moment, I felt small and mean to be standing here on the edge of the pit, urging the dogs to finish their business. For their part, the other six dogs backed away and studied the monster quietly, sniffing the air, wondering at this awe-inspiring sound that it made.

A biting gust of wind hit my face, and for the first time during that fight, I realized just how cold I was. The storm was blowing in warmer air. Indeed, I looked forward to the next few days under the cloud cover. But the wind was brutal. It felt as if ice water were running in my veins, and the bitter weather drove the breath from me. I hunched against the cold, saw how the dogs quivered with anticipation in the pit, the breath steaming hot from their mouths.

I wanted to turn, rush inside to the warm stove, forget this grisly battle. But I was held by my own bloodlust, by my own quivering excitement.

There were six strong dogs in the ring, dogs bred to a life of toil. They growled and menaced and kept their distance, and the Martian retracted its horn back under that peculiar V-shaped beak, and flung open the doors of the bear cage, surging forward.

Its appetite for blood had been sated, and now it was ready for battle.

In a pounding, quivering mass it rolled forward over the ice, staring into the eyes of the dogs. There was a look of undaunted majesty in the Martian's eyes, an air of mastery to the creature's movements. "I am king here," it was saying to the dogs. "I am all you aspire to be. You are fit only to be my food."

With a coughing bark, Grip lunged for the Martian, its gray body leaping silent as a specter over the snow. It jumped in the air, aiming a snapping bite at the Martian's huge eye. I was almost forced to turn away. I did not want to see what happened when that pit bull's monstrous, vise-like jaws bit into that dark flesh of the Martian's eye.

In response, the Martian dropped down and under the dog with incredible speed. It became a whirling vortex, a living force of incredible power. Reaching up with three tentacles, it caught the pit bull by the neck in mid-air, then twisted and pulled down. There was an awful snapping as the pit bull hit ground, bounced twice. The pit bull slid a few feet over the snow, its neck broken, and lay panting and whining on the ice, unable to get up. Somehow in this brief encounter the Martian had ripped out the pit bull's eyes, punishing it for its own vicious intent.

But the huskies were undaunted. These were the cousins to wolves, and their bloodlust, the primal memories passed through generations, overcame their fear. Four more dogs lunged almost simultaneously, undaunted by the spectacle of strangeness and power before them.

As they latched onto a tentacle, twisting, trying to rip and tear at the Martian as if it were some young caribou on the tundra, the Martian would convulse, pull its limb back rapidly, drawing each dog into its clutches.

In seconds, the Martian had four vicious, snarling dogs in its grasp, and its tentacles wound about their necks like a hangman's ropes.

There was a flurry of activity, of frantic writhing and lunges. The growls of attack became plaintive yelps of surprise and fear. The eager savage cries of battle became only a desperate pawing as the four worthy huskies tried to escape.

The Martian gripped with several tentacles to each dog, as a squid might grasp small fishes, and choked the fight and life from them while we ogled in horrid fascination.

Soon the startled yelping, the labored breathing of dogs, the frantic tussle as the huskies sought escape, all became a stillness. Their heaving chests quieted. The wind blew through their gray fur.

The Martian sat atop them, slavering from its exertions, heaving and pulsating, glaring up at us.

In that moment, we saw that we were beaten. The Martian saw it too and perhaps knew too well what would come next.

It slithered to a dead dog, crawled atop it, and used its tentacles to grab the dog's feet. Suddenly the dead husky rose, as if it were a marionette, and did a gruesome jig, the Martian astride its back, mocking us.

One dog was left. Old Tom King's husky, a valiant fighter that knew it was outmatched. It paced on the far side of the pit, whimpered up at us in shame. It was too smart to fight this strange monster.

Tom King hobbled over to the dog run, grunted as he lifted the gate that would let his dog escape the pit. Under normal circumstances, this act of mercy would not be allowed in such a fight, but these were anything but normal circumstances. We would not be amused by the senseless death of this one last canine.

Klondike Pete raised his .30-30 Winchester, aimed at the Martian's head, right between its eyes. The Martian dropped its morbid puppet and stared at us fiercely, without fear. "Kill me," it seemed to say. "It does not matter. I am but one of our kind. We will be back."

"So, mah fren'," Pierre called to the Martian. "You have won your laif. As Ah promis, Ah weel let you go now. But mah companions here," he waved expansively to the rest of us around the pit, "Ah no t'ink weel be so generous, by Gar. Mah condolences to you!"

He turned his back on the Martian, and I stared at the indomitable creature in the pit, lit only by the frantic wavering of our oil lamps. The storm was blowing, and the fierce cold gnawed at me, and for one moment, I wondered what it was like on Mars. I imagined the planet cooling over millennia, becoming a frozen hell like this land we had all exiled ourselves to. I imagined a warm house, a warm room, and I thought at how I, like the Martian, would do anything for one hour of heated solace. I would plot, steal, kill. Just as the Martian had done.

Time seemed to stop as Klondike Pete took aim, and I found myself croaking feebly, "Let it live. It won the right!"

Everyone stopped. One-Eyed Kate peered from across the pit. Pete cocked his head and looked at me strangely.

The Martian turned its monstrously intelligent eyes on me, and gazed, it seemed, into my soul. For once there was no hunger in that gaze, no disconcerting look of malevolence.

What happened next, I cannot explain, for words alone are inadequate. There are those who assume that the Martians communicated through clicking sounds of their beaks, or through the waving of tentacles, but the many witnesses who observed the

monsters in life all agree that no such sounds or motions were evident. Indeed, one reporter in London went so far as to suggest that they may have shared thoughts across space, communicating from one mind to another. Such suggestions have met with ridicule in critical circles, but I can only tell what happened to me: I was gazing into the pit, at the Martian, and suddenly it seemed as if a vast intelligence was pouring into my mind. For one brief moment, my thoughts seemed to expand and my intellect seemed to fill the universe, and I beheld a world with red blowing desert sands so strikingly cold that the sensation assaulted me like a physical blow, crumpling me so that I fell down into the snow, curling into a ball. And as I beheld this world, I looked through eyes that were not my own. All of the light was tremendously magnified and shifted toward the red spectrum, so that I beheld the landscape as if on some strange summer evening when the sky shone more redly than normal. I looked out across a horizon that was peculiarly concave, as if I were staring at a world much smaller than ours.

A few red plants sprouted in this frigid waste, but they were stunted things. Martian cities—walking things that traveled through great maze-like canyons as they followed the sun from season to season—were marching in the distance, tantalizing, gleaming. I craved their warmth, the company of my Martian companions. I hungered for warmth, as a starving man might hunger for food in the last moments of life.

And above me, floating like a mote of dust in the sea of space, was the shining planet Earth.

One. We are one, a voice seemed to whisper in my head, and I knew that the Martian, with its superior intellect, had deigned speak to me. You understand me. We are one.

Then above me—for I had fallen to the ground under the weight of this extraordinary vision—a rifle cracked, the sound of it reverberating from the cabin and the low hills.

Klondike Pete cocked the gun and fired three more times, and the stinging scent of gunpowder and burnt oil from the barrel of his gun filled the air.

I got up and looked into the pit at the Martian. It was wriggling in its death throes, twisting and heaving on the ground in its inhuman way.

Everyone stood in the freezing, pelting snow, watching it die. I looked behind me, and even Doctor Weatherby had come out to witness the monster's demise.

"Right then, I say," he muttered. "Well, it's done."

I got up, brushed the snow from me, and looked down into the pit. Tom King was watching me with rheumy eyes that glittered in the lamplight. He pulled at his beard and cackled. "'Let 't live,' says he!" He turned away and chuckled under his breath. "Young whippersnapper thinks he know ever'thing—but he don't know gol'-durned nothin'!"

The doctor stayed out to examine the Martian, measure its body temperature with the thermometer that normally rested outside Kate's window. The others hurried into the warm lodge for the night, and in moments I was forced to follow.

☼

That was on the night of January 13, 1900. As far as I know, I was among the last people on Earth to see a living Martian. In warmer climes, they had all passed away months before, during that hot August. And even as we suffered that night through the grim storm, the huge walking city in Anchorage began a tedious trek north, and was never seen again. Its tracks indicate that it came to the frozen ocean, tried to walk across, and sank into the sea. Many believe that there the Martians drowned, while others wonder if perhaps this had been the Martians' intended destination all along, and so we are forced to wonder if the Martians are even now living in cities under the frozen polar ice, waiting to return.

But on the night I speak of, none of us at Hidden Lodge knew what would happen in the months to come. Perhaps because of the Martian's malevolent gaze, perhaps because of the nearness of the creature, we feared more than ever an ignoble death in the tentacles of the Martians.

After we had warmed ourselves for a few moments in the lodge, we all scurried away. Doctor Weatherby agreed to accompany me to my cabin under the cover of the storm, so that he might look in on Bessie. More than anything else, it was her need that had driven me to the lodge that night.

We left Hidden Lodge during the middle of the storm, let the snows cover our trails until we reached the cabin. The doctor brought the Martian's corpse for examination. He spoke in wonder all the way, "Minus-fifty degrees! How could the thing survive with such a low temperature? No wonder the bacteria isn't growing in them!"

Once we reached the cabin, we found Bessie gone. The front door was open, and an armload of wood lay on the floor just inside. I knew then that the Martians had gotten her, had snatched her as she tried to warm herself. I tramped through the snow until I found her frozen, bloodless corpse not far outside the cabin.

I was overcome with grief and when the storm had passed I insisted on going out, under cover of darkness, and burying her deep in the snow, where the wolves would not find her. I did not care if the Martians took me. Almost, I craved it.

The Arctic night was brutally cold, the stars piercingly bright. The aurora borealis flickered green on the northern horizon in a splendid display, and after I buried Bessie, I stood in the snow for a long hour, looking up at the shimmering display.

My thoughts were cloudy, but I wondered at all I had seen. The Martians wanted this useless tundra, and I tried to imagine a world where we lived in peace, sharing it.

Could it be that the two species, man and Martian, each bred to savagery and domination over the millennia, might coexist?

I tried to imagine the wonder of such a strange brotherhood, the gifts that our two civilizations might exchange. But I could not entertain such thoughts for long, not while standing above Bessie's grave.

My dogs, perhaps from their own sadness at the loss of Bessie, perhaps sensing my mood, began to howl, their eerie voices mingling with the sigh of a small wind that sent some crystals skittering over the ice.

Doctor Weatherby must have worried at why I stayed out for so long, for he came out, silenced the dogs, and put his hands on my shoulders, then stared up into the night sky.

"I say, there it is—isn't it? Mars?" He was staring farther south than I had been watching, apparently believing that I was studying events elsewhere in the heavens. I had never been one to study the skies. I did not know where Mars lay. It stared down at us, like a baleful red eye.

After that, Doctor Willoughby stayed on for a week to care for me. It was an odd time. I was brooding, silent. On the woodpile, the good doctor set out petri dishes full of agar to the open air. By watching these, he hoped to discover precisely what species of bacteria were destroying the Martians. He insisted that cultures of such bacteria might provide an overwhelming defense in future wars. I was intrigued by this, and somehow, of all the things that happened that winter, my numbed mind remembers those forlorn and empty petri dishes better than just about anything else.

After the doctor left, it was the most difficult time of my life. I had no food, no warmth, no comfort during the remainder of that winter. Sometimes I wished the Martians would take me, even as I struggled to stay alive.

Before the end of the cold weather, I was forced to eat my dogs, and ultimately boil the gut strings from my snowshoes to eat there at the last. I struggled from day to day under each successive frozen blast from the north.

I managed to live.

And slowly, haltingly, like the march of an old and enfeebled man, after the lean winter, came a chill spring.

Copyright © 2011 by David Farland.

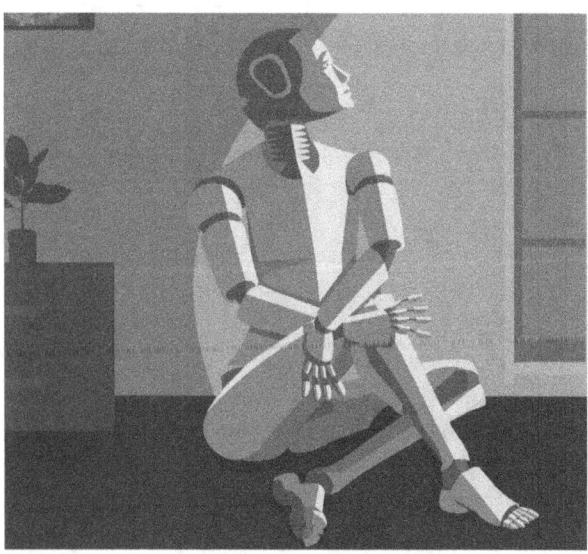

Scott lives with his husband, Mark, in Sacramento. He started reading sci-fi at nine, and as he grew up, he wondered where all the queer characters were. Eventually he decided to write them himself. A Rainbow Award–winning author with thirty-five publications, he runs QueerSciFi.com and is an associate member of SFWA.

PING

by J. Scott Coatsworth

"Remember that crazy lightshow last week over the Space Needle?" I sipped my Red Hook, watching my date—a cute programmer from the 'zon—carefully for his reaction.

Jayson nodded. "Trevor Noah had a field day with it. 'Maybe the aliens have come to save us. Erp Urk Ewwwww.'" He did his best alien face, eyes bulged out and barring his perfect white teeth.

Geekily adorable. "Yeah." It felt good to finally tell *someone.* Why him? Alien contact wasn't exactly normal first date material, but we'd been talking classic sci-fi—and he *really liked* it. Call it a feeling. "That's not what really happened."

"Yeah?" Jayson leaned in, his face inches from mine. He was just twenty-five, and cute as hell.

I'd hit my thirties in May—senior citizen in gay circles. Still, five years wasn't *that big a deal.* That was the loneliness talking. I took another swig and nodded. "I was there."

Jayson grinned, making him even more attractive. "What happened?" He had the cutest dimple when he smiled—my boss Marlee had good taste.

I readjusted my jeans. "You sure?" I didn't want to scare him off, but if he passed the test… I touched the little sphere in my pocket. It was still there.

His hand touched mine, sending a thrill up my arm. "Hit me."

I chuckled. So many ways to respond to *that.* "I just might, later."

He blushed. Not quite as brave as he wanted me to think.

I bit my lip. It was tempting to take him home, *now,* but I really needed to get this off my chest.

Jayson sat back and grinned. "You gonna tell the story, or what?"

Zlim was safe, a thousand light years away by now.

I looked around, then leaned forward and dove in. "It started with a little *ping* in the back of my head…."

☼

I'm a sci-fi nut. Always have been. When other kids in first grade were reading Dick and Jane, I was working my way through the classics—Pern, Rama, Majipoor, the Foundation. I mean, how cool was that when R. Daneel Olivaw suddenly showed up, all those millennia later?

While my friends watched *Survivor*, I was engrossed in *Trek*. Classic. Yeah, I got the shit beaten out of me in high school a lot.

I freaking love science fiction. Which is why they chose me. Well, sort of. I'll get to that later.

At thirty, I live alone—never managed to find my Doctor Who or Captain Jack. Sure, I've dated, but the gay sci-fi dating pool in Seattle is *microscopic*.

I work weekends at MoPOP, away from my evil day job as a real estate assistant. You know it—that weird Museum of Popular Culture by the Space Needle? Rock and roll and sci-fi history in one warped Frank Gehry building. Dream job. We're both outcasts, but the Gehry's the cool kind, the James Dean of museums.

I'm so *not*.

I hang out at the museum, pointing patrons the right way and soaking up all the little bits of book and film history. My boss Marlee lets me help out changing the exhibits too.

I write a little too. I'm always searching for my next story—I never thought it would find me.

Not that I'd ever really *sold* anything, but that hasn't stopped me from trying. If you're meant to be a writer, it's like this itch in your balls. You're not really happy until you reach down and scratch it. We writers are also fucking *masters* at the art of procrastination. You'd be amazed at how far some writers will go to avoid actually *having to write*. Like taking second jobs at sci-fi museums.

Anyhow, it was a rainy mid-winter day at the Mo-PoP when I first felt it.

I was explaining Golden Age Sci-Fi to a befuddled lesbian couple from Dallas—one tall with long red hair and one short with a buzz-cut—and their kids, who apparently had wandered into the sci-fi side of the museum by accident. They train us to notice visitors' physical characteristics—size, hair, clothing—to be able to describe patrons when needed.

"Clarke was gay, but you couldn't come out, back in the dark ages…" A strange buzzing sensation arched up my neck, landing in the back of my skull. Wincing, I reached up to scratch it.

"Tyler, knock it off." Buzz-cut pulled one of her kids away as I felt pain lancing through my shin.

I glared at the little monster. "He *kicked* me." I took a deep breath. "It's all right, ma'am." You suck it up a lot in a job like this.

Long-red's face registered a strange combination of anger and regret. "I'm sorry. It won't happen again." She ushered her wife and kids away, and Buzz Cut shot me a dirty look.

What was that for? Now both my shin and my neck hurt. I rubbed the back of my neck absently. *Did something bite me?* Were the murder wasps finally here?

It was pouring outside. After they left, I had the hall to myself, so I wandered around, looking at the works of the greats.

Asimov died of AIDS. Clark was gay. And Marion Zimmer Bradley? I shuddered. *The Mists of Avalon* was brilliant, life-changing for me. Best not to think about that one too long.

I felt the strange ping again, this time in my temple. I turned my head, and the sensation shifted, running across my forehead. *What the hell?*

I'm gonna stop right here. This gets into some Twilight Zone–level *weird*, stuff you'd find in the deepest, darkest hidey holes of *4chan* or *reddit*. You're not going to believe a word of it. I know, 'cause I didn't believe it either.

Anyhow, I turned, and that weird *ping* was right in the middle of my forehead. I started across the room, using it like a homing beacon. Did I mention I'm a sci-fi nut? It came naturally to me.

I passed the display of golden-age paperbacks, fixated on the women in science fiction exhibit…

sci-fi greats like Shelley, Russ, Le Guin and Springer. *There.*

Between *The Left Hand of Darkness* and *Larque on the Wing*, a tiny red light flickered. I peered into the darkness.

It vanished, imprinting the afterimage of a tiny man standing there, staring at me with huge eyes. I blinked and it was gone.

Too much Red Hook. I swore to myself I wouldn't have my usual celebratory after-work beer that night. So I had two.

☼

By the next weekend, I'd forgotten all about it. I'd been tired, a long day after a long week—I made excuses, like you do when the impossible happens.

I was busy at the day job, with three townhome sales and the purchase of a downtown condo with views of Puget Sound to die for, and hadn't hit my pillow until after midnight all week.

By Friday night I was an exhausted wreck. I collapsed into bed at nine. Sam and Winn had invited me out to the Lumber Yard, but I was in no mood for the inevitable night of sipping on craft beer in a dark bar while everyone else hooked up and went home.

Just after midnight it happened again.

I was having the strangest dream—my ex Jordan was an extra in a new live-action version of *Dune*, but he was also Arianna Grande, and damn could he *sing*. The sandworms rose from the desert and wiggled and writhed to the beat as he belted out that old Bonnie Tyler song "Holding out for a Hero."

I woke with a blazing headache. I stared at the blinking lights of my alarm clock—the tall green numbers said 11:07 a.m. I glared at it—somehow the old plastic CD case I had propped up against it to block out the light had fallen over, flooding the room with a creepy glow.

"Hello."

My hand froze in midair. *What the hell?*

Something was standing on my nightstand.

My eyes slowly focused.

It *looked* like a bug, but it was hard to make it out in the dark. *Please, let it not be a cockroach.* I didn't want to have to call the landlord to fumigate the apartment. Again.

I reached over it and flicked on my TARDIS lamp and stared at it.

"Hello!" it said again in a tiny voice, raising what could only be described as a tentacle.

"What the frak?" I scrambled backward across the bed. That was no *bug*. I was hallucinating—that must be it. *What did I eat last night?* Mac and cheese and hot dogs. Oh, and Cherry Coke with a chaser of Oreos. Nothing out of the ordinary. I know, my diet's crap, but I *hate* cooking. "Helllllo?" I managed, staring at my visitor. I wasn't sure what the protocol was for this situation. *What is this situation, exactly? Swamp Thing? Rats of NIMH? Stargate? Or maybe Stranger in a Strange Land?* I knew them all, but none of them had prepared me for this. I wished I'd stayed asleep on Arrakis with Jordan/Arianna. At least that was *normal* weirdness.

"Day-vid." It said my name like it was using one of those old Hooked on Phonics things to translate.

My eyes slowly adjusted to the light. The bug was dressed in some kind of black uniform, complete with little patches on the "chest." *Captain* Bug? "Yes, I'm David." It sounded inane, even to me. Don't laugh. I was in uncharted waters.

It waved one of its three tentacles at itself and opened its mouth, a long gash between its eyes, which was just weird. "Zlim." I supposed the strange body made sense. Why would an alien race—or whatever it was—be like us? "Need yir halp." It flicked its comically large ears at me, and I felt an unexpected wave of compassion for its situation. Wherever it was from, my bedroom must be a strange and daunting place.

"We?"

Zlim waved its tentacles again, and three others like it emerged from behind my alarm clock. Had they been there the whole time?

Two were similar height, but unlike Zlim's pale pink "skin," one was as black as its uniform, and the other was a pale green. The last one was even smaller.

I pointed and they shrank back. "Sorry." I pulled my finger back—it was as big as one of them. "Child?"

Zlim's eyelids half closed, and then it responded. "Yes. Child." It pointed to each of its companions in turn. "Leyl, Crill, child Alyn. We *emmins*."

Emmins? I sat back, feeling less alarmed. I don't know why—here I was facing a tiny alien horde in my bedroom—but the fact that they had a child made me feel better. But whose child was it?

I shook my head. I was getting ahead of myself. Establish communication—that's what they did in first contact books, right? Find out if they meant harm.

I laughed. What could they do? They were so tiny. They waved their tentacles wildly in alarm. Alyn turned tail and ran behind the clock again. And yes, he had an *actual* tail.

Space mice. My apartment had been invaded by space mice.

"It's okay!" I held out my hands, palms up, hoping it was a universal symbol of peace or submission.

Zlim looked at its own tentacles, and then held two of them out in a rough approximation of my gesture.

Alyn popped its head out from behind the clock, watching me avidly.

"Need…help." Its eyes blinked at me from either side of its mouth. It was creepy as hell…and weirdly moving. I wanted to 'gram the whole thing, but I was afraid grabbing my phone from the nightstand would scare them.

I sat up slowly, pulling my sheet over my torso and adjusting myself as discretely as possible. Not that it mattered, but I didn't want history to record that I met humankind's first alien contact stark naked. I yawned, stretching my arms, and Zlim stumbled backward. "Sorry. We do that when we're tired."

Poor little thing was shaking. "Big teeth."

"I won't hurt you."

"One…hoomin…sprayed us. It tasted *grmlgggt*." He shuddered.

I stared at the little creature. "He sprayed you with *bug spray*?" Uncomfortably aware that the same thought had crossed my mind.

Zlim moved his mouth silently, tasting the word. "Yes. Think."

"Asshole." That ruled out *mutated cockroach*. "So… I'm not the first? Why me?"

Zlim digested that. "Only a few help."

A burst of warmth filled my chest. "You mean, only a few can hear you? See you?" I felt a burst of warmth. I was *special*, after all. All my life I'd thought so, even when everyone else told me I wasn't. Steady as a rock, they said—

"No. All can hear."

And poof, the warmth was gone. I sighed. "Then why?"

"Work at mooseum."

I laughed again. There it was. They wanted me because of where I worked. The universe loved to bring me down a peg.

Maybe the Space Needle was their spaceship, and they needed my help to get to it? Nah, that made no sense. It was too damned big, for one. They were tiny! And if they could reach me here and at the museum, why couldn't they get in there? It was *right next door*. I sighed.

Suck it up, buttercup. That's what my nonna used to say when I was feeling down. They chose me. *Eventually.* That's what matters, right?

And I'd always had a soft spot for strangers in strange lands. "What do you need me to do?"

☼

I took a Lyft—it was late, and I didn't feel like walking the forty-odd blocks in the cold Seattle rain. You laugh, but I'm about ready to move back to Phoenix—at least it's dry there.

The driver dropped me off on Fifth, just across the street from MoPoP. It was eerie at night, the building's strange angles appearing and disappearing like ghosts in the heavy rain.

Zlim rode in my pocket, nibbling on a piece of old cheddar cheese I'd found in my pantry. I mean, of course space mice liked cheese, right?

Look, I have a pic…yeah, I know, it's fuzzy. It was dark out and I was in a hurry.

The others were tucked in the pocket of my backpack.

I ducked out from under a tree and made a dash for it, reaching the overhang without getting soaked.

I miss the thunderous monsoon rains in Arizona. In Seattle, you get two kinds of rain—warm and cold—and both boring as hell. They say you got used to it. They said a lot of things when I moved here.

Zlim chittered excitedly in my pocket. I didn't catch much of it—alien words, mostly, interspersed with a few I did recognize. Architecture. Curves. And cheese.

"Hey there!" A flashlight beam cast my shadow across the front of the museum.

Zlim's head slipped down into my pocket.

"Hey, Harry." I turned slowly, making sure my passenger was out of sight. "It's just me. David."

"Oh. Hey there, David!" Harry slid his stun gun back into his holster. "Sorry to scare you. We had a couple hoodlums here last night, trying to break in. They put me on high alert." He turned off the flashlight.

Hoodlums? Harry is older than my father, but a lot less cranky. "Just getting ready for a new exhibit, and inspiration hit."

"Ah." Harry scratched his white beard. "What's it this time?"

"The exhibit?" I'd forgotten to prepare a good lie—rookie mistake. I cast about for something. "Um… alien invasion. *War of the Worlds.* That sort of thing." I wondered if Harry had heard the original on the radio. Surely, he wasn't *that* old.

Harry nodded. "Wasn't that a movie? I don't follow much sci-fi."

"Yeah. Tom Cruise." I pulled out my key. "Well, better get to it. I want to get this done and get back home to bed."

Harry patted me on the back. "I'm on all night. You know how to reach me if you need me." Harry tapped his cell phone holster.

"Thanks, Harry." I waited until he was gone and then opened the door, slipping inside to disarm the alarm. I really *did* help with the show changes, and Marlee gave me the key and the code to the alarm last year. "Coast is clear."

Zlim popped up from my pocket, ears flicking. "Coost…?"

"It means he's gone."

"Okay." He made a loop with his tentacles again.

I grinned and flipped on the lights to the main hall. This month it was dedicated to spaceships. Not the *real thing*, of course, but a traveling exhibit of models made for films over the decades. I loved this exhibit, even if the tiny ships didn't look as *real* as they did in the films. I ran my hand along the first glass case, admiring them.

Battlestar Galactica (the original) sat next to a mock-up of her counterpart from the 2004 series—many shows didn't bother with real models anymore.

Next was the alien ship from *District Nine*, followed by the USS Cygnus from that cheesy seventies film *The Black Hole*. Never trust Disney to get sci-fi right.

The *Nostromo*, *Alien*'s blocky mining ship from the same year, occupied a pedestal of its own in the middle of the case.

On the far side of the room, one case was devoted entirely to various versions of the *Enterprise*, and another to ships from the Star Wars universe, including two *Millennium Falcons*—*A New Hope* and *Return of the Jedi*.

But it was the small case in the back I was after. It held all the ships from fifties TV shows and films, including the one my little friends wanted. "Danger, Will Robinson!"

Zlim became visibly excited as we approached the case. "Go home. Go home!"

I glanced around, worried that someone else might be in the building. "Keep it down, will ya?" I'd turned off the cameras in the room, but what if Marlee decided to stop in to pick up something she'd left in her office? She was a night owl.

What if Harry called her to check on my story? Great, *now* I was nervous. "Let's get this done. Tell me again why your spaceship is with all the models?"

"Not ours. *Like* ours. Ours broke."

I set my backpack gently on the glass and opened the back pocket. His mates—in whatever sense of the word applied—climbed out, followed by little Alyn. Well, they were *all* little, but you know what I mean. "Where is home?"

"Two star. Bigger than this."

I nodded. That tracked. They were probably small because the gravity was heavier where they came from. "What color is your sky?"

"Green." Zlim waved his tentacles animatedly. I got the message: *Can we get on with this?*

I put my hand up to my shirt pocket and he climbed out and landed softly on my palm. I set him down on the glass, and he rejoined the other emmins. They all touched tentacles, a gibbering sound raising from the group that was almost musical.

"David?"

I spun around, deer in the headlights, to find my boss staring at me. "Marlee! How surprising to see you." Behind my back, I gestured for the emmins to slip into hiding. I could lose my job if she found out what I planned. Or worse. And the poor emmins might get *NIMH*'d.

She peered around the room, pulling her purse strap back up on the shoulder of her black blazer. "Yeah. I got a call from Harry. Were you talking to someone?" Her voice had that lilt she got when she'd been out drinking.

"Just myself. You know how I am." I tried to keep my breathing calm.

"Sure? Harry said you were working on a new exhibit." She frowned. "I don't remember authorizing overtime."

I shook my head. "Of course not. Harry must have misunderstood. I was working on an *idea* for something new. Alien invasion. *V, Body Snatchers, War of the Worlds*…all of that."

She nodded, teetering a bit and catching herself on a display case. "I like it. Bring me your ideas… tomorrow."

"I will. Just…gathering inspiration. Sorry to wake you—you should get to bed. You look…tired." I'd almost said *drunk*.

Marlee nodded. "Just hanging out with some of the 'zon boys at a wine bar in Lake Union. You should come out with us sometime. There are a couple cute single gay geeks. Like you. I could set you up."

Like me? Gay or geek, or both? "Um, thanks?" I breathed easier—I was going to get away with this.

"Oh, and David?"

My heart pounded in my chest. "Yeah?" Zlim was peering out from behind me. I leaned sideways to hide him.

"You're an odd duck." She laughed. "Don't stay too late. See you in the morning." Then she was gone.

I waited to hear the click of the front lock echo through the quiet building and let out a sigh of relief. "Okay, let's get this over with before we get caught. Which one is yours?"

Zlim pointed. "That one."

I whistled. "The *C57-D* from *Forbidden Planet*. She's a beaut. But how are you going to make a model fly?"

"Not model. Turn on, go whoosh." Zlim's tentacle extended into the air.

I'd believe it when I saw it. Then again, I'd seen stranger things in the last two hours. Another

thought occurred to me. "Hey, how did you get to my house from here?"

"Like this." He pressed something on his belt, shimmered, and reappeared on the far side of the case.

I looked at him, then at the ship, and back at him again. "So what do you need me for?" I felt like a fool. These little aliens were messing with me. It was high school all over again, but instead of Billy Smith it was Zlim and his little crew of emmins.

The alien's tentacles sagged. "Can't pass." It tapped on the glass.

Can't pass through glass? Well, technically, acrylic. "You can't go through plastic?"

Zlim shivered. "No. Poison."

"You're right about that." They needed *me* to open the door. I laughed at the absurdity of life…that this tiny alien race could flit across miles as easily as a thought but were stymied when it came to a simple pane of acrylic.

Still, if this was all true—and I was way too far into it to start second guessing now—what would happen tomorrow when someone noticed that *C-57D* was missing?

You know that lightbulb feeling? This one almost blinded me. "One sec." We had a few extra ship models in storage. By the time the exhibit moved on next month, I'd be in the clear—I could claim plausible deniability.

I opened the storage room and flipped through the crates. There had to be *something* that would work.

I found it in the third one, covered in packing peanuts. I lifted the saucer up—Klaatu's ship from *The Day the Earth Stood Still*. It was close enough that most folks wouldn't notice the difference. At least until I could print out a new sign.

I closed my eyes. Was I really gonna do this? Was it worth my job?

Then I thought of Alyn, Zlim's child, and what scientists might do to the lot of them if they were found out. I made up my mind, dream job be damned. Some things were worth it.

"A decoy," I explained proudly to Zlim.

Its tentacles fluttered, and then its vertical mouth split open in what I hoped was the emmins version of a grin. "Ahhhh." He must have a universal translator on his belt. So many questions… "Are you ready?"

"Yes."

I opened the case. Carefully I eased the little *C-57D* out and set it on top—it was heavier than I expected. I replaced it with Klaatu's ship, which fit perfectly.

Zlim ran up to it and passed a tentacle over the edge, and damn if the thing didn't light up and extend a tiny boarding ramp, bordered in blue light. I tried to peer inside, but the light was too bright. Hey, do you think they had a miniature Robbie the Robot in there?

I suppose I was lucky that the emmins had an aversion to plastic. If not, I never would have been witness to this strange scene.

The others boarded the tiny vessel. Alyn ran back and gave me a three-tentacle wave before vanishing inside after the others.

Zlim popped open a tiny access panel. The top of the ship rotated and opened.

"Fuel?"

"Right here, buddy." I unzipped the backpack and pulled out a couple of bottles of Kirkland water—I wasn't sure how much I'd need. "This will take you all the way home?"

Zlim waved his tentacles up and down, a gesture I was learning to interpret as a *yes*. "Water most strong."

I closed up the case and pulled on my pack. "You sure you don't want to stick around for a while? We could learn so much from you."

Zlim's tentacles sagged a little. "Crill hurt. Crash. Must home."

How had they ended up here? What happened to their original ship? And how had good old Fred Wilcox—the *Forbidden Planet* director—gotten his hands on one of the emmins' actual spaceships? I figured I'd probably never know.

The water tank cycled closed.

"So…what now?"

Zlim's tentacle reached into its belt and pulled out something. He held it up to me.

It was a tiny sphere the size of a marble. I took it. "What is it?"

"*Knowing*. In water. Drink."

Knowing what? "Thank you." I stuck it in my pocket. "What now?"

"Outside. Then go."

I wasn't sure if he meant for me to leave, or that they would go away. Or both. "Okay. All aboard!"

"Aboard?"

I laughed. "It's something you say…never mind."

He waved his tentacles at his side. "Thank, Day-vid."

I grinned. "My pleasure."

With one last wave of his tentacles, he vanished inside.

I stared at the ship for a long moment. The most momentous moment in human history—meeting an alien race for the first time—and I was the only one to see it. I squinted at the ship. *Or was I?*

Maybe me and Fred Wilcox would've had something to talk about. I'd have to stream *Forbidden Planet* again—I hadn't watched it since I was a kid.

I took a picture to commemorate the moment. See the lights?

Then I closed up the case. I lifted the *C-57D* gently—it was even heavier now with the water inside—and carried it out into the main lobby. It was past one o'clock—I wondered if Marlee had made it home yet.

I shut off the lights and unlocked the front door. I pushed it open and set the ship down to lock it. Then I stepped out under the open sky.

The rain had passed, and the heavens were clear. I carried the *C-57D* under the monorail tracks and out into the grassy area below the Space Needle, setting it down beneath that jet-black sky, and looked up at the shimmering stars, wondering which one belonged to the emmins.

I stepped back, waiting for something to happen.

The ship sat there still and dark as a rock for a moment. Then a series of blue lights encircled it and it lifted up into the air under its own power. It hovered there for just a moment, and I imagined Zlim and his team waving their tentacles at me in farewell.

Then it shot into the sky like a rocket and vanished into the vast darkness.

"Hey, David, all done with your exhibit?" Harry came up behind me, patting me on the back. "Sorry about calling your boss. Standing orders."

I nodded, a tear in my eye. "Not a problem."

"Beautiful night. Chilly. Can't remember the last time the stars were so clear from here."

"It's the new moon." Though it *did* seem darker than normal. "I wonder if—"

The sky lit up, a flash brighter than sunlight washing over the city, filling the sky with a twisting rainbow of light. Car horns went off all around.

I blinked, trying to clear my vision.

"What in tarnation was that?"

The emmins. "They're going home."

"What?"

I could see Harry's outline now as the aftereffect of the flash faded. "I said I'm going home. Night, Harry."

"Night, David." He was still staring at the sky.

I called a Lyft, wondering if I would ever know the truth.

✧

I blinked. Jayson was staring at me.

"You know that's like stone-cold crazy, right?" He sipped his vodka sour.

"I know, right? If I hadn't seen it…"

Jayson sat back, staring at me. "I've never had a first date quite like this."

Time to play my ace. "I can prove it."

Jayson leaned forward. "Yeah? 'Cause I'm kinda into you. It would be nice to know you're not totally crazy." He laughed. "I've had *enough* crazy."

I reached into my pocket and pulled out the marble-sized sphere. I'd considered trying it myself, but I didn't want to do it alone. I was sick of being alone.

Jayson's eyes widened. "Is that…?"

I nodded. "*Knowing.*" I grinned.

Jayson snorted. "Can I see?"

I hesitated, but then handed it over.

Jayson held it up. It sparkled with its own light. "Oooh."

I leaned forward. "You in?"

"Sure. They say knowledge is a powerful drug."

I laughed. "See? I knew I liked you." I called the bartender over. "Two waters please?"

"Coming right up."

Jayson's eyes twinkled. "You're serious."

I nodded. "I'm always serious about sci-fi."

"A man after my own heart." He handed the sphere back to me.

I grinned. "You can be Apollo to my Starbuck."

"Hey, I get to be Starbuck!"

I laughed out loud. I could really get to like Jayson. How many of my dates had even known who Starbuck was? Especially 1.0? Most of them thought I was asking them out for coffee.

The glasses arrived. With a flourish, I dropped the sphere into the water and watched in fascination as it frothed and glowed, sending a blue mist over the rim. When it settled down, I poured half of it into the empty glass and handed it to Jayson. "Ready?"

His eyes met mine over the steaming glasses. "Now or never."

We downed them in one long gulp.

Jayson reached out and took my hand, warm fingers closing around mine. *Some first date, indeed.*

My thought before my mind exploded with *knowing*?

Tastes like cheese.

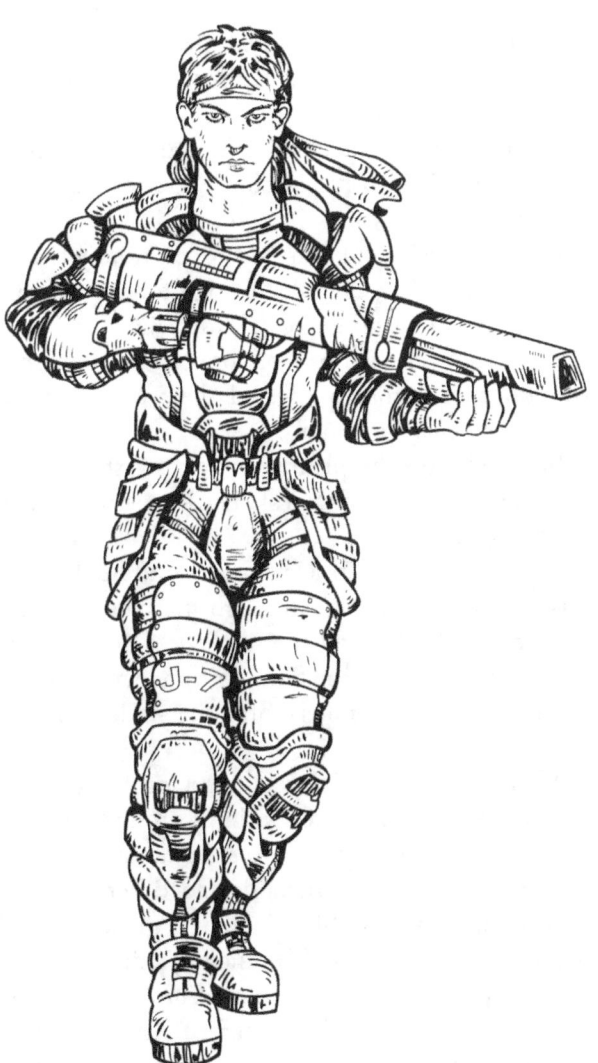

M. O. Muriel is the double-contest winner of the International Writers (2012) and Illustrators (2011) of the Future Contests. She is the first and only woman to win both contests and do it in back-to-back years. Due to an ongoing domestic violence situation, this is her first publication since 2014.

A MATTER OF TIME

by M. O. Muriel

"You're such a Seven," Gebriele accused Mada, fussing with the baby palm as she did every time she swept into Mada's office and into her train of thought. She angled the potted plant this way and that, until it caught the pinkish light percolating through the stained-glass oriel window. "In Arithmancy, Seven Life-Paths either thank God or think they're god."

"Funny thing." Mada smoothed an unruly lock of auburn hair into her coiffure. "We're *both* Life-Path Sevens."

Only Gebriele could distract Mada from writing her dissertation on Complex Design for the University Review Board. The blond Arithmancy Professor was so bubbly, and her passion for how the energetic vibrations of numbers affected the world around them was *usually* infectious.

Satisfied with the plant, Gebriele swashed from the oriel over to Mada's desk, her honeysuckle day skirts flouncing.

Really. The lace Gebriele wore around her bodice was frankly scandalous (although the menfolk had an affection for it), and she smelled of apricot preserves. In Mada's estimation, Arithmancy wasn't a practical study of numbers. Still, the students filled the registers.

"Unlike you," said Gebriele, plucking her pocket watch from her bustier to twirl idly around a finger, "I enjoy my *desperate* quest into the unknown."

"I enjoy what I do," Mada defended her dissertation in an arch tone. She chanced a glance at the plant and watch in turn. "Conflicting points of view have simply intensified the conundrum of Complex Design over the years." She sighed. "It really is a riddle, you know."

"A riddle you're determined to *solve*." Gebriele winked appreciatively at her friend's doggedness.

Mada ignored her. She drummed her fingers on the desk. "One side argues that the extensive cataloging of living organisms and their characteristics has finally generated enough evidence to substantiate the existence of Intelligent Design," she explained. "They claim that biological complexity *proves* that an Intelligent Designer exists. And, point taken: Even the simplest of organisms are much more intricate than anything manmade. Say a watch." She pointed at Gebrielle's. "Even if that were perfectly maintained for eternity, it will never amount to more than a mechanism engineered by humans for measuring the flow of time."

"Naturally," Gebrielle sympathized.

"Yet, the other side argues that no matter how advanced we engineer our clocks, we human beings, who are the highest form of sentient biology, are ironically only equipped to observe processes that take place within our limited frame of reference."

Gebrielle admired her reflection in the back of the watch. "Well, we do possess the ability to *appreciate* our observations," she agreed.

"Yes," said Mada. "But it's still a riddle. See? It's a cog within a wheel within a greater cog. Individually, the slow, cumulative processes are escaping us. The older points of view are becoming dated, only to be replaced by the newer points of view, and so on and so forth into infinity, causing subjectivity and skepticism to misfire by huge margins and compounding even the most fundamental of questions. Don't you see? I've found the answer! The flow of time must be rooted in the flux of *human perception*, just as the notion of an Intelligent Designer must also be a function of *human perception*."

"You've stunted the baby palm with your boringness," Gebriele accused. She twirled her pocket watch counterclockwise. Its chrome enamel glinted on the upswing. "Ace gave you that baby palm for a gift, I hope you remember. Do you know, the minute he planted it, it sprouted and grew like a weed? My, but just look at it around *you*. It's half alive!"

"I've *tried* everything." Mada surrendered her dip pen to its inkwell. "Sunlight, fresh air, music, mineral water." She held up her digestif suggestively. "Sweet vermouth."

Ace was Gebriele's baby brother, and *he* was a Life-Path Five. Always the adventurer, always on the go.

Gebriele's pocket watch whistled softly as it zoomed around and 'round…

And oooh! Snatching it out of the air for reference, Mada rewound the smallest hand on her carved-ivory wristwatch by twenty-nine units. Remarkable. Just like her bedside digital at home. Both timepieces were getting progressively worse. What could possibly be wrong with them? They were becoming almost as vexatious as her dissertation. Perhaps Pa could re-tinker with them. Or…Mada was loathe to replace the pieces altogether.

A chrome cylinder the size of her forearm, attached to a little white parachute, fluttered past the windows with a clink. The sound of a biplane and more falling cylinders followed.

"Speaking of Ace." Mada rose from her desk (perhaps a bit too abruptly). Reproaching her wristwatch with a shake, she brushed smooth the chocolate damask fabric of her overskirt. "I've to collect the mail for Pa. He'll be needing my eyes."

"Well, don't tell Ace you've been neglecting his gift, and no mistake. He'll only get you another one." Gebriele opened the office door for Mada—and sighed dramatically. "We should stop for libations and a show tonight on Lagoon Platform Nine. I've a Worshipful meeting in an hour in East End City, right across the bridge. We could make it a night."

"I've not been neglecting the palm," Mada defended, shaking her watch again as they both skittered out of the office, down the spiral staircase beyond the door—Mada on a mission, Gebriele intent on predicting her friend's every move based on her numerological blueprint.

"Oh don't be such a wet blanket. "You're so *slow*! You never have enough time for fun," Gebriele insisted.

It was true, thought Mada. Escapist to the core. But then, so was Gebriele, in her violently contrasting way. If time travelers were ever to turn up on the steps of City Hall, Gebriele would be the first aboard the ship.

✿

It couldn't be helped. Mada stopped by the Five and Dime near the University to replace her digital

from home. Then she caught a gondola down the canal to the jeweler on Poets Isle in Central Town to replace her wristwatch. When she finally wound her way back to the Atomic Clock to collect the mail, Ace was nowhere in sight.

Drat. She had hoped not to miss him. Mada had even surreptitiously disguised her jog as a brisk walk (scandalous). She had never been late before. It's simply that it wouldn't do for Ace to catch her out of countenance with a broken wristwatch.

Hiking the stairs to the top of the Atomic Clock, she entered her father's observatory. "Pa, I've replaced my timepieces."

"Oh, why I thought I fixed those," he replied, bent over his stylus. Plugging the tiny computer into a main conduit for the Atomic Clock, he made some calculations on it…and his brow creased over.

"What's wrong?" Instantly Mada was worried. The Atomic Clock was the generator for all of Lagoon City. While some of the floating city's infrastructure ran on cogworks autonomously, the electricity generated by the Atomic Clock powered most of the buildings, machines, and vehicles. More importantly, it kept exact Universal Time to the micro-unit. All other clocks were set by it. As one of the City Founders, Pa had charge of the workforce of Coggies who maintained it and kept it running smooth as a whistle. Unfortunately, Prof Truing (so named, because he also taught Quantum Mechanics at the University) was going blind in his old age, and as of late, he'd been relying more and more on Mada to run things. She feared he had a mind to groom her as his replacement.

Which worried her even more. Collecting Pa's correspondence and assistant-managing Coggies was one thing. Complex Design—what she taught at the University—was entirely another. The studies of Complex Design and Quantum Mechanics were as far from each other as the timekeeping processes were between analogs and digitals. Mada had no interest in taking over for Pa.

Etching an invisible calculation in the air with a finger, Pa plugged it into the stylus.

"It seems that the on-duty representative of the Horology Guild has discovered a discrepancy with the Atomic Clock," he said. With an agitated hand motion, he wiped the stylus's face clean, cranked a lever over the conduit to reset the connection, and scratched his snow cloud of a beard. "Likely it's only our monitoring equipment. But one of our airmail pilots just now returned from his mail run across the sea to Jade City, and he's reporting that the chronometer in his biplane is off by 1 micro-unit."

"Odd." Mada wondered if the phenomenon had something to do with her own faulty timepieces.

"Highly irregular." Pa was clearly flustered. Mada had never seen him this way before. "The Atomic Clock is the heart!" Patting down his double-breasted vest for his spectacles, he unearthed them from an inner pocket. "Were it to stop running, even for *One Planck time,* the city would be plunged into darkness!"

"I know."

"Industry would come to a screeching halt!"

"I know. Pa—"

Outside the observatory's half-moon cordon of bubble-shaped windows, a plane zoomed overhead. Mada wondered if that mightn't be the selfsame pilot with the unsynchronized chronometer flying back across the sea, to confirm his discrepancy with Jade City's Atomic Clock.

She hoped it wasn't Ace!

In a supersonic boom, the plane punched a hole in the clouds.

"Oh, Pa." Mada squeezed his shoulders before hunting for his daily reports in their usual place. "Likely it's the chronometer in that pilot's plane. The Atomic Clock has never been out of sync with the rest of the Planetary Continuum before. Or the Arch Regulator."

"No indeed." Sliding his spectacles onto his nose, Pa thumbed their catch release and they folded outward into a set of oscilloscope goggles. The greenish graticule crosshairs superimposed behind their lenses flickered on with a stuttering zap-*spark!*

"There shouldn't be anything to worry about," Mada assured him, watching him jigger the stylus. He scrutinized the ropy umbilical that connected the stylus to the main conduit. Eyes blinking through his oscilloscopes, he ran a thumb and forefinger along the connection, feeling for kinks.

He jiggered the stylus by his ear.

Watching him, Mada tidied up a single nonconforming mound of clutter on the observatory's maze of metal apothecary shelves. They were packed solid with uniform rows of beakers and stills, gadget, alembics and aludels, electronic hardware, and secret keyhole compartments.

More and more, Mada had been observing how her own timepieces had begun to slow down if she didn't reset them regularly. The ones she had replaced only this afternoon had deteriorated to the point of requiring a daily resetting. Still, only her personal timepieces seemed to do this—until now, that is, with the news of this pilot and his chronometer.

She hoped it was only a coincidence.

Inhaling, Mada detected an orange-metallic twinge of ozone ballooning through the customary scent of cleaning agents. A faint, underlying screech had begun filtering through the normal ticking and whirring of gizmos.

"Pa, you haven't even touched your lunch!" Mada was aghast at the sheer *bedlam* in the observatory today! No wonder she couldn't find anything. Normally, Pa was so orderly. He ran his day…well, like *clockwork.*

"Pa you're an Interminable, one of the Twenty-Four City Founders!" She stamped her foot. "You've existed since time immemorial, a living testament to your life's work!" Fists on hips, Mada scoured the nearest shelves for those reports. Typically, Pa sent them through the mail to his official channels in the Planetary Continuum via Ace. Which, of course, was her whole purpose for this visit. They had to be *somewhere.*

"Don't tell me you've given up a measure of immortality," she said, and almost knocked her head on the large, hanging lens Pa had neglected to snap back into its proper place on the ceiling.

Mada rubbed the almost-bump.

"I will if this infernal clock is off," Pa promised darkly, blinking at her large-eyed through his oscilloscopes.

"Oh baloney." Anyone halfway educated knew that the Interminables possessed several measures of immortality. It consisted of bits of their Body Electric (their life force), which they could bestow on another person or situation to jumpstart or reset them, like a living set of sparkplugs. Only problem was, doing so aged the Interminables. Not to mention, there wasn't a single Interminable who remembered anything before founding the cities. Nor did they recall from where they had originated. Rumor had it the Interminables themselves had been "reset"—their memories wiped. No one knew exactly why, how, or by whom—a concept that made Mada's dissertation all the more irksome to solve, but important to prove.

Of course, the Order of the Worshipful Clockmaker believed that God had done it as punishment for some unimaginable crime. And the Time Dilation Cult, well, they had started a war…

"Confound it all." Pa bobbed past a window. "Word's already leaked out. Blast that rabble."

As if on cue, the subtle booming of drums from outside morphed into hearing. At once, Mada knew the Order of the Worshipful Clockmaker was picketing again.

"Oh, they're a lot of chin music," she said. Although, she kept it to herself that Gebriele might be down there. *Gebriele* would know where Ace had scampered off to. Usually he had an hour lunch break in Lagoon City before he took off again to deliver the rest of the airmail.

Ah! Gotcha. There they were, Pa's daily reports, right under his titanium tray of untouched tea sandwiches of cucumber spread on marbled rye and chocolate dacquoise. Mada pushed the button for the conveyer on which the tray was perched, and the sprocket inched it off the reports enough for her to pluck them up through the teeth of the metal roller chain.

No time to waste, Mada kissed Pa on the brow. With his correspondence in hand, she tucked out the door to go catch herself a pilot.

Big news, this! Mada shook out her parasol on the boardwalk outside the Atomic Clock. And how! Word had already begun to spread about the discrepancy (although not through any permission of Pa's). The city's PA system was broadcasting the news like it was a raid.

A runner from the Craftsmans Guild passed her up. *Whoosh!* Another.

One for every island in the floating city, off to compare each isle's master clock to the Atomic Clock.

Like the pedestrians who were milling about the whitewashed gazebos and bridges that networked together the floating islands of Lagoon City, Mada simply couldn't hide her skepticism that something as indestructible and everlasting as the icon of their civilization, the Atomic Clock, could be *broken*. Certainly Pa had the right of it. It must be a glitch. Something to do with his monitoring equipment.

Drat this concourse. Pushing through the approaching assembly of blue frockcoats and picket signs which composed the Order of the Worshipful Clockmaker on their umpteenth circuit around the Atomic Clock, Mada searched for Gebriele.

"Excuse me. Pardon me. Have you seen Gebriele?"

Salt spray from the lagoon peppered her parasol over the balcony railings. Longingly, she glanced over signs and heads at the shadows cast by the conical, tree-covered cliffs, as they saturated the suburbs of East End City, wondering if Ace had gone to lunch. The sun was shining bright and clear—and *hot*—over Central Town, where she was.

"The Atomic Clock has sped up by one micro-unit!" the montage of voices shouted around her. Feet stomped. Signs bounced in the air. "The Worshipful Clockmaker orders time! And we are the components who keep it! Yet the Atomic Clock has sped up! It is a sign. The end is nigh! Time is running out! You MUST be prepared for the afterlife! Where will you spend eternity…?"

"Hi there, Mada." Ace touched her by the elbow, and she whirled.

Same as ever, Lagoon City's own Top Gun was dressed head-to-toe in his sharp white aviator coveralls, white leather flight jacket with a lamb's wool collar, jump boots, parachute, goggles, and the dog-ears of his leather flight helmet flapping. He had a silver mail cylinder tucked under an arm, and the smell of the wind was on him.

It must be the difference in the setting, Mada decided. The confusion. Her *lateness*. An uncustomary glow prickled over her chest, making her tug on her collar with a finger.

She pulled out her fan.

As soon as the press of picketers moved off, Ace held out the cylinder. "What's the idea, Mada? You didn't meet me at the usual time."

He shrugged when she didn't reply. "Gebriele told me about your palm tree. Guess I figured when you didn't show, I'd buy you some minerals."

He flashed her a smile and held out a baggie of plant food tied with a yellow ribbon and the slogan "Time is of the Essence" scrawled on a little golden tag. "It's for luck."

"I'm sorry, Ace." Mada couldn't help feeling guilty. Ace was always acquiring her favors from the various cities in the Planetary Continuum, bringing her tidbits from exotic locales to slip to her under the Clock. "I've never missed a meeting before. It's only that…" She glanced down at her wrist. "I had to attend to a matter of import."

"More important than the mail?" Ace cocked his head at her.

Reddening, Mada closed her eyes. He had the right of it. An Interminable's mail was far too sensitive to be dropped via biplane. As such, for the better part of a year, Mada had been meeting Ace under the Atomic Clock on Pa's behalf at exactly twelve-noon every day, to receive his correspondence in person.

And to think, today she might have missed it!

Strolling by, a bespectacled oriental gentleman in a tan trench, holding a beaver's-head cane, touched the lip of his top hat at them.

Ace saluted. Mada dipped her chin in greeting.

Likely the Chief of the City Guard was keeping an eye on the Worshipfuls as he continued along his peacekeeping route. Hot Fudge Sundae, as the locals called him, often took strolls by the Clock at this hour.

Mada grabbed Ace's wrist. "Ace, you don't really believe Lagoon City is off by *every* Atomic Clock in the Planetary Continuum, do you? The Arch Regulator? Jade City might be the one with the discrepancy."

"Negative." Ace exchanged the mail cylinder and plant food for Pa's daily reports. "That pilot who flew in after me—that'd be Hot Box, one of Lagoon City's. He sets his gizmos off our time. Musta tracked just fine with Jade City on his run this morn. Naw, the difference would be on our end."

He pointed at the cylinder. "You just give that there message to Prof Truing. Might be important, considering." A lick of frustration furrowed his brow, but he exchanged it for a smile. "Besides, I'll be out of a job just as soon as the Craftsman Guild finishes up that mail system of pneumatic tubing under the cities, anyhow."

For a moment, Mada considered him. Ace was one of the best combat pilots from the Time Displacement War eight years back (and how). After the Time Displacement Cult had taken over the cities of Char, Flow, and Eternity, hell-bent on rewinding every Atomic Clock in the Planetary Continuum to the time before the Reset to uncover the true origins of society and who the Interminables really were, Ace had been a wing leader in the strike force for the Planetary Continuum. A crackerjack in a dogfight, he'd scored a whopping seventy-eight victories against enemy aircraft, and had flown reconnaissance through TDC territory.

"You're a true hotshot, Ace," Mada noted.

"Pilots are being phased out, Mada." Ace mock-smiled. "Daggonit, I'm a decorated veteran flying mail sorties with the rest of the war veterans, but that's all I got." He snapped his fingers playfully. "Say, you know I keep tellin' you I'm considering this retirement, though I'm only thirty-two?"

"I don't think anything can ever ground you, Ace." Mada loathed herself for blushing.

"Gee wiz, I'm late!" With a salute, Ace sprinted off to the air docks. "See you later, Mada!"

Stepping out from the midst of the picketers on their latest circuit, dressed in her blue frock coat, Gebriele whistled. "Oh boy, does *he* carry a torch."

Mada was about to heartily disagree, when she looked down at her new wristwatch again. Frowning, she cast a glance at the circular face of the Atomic Clock, as a portentous feeling tickled over her skin, up her arms.

Drat. Her brand-new timepiece had already slowed down by several units.

☼

"Oh, this is vogue," Gebrielle gushed to Mada on the balcony of Lagoon Platform Nine's outdoor amphitheater that evening. She saluted the performance with her glass of Spumante.

Packed to the nines with worried citizens too anxious to go home, the Operetta had overflowed beyond all five of its bridges. Gondolas, yachts, and private submersibles had parked nose to dorsal fin, bubble cockpit to pump-jet-propulsion turbine, along the canals by the floating island, their lanterns and underwater phosphorescent tubing illuminating the water with a radiance of greens and silvery oranges, soft violets, and every shade of red from candy apple to carmine, creating what looked like underwater poinsettia leaves. The hanging lanterns across the bridges cast a velvety golden glow across the show's peripheral spectators. Although, the real catchall were the Operetta's multi-colored stage lights and fan-blown ribbons.

Gebriele blushed expertly at a gentleman who passed their table.

"Aristocrat," she labeled him. "By the looks, I'd say a Life-Path Six. Too bad. We'd be a toxic match." She giggled behind her fan.

"Are you ever serious?" Mada's mind was full to bursting with more pressing concerns.

"About numbers?" Gebriele said in a mocking timbre. "Always."

A perfume of wood smoke and dry ice blanketed the random fishy whiffs from the lagoon and the occasional retort of motor oil from the gears of the city. Mercifully, Mada hardly registered the disagreeable scents; they had faded under the sweet taste of the sparkling wine on the back of her palate as she swilled the last sip of it around her mouth.

"I can't believe you dragged me here tonight." She set her glass down. "You know I'm infernally behind on—"

"Tonight is the *perfect* night for a show," Gebriele arbitrated, pouring Mada another glass from the bottle service they'd ordered for their little table. She held a lace napkin around its neck to catch the drops. "People need a show to take their minds off their worries. Especially when they can do nothing about them. And tonight's theme of hope just happens to be perfect!"

"Hope, yes. And war." Mada glanced beyond one of the several populated bridges spanning the lagoon to the boardwalk isle, to Ferris Quarters, a residential area lined with six-story-high apartment buildings, skirted by trolley tracks. Since the beginning of the show, troopers and a mess of Navy Bell Bottoms had been hauling in back-up generators all over the city from the mainland garrisons and Lagoon City's underwater base.

"Now, keep it a secret," Ace had whispered to Mada once. "I could get in real trouble, you know. But the mainland garrisons are just a ruse to disguise Lagoon City's true military force. Most citizens think they're diving above an underwater garrison in their submersibles. No one supposes that the surrounding tropical cliffs are really hollow, bristling with nukes. Or that the coral reefs below their feet house a whole flotilla of the city's submarines."

"Oh, is this really necessary?" Mada rested chin in hand, as she watched the telltale lights of a Naval submarine emerge like a shark in the water, just offshore.

As usual, Gebriele was right. In no uncertain terms could she concentrate on her dissertation *tonight*, what with the lock-down of all major institutions, including the University, ordered by the Prime Minister of Lagoon City himself. Only the Guilds had access, and they were in pandemonium. In the midst of performing drills, campus security had escorted Mada bodily from her office, pen in one hand and the baby palm in the other.

Worse, the PA system hadn't let up yet. It was *still* blaring the news about the Atomic Clock all over the city, so she could hardly work from home. As it was, the distant echo of it occasionally punctuated the music of the Operetta below.

Next to her, Gebriele clapped enthusiastically as a hydraulic replica of the rocket ship, *Time Runner*, wheeled onstage to a chorus. The theatrical reenactment of the Planetary Continuum's first manned space expedition boasted high-wire stunts and panels of bubbles to represent the stars tumbling by.

In entered the Baritone, right behind the *Time Runner*, costumed in white coveralls. He sang of the era before the Time Dilation War, when the *Time Runner* had flown there and back again to Numeral XIII, the nearest planet in the solar system. Though the round trip had taken only 18.967 light-minutes, traveling at near relativistic speeds, upon the astronauts' return, everyone else in the Planetary Continuum had aged by almost a week. Naturally, the Spacing Guild had accounted for the time dilation by calculating the astronauts' return through detailed measurement, to the micro-unit. Via a prearranged set of adjustment programs, the astronauts had been welcomed back in an appropriate fashion and reintegrated into society without a hitch.

And yet...

...onto the stage dropped a band of Sky Troopers from ribbon cables, attired in indigo-violet. In opposition to the Baritone's narration, their Soprano sung a challenge aria, while the Sky Troopers chorused against the astronauts in white. The time dilation experienced by the astronauts had sparked a brainwave of speculation. Time could be reversed if all the Atomic Clocks were...

Rewound.

Steaming and hiccupping, *Time Runner* wheeled off stage to the escalating chorus.

In an elegant ballet, the Baritone and Soprano melded into a dance of white on indigo-violet. A bounce-lift. And the Baritone lifted the Soprano on high, dipped her, then spun her. The soprano spiraled around his chest headfirst, down, down, until her nose brushed the floor.

Yes! Time could be reversed if all the Atomic Clocks were rewound to the time before the Reset.

"Listen to reason!" sang the Sky Troopers. "In the name of the newly formed Time Dilation Cult, we pledge to find out what happened before the Reset. For the betterment of all humanity," they rose in crescendo, "we *will* find out what caused it!"

"You look a million worlds away." Gebriele snapped her fingers in Mada's face. "What *is* so important about that dissertation of yours, anyway, that you're this deep inside your head tonight?"

"What? Oh, um." Actually, Mada hadn't been thinking about that at all. She was wondering if somehow her Body Electric was producing a temporal vortex, causing time to slow around her—in essence, creating a time dilation effect on her timepieces.

An earsplitting roar suddenly rent the sky as a plane zoomed overhead, coming in low. The night swathed the cockpit and its pilot in a blanket of darkness, but the lights of the Operetta momentarily reflected off the red numbers 555 painted on the plane's metallic underbelly.

"It's Ace." Mada nearly knocked over the table, as she rose. "He'll have news."

Gebrielle followed her through the audience, and they ran to the air docks.

"Higher Command radioed in." Ace leapt from the cockpit, the flashing lights of his biplane making his movements look surreal. He grasped Mada's hands and took in the baby-blue lace around her collar. "Gee, don't you look swell, Mada. Say, the Guilds are petitioning all the surrounding cities for a Universal Consensus on their Atomic Clocks."

"Sure," Mada agreed. "They'll want to reset them accordingly, lest civilization come to a screeching halt."

Maybe lace didn't hurt after all, she thought. Gebriele did have an I.Q. of 142, even if she was a flirt.

"Sorry, old girl. I'm being sent as part of the sortie to the other cities to synchronize the Atomic Clocks." Ace looked from Mada, to his sister, then back again. "I won't be delivering the mail for a few days."

"That's all right, Ace," said Mada, "we'll work something out."

Taking Mada's chin between thumb and forefinger, Ace measured her with a look.

No, no, definitely not! Mada stemmed an errant rush of adrenaline. Ace was in his element, that's all. Nothing more. Nothing at all.

"Rumor has it that the TDC might take advantage of a situation like this," he warned them. "Might be there're even spies in the city."

"Oh, I hope not." Gebriele shucked her gloves from her hands. Strands of her blonde hair whipped out of her coiffure from the blustery sea breeze. "I ran the numbers on tomorrow and they're eights and fives all across the board. *Drama* and learning lessons the hard way." She wiggled her brows at her brother. "Although you might be in your element, fly boy. Best be prepared, and no mistake."

"You girls just take precautions," Ace replied, his trademark debonair attitude soundly replaced by the staunch determination he was famous for in the TDC war stories. He saluted them with two fingers. "Keep your chins to the sky."

✧

Bother.

If the PA system had been giving Mada unproductive nights before, the klaxons that had started going off in one-hour intervals, as the military performed drills and set about securing Lagoon City in case the Time Displacement Cult attacked, were giving her a real brain thumper now.

For the time being, classes at the University had been canceled outright.

It was currently morning, and while Mada brushed out her hair before the vanity's pewter mirror in her apartment's diminutive master bedroom, she studied the baby palm.

Once more she turned her gaze out the window. In the two days since Ace had gone, she'd fed the palm the new minerals he'd given her. Little good they did. Poor thing. It just wasn't growing. More now than ever that made her nervous.

She harrumphed crossly at her bedside digital. Again, slow. Guild runners had already tested and reset all the clocks in the city (public and private) against the Atomic Clock. Which, thanks to Ace's sortie, had been newly reset off of neighboring cities' Atomic Clocks.

Well, until it had started running *backward*!

Oh boy, and hadn't that gone and done it. Now rumor had it that Pa was running things manually.

As ever, Prof Truing was sequestered, nose-deep in his work, surrounded by Coggies. He'd reset the Atomic Clock again all right, and it was currently keeping proper time. But pa was a *person*. He was subject to physical limitations, like the need for food and sleep and—Mada stomped her foot! Forget his old age. Interminable or not, Pa was a living, breathing, *thinking* person, not an automated process. Or a magician.

"If I could only get in to see him!" She had haggled with the Prime Minister upon an emergency appointment, after using her status as Prof Truing's daughter to squeeze by the secretary. That, and after she had called in favors with two cabinet members who had sons in Gebriele's Arithmancy class. "I could help. I'm only his *heir apparent*."

Incorrigibly, the Prime Minister was in the midst of directing all citizens via the PA system to "cooperate for the good of the Planetary Continuum and the assurance of a smooth and painless operation." He turned to her, clutching his double button carbon microphone in both fists, and continued broadcasting, his every rebuttal to her every reasonable and sound argument blasted all over the city.

Fact of the matter, Mada was *not* an Interminable.

So. Even someone of Mada's stature couldn't get in to see her own father.

Oh, I do hope he hasn't given up a measure of immortality, she thought direly, slipping out of her quilted silk morning robe to dress for the day. What else was there to do? Already, the Guild runners had hassled her twice in her residence yesterday—once in the morning and then again in the afternoon—performing their scrupulous checks of every timepiece she owned.

"Cooperate," she retorted.

The doorbell chimed. Re-cinching her robe, Mada quested tentatively through the voice-tube by the front door: "Yes? Who's there?"

She peered out the peephole. Two uniformed city patrolmen and a Guild representative stood outside.

Her crest fell.

"Sergeants Baume and Mercier with Journeyman Longines from the Horology Guild," twanged the reply through the tube. She cranked down the volume. "Prof Truing, Miss, please unlock the door."

"Half a moment, I'm not presentable." Scowling, she murmured "horsefeathers" under her breath. There was hardly time to throw a pair of knickerbockers over her chemise. She didn't even bother plating her hair. Let the old boys be scandalized. Today she was feeling unusually Gebriele-like.

"All right. What can I help you with now? Oh—!" Without a moment's hesitation, the patrolmen and the Guild rep stormed into her tiny apartment with a squad of armed troopers.

"What's the meaning of this?" Mada backed up against a wall.

"We insist you come with us, Prof Truing, Miss," said the young patrolman with the name badge "Mercier."

"Why? Is it my father? What's happened?"

"No, ma'am." Looking solemn, Mercier managed to tip his bell-style cover at her respectably. Baume did the same—and blushed with embarrassment at her long, unbound tresses. A bit late for formalities, Mada thought, quite affronted. "My deepest apologies. I'm afraid we have to take you in for questioning."

"Questioning? Why, what for? My father is head of University, along with the upkeep of the Atomic Clock!"

"That's just the thing—" Baume started.

"Now see here, don't scare the girl!" A familiar voice at the back of the press cut through the hubbub.

"Oh, Ace!" Mada rushed to him. But she found that he couldn't hold her. "You're in handcuffs!"

"Prof Truing, Miss, your bedside digital was found to be several units behind after we reset it the day before," Guild Rep Longines informed her.

"I'm sorry, Mada," Ace confessed, jiggling his cuffs around so that he could stroke her hair awkwardly with a hand. "I'm suspect too. I came back with my chronometer a full 13 units ahead of the other pilots. Told my commanding officer you'd never agree to come in for questioning unless I was here with you. It'll be all right."

"As you can imagine, the City Guard still has jurisdiction in civil matters," inserted Guild Rep Longines. "At least for the time being. But they've agreed to take you both in together."

"The hero of Lagoon City has some sway, ma'am," added one of the troopers about Ace. "And how!" A look from his squad leader clamped him up quick.

Ace looked down at Mada. A lock of his wavy brown hair fell into his eyes without his helmet to keep it tight under cap. By now, his five-o'clock shadow looked more like a forty-eight-hour Brillo Pad, and his normally playful brown eyes were haggard and worn. "Will you come with me, Mada? I'm sure Prof Truing will be all right."

"Oh, I suppose," she replied, just to throw them all off the scent. The daughter of Prof Truing, worried, at a time like this? That would *not* help the situation. Pa might not be a hat for politics, but Mada was, and the last thing she needed was for Lagoon City to lapse into total shutdown, raise the seals and blast domes, and retreat under the water like a bunch of oysters, all because of something she said.

"But I hope they find out what's happened to the Atomic Clock soon, so we can go back to normal," she said. "This rumpus is really starting to wear, in my opinion. Really, Lagoon City's acting like an off-key orchestra." She batted a hand, nonchalant. "Like a room full of unsynchronized cuckoo clocks!"

With one last accusing glare at her bedside digital, Mada stepped out onto her apartment's landing and secured the door behind them. Flanked by the military personnel, the patrolmen proceeded to escort her and Ace into Central City, through the suburbs of South End City, all the way to the Department of the City Guard.

On the way, Mada observed members of The Order of the Worshipful Clockmaker, likewise, being rounded up.

"Oh, Ace," she said, "what have they done?"

"The Guilds think they've been tampering with the Atomic Clock." He leaned in to her, indicating Longines.

"Tampering!"

"Shhh."

"I know they've always been sympathetic to the TDC," Mada whispered, "but they're perfectly harmless. Oh, I hope Gebriele isn't with them."

"Hello, you two. Out for a stroll?" Gebriele joined them with her detainers in short order, as the patrolmen whisked their questionables across Hour Glass Pavilion, a posh, whitewashed manse on Platform Fourteen and Seven-Eighths.

In the adjacent canal, a gondola rowed past, filled with several city roundsmen and two Worshipfuls preaching the end of time to the pedestrians along the bridges and boardwalks.

"Boy did we get the bum's rush today. Right out of our meeting!" Gebriele said. "Figures. Today's a nine day, anyhow: clearing spaces for new beginnings. But they won't easily get inside my head, or yours, Mada. We're impenetrable, contemplative, mysterious Sevens!" She looked slyly out of the corner of her eye at one of the troopers escorting them. He missed his step, and with a curse, the fellow behind him tromped on his boot.

Gebriele winked at Mada.

"Say, you finish that dissertation of yours yet? As you can clearly see, we're on the lam." She smiled winningly at Baume. "So I hope you're mind's free and clear for all the fun we're about to have downtown."

"Not exactly," Mada confessed, in a right state by all the submarines she could now see surfacing outside the lagoon in the distance. By the way they were diving, they looked to be maneuvering into defensive positions along the mainland.

Overhead, a squadron of biplanes escorted a flight of bombers out to sea, followed by a sound wave that rocked the floating clockwork islands of the city.

Shielding her face from the windblast, Gebriele leaned in close to Ace. "She's been losing herself in her work. That's why she's *such* a killjoy."

"No, I've been trying to solve the riddle of Complex Design!" Skirting another blue clot of Worshipfuls headed in the same direction, Mada retorted, "The whole premise involves the idea of a watch that washes up on the beach of a deserted island—"

"Here we go." Gebriele winked.

Mada barreled right over her: "No one knows where the watch came from or who made it, if indeed 'someone' did make it, as it appears to be 'made.' After all, an object like a watch is so intricate in design that it *must* be proof of a designer, right? Not necessarily. Setting aside the fact that the function of anything 'made' is to improve upon the capabilities of its maker, the riddle still lies in the fact that the watch—which is a 'created' object—can ironically keep longer and more accurate time than its human 'creator' can."

"Prof Truing's an Interminable, Mada," Ace pointed out.

"What does that matter?"

"Well, he can live forever, can't he? And you're his daughter."

They hurried past a large broken-out clock face and a temporary fallout shelter constructed of spare clockwork components, newly assembled.

Thinking ponderously, Mada rebutted, "At best, the Interminables only represent borrowed time, Ace. No one knows where *they* came from, either, or who they really are, including the Interminables themselves."

Even in handcuffs, Ace managed to help her around a puddle of saltwater.

"Gee wiz, it sounds to me like you're questioning your own existence," he said.

"No, my dissertation proves that there *is no* Intelligent Designer! That everything truly does happen by random chance."

But Ace had caused Mada to stop—literally, right there, on the Isle of Circuits, with its gazebo and whitewashed wooden parquetry made to resemble a motherboard. She'd never thought about the problem quite like that before—on a *personal* level. That Ace. Inserting a new variable into her equation.

Maybe it took an outside observer to spot it.

In the most secluded recesses of her being, Mada heard the real reason for her dedicated quest chime like a Grandfather Clock: If she could prove that there was no Intelligent Designer, then it would make her feel much better about everything she didn't know about her Pa. Which would make her feel much better about what she didn't know about *herself*.

"Ho ho!" Mercier made to prod Ace along with his nightstick, but stopped short and came promptly to attention. He popped a spring-loaded salute at the bespectacled Chief of the City Guard, who was strolling across the bridge before them, twirling his beaver's-head cane.

"What is this?" Hot Fudge Sundae's round lenses glinted like a violent oil slick in the sunlight. He thumped his cane on the wood.

Out of respect for the oriental Interminable, the troopers came to attention.

"The hero of Lagoon City? In handcuffs?" Sundae's accented high-pitched tenor voice brokered no room for dispute.

Steepling his fingers, Guild Rep Longines approached the Chief of the City Guard. A bold move, in view of the fact that everyone knew how Hot Fudge Sundae was also a master aikido martial artist.

"They're being audited, Sundae," defended Longines. "No long-term damage. As you can clearly see from the citywide emergency, there are questions that need answering about the Atomic Clock. These citizens are suspect."

Overhead, a red tockgull called and dove for a fish. Inside the artificial lull between looped PA announcements, the quiet lapping of the water against the support columns of the island platform momentarily drowned out the blanket murmur of city life elsewhere.

"Is this how you treat the daughter of our own Prof Truing, and Lagoon City's Top Gun from the Time Dilation War?" asked Hot Fudge Sundae. "Release them."

"I'm afraid I can't do that, sir." Longines grimaced. Although the Lagoon City Guilds had martial authority in matters of time, the city patrolmen were already hands-off the prisoners. At best, the troopers looked uncomfortable. "Despite their elevated statuses, they're under suspicion for tampering with time. We're taking them in precisely *because* of who they are in lieu of certain evidences which have recently come to light. The Guilds need to be sure they're not TDC spies."

"Spies!" Gebriele was indignant. "You can't be serious!"

"I say," Ace replied.

"Oh, this is so ridiculous." Mada pinched the bridge of her nose. The Guild Rep might have told them the ocean had just turned to orange pop.

Hot Fudge Sundae cocked his head at Longines, leaned both hands on his cane. "As you must be aware, my son was one of the original astronauts aboard the *Time Runner*, later killed in the war? So I have personally been witness to time dilation." He turned his head toward Ace and Mada, his lenses glinting into the ultraviolet spectrum. "I have a good notion about what is going on with the Atomic Clock."

"Oh really, and what might that be?"

"Release them." Hot Fudge Sundae waggled his cane at Longines. "I'll give you a measure of immortality. Release them. And I'll throw in a barrel of hot buttered mead for the exchange."

Longines gave him a lengthy stare. "Are you—" he squinted "—bribing me, sir?"

Slowly, unnervingly, Hot Fudge Sundae grinned. "Not at all."

"But—"

"It doesn't work that way, my friend. I am the hour hand, not the chime. It's not my place to give the answer." The Chief of the City Guard turned to Mada. "This 'riddle' is not mine to solve. But I can assure you, the TDC have nothing to do with this." He tisk-tisked. "Why are you all thinking so logically? None of these heroes are spies. And neither am I. Why else would I offer you a measure of Immortality as collateral for my honest observation?"

"You mustn't!" Mada surged toward Hot Fudge Sundae. Gebriele grabbed her skirts. "You only have one-and-three-fourths measures of immortality left! Why, with only three-fourths, you'd be so old as to lose your mobility. And if you lost all your measures, you'd turn to dust!"

The Chief of the City Guard merely held up his free hand.

"Why indeed?" A dubious expression spread across Guild Rep Longines's countenance. He stroked his chin with two fingers. "A measure of immortality *would* gain the city enough power to function off-

line for about two days without the generators, in an attack."

"No!" Mada repeated.

"That's a pretty hefty fine," Ace inserted with a belligerence that shocked Mada. He made to muscle his way past the patrolmen and step protectively in front of the Chief of the City Guard, but one of the troopers pulled him back.

Ace yanked his elbow out of the other's grip. "A measure of immortality isn't worth a little time behind the eight ball." He gestured with his chin in Hot Fudge Sundae's direction. "We'll take the questioning. Gladly."

"Ace, don't let him do it," Gebriele insisted, pulling on the sleeve of her brother's uniform.

Casual as you please, Hot Fudge Sundae threw up his beaver's-head cane and caught it one-handed. In long, deliberate strides, he circled the detainees, nodding almost imperceptibly at Mada.

"Each person has their own internal clock. Each person runs on time, just like the city does. And in turn, so does all of industry."

Turning back to Longines, he tripped him up a bit with his cane.

Longines shrieked and the troopers exchanged glances, trying not to laugh.

"I am an Interminable," said Sundae. "If you will not take my immortality, then take my word for it that the Atomic Clock and all of the city and its inhabitants will go back to normal by tomorrow."

"Riddles, Sundae, that's all you have to offer?" Brushing himself off, Longines realized with a start where loyalties lay. He backpedaled away from the aikido master as if the other might do something tricky.

Hot Fudge Sundae held out his free hand, palm up. He financed Longines with a wiggle of his brows. "At least take my mead."

"Sundae, you're going too far! How can we know that the Atomic Clock hasn't been sabotaged?" He pointed at Ace. "Be serious. How can we know they aren't spies?"

Sundae merely touched the lip of his top hat. "I am serious. And very observant."

It was true.

Mada's eyes popped wide open.

Oh, it *was* true!

The Chief of the City Guard was always present at the Atomic Clock around the time that she and Ace met up for the mail!

"Ace." Mada grabbed his wrist. "You told me that the chronometer in your biplane sped up by 13 units during your mission, right? That's why the Guilds want you for questioning?"

"That's right."

"Indeed," inserted Longines huffily.

"Have you ever noticed time speeding up around you before?"

Ace ran a hand through his hair. "As a matter of fact, I have," he said. "Just thought my clocks were all jiggered. Though, I've never been in the cockpit so long as to notice my chronometer going haywire before. Never made the connection."

"Oh!" Mada was close to bursting. "Ace! Don't you see?" She turned to Longines. "We *did* cause all this chaos! It *is* our fault that the Atomic Clock sped up by one micro-unit!" Anxiously she added, "Indirectly, at least."

Then she said, "It's our *Bodies Electric*!"

Subtle intrigue overwrote Longines's scowl while he eyed the troopers. "How do you mean?"

Behind them, the squad leader's talkie beeped and sputtered.

Mada explained. "Lately, I've been noticing that clocks tend to slow down around me if I'm in physical proximity to them for long enough. My wristwatch, for example, and my bedside digital. I could never figure it out. Even after Pa resets them, eventually they all start running slower and slower." She turned to Ace. "But if the opposite has been happening for Ace…"

"You forgot to meet me under the Atomic Clock at our usual time to collect the mail," Ace filled in the blank.

"You two!" Gebriele ribbed her baby brother. "You've been meeting under that old Grandfather for a solid year. Come rain or shine."

"The Atomic Clock sped up by one micro-unit on the day I went to replace my time pieces and missed Ace at our usual time!" Mada elaborated excitedly.

"Roger that. It *was* the first time you ditched me since I've been delivering the mail in person to Prof Truing." Ace cocked his head at her.

"So then, if I slow down time, and you speed it up, when we meet…" Mada mirrored him with a head-cock of her own.

"Time stands still." Tipping his top hat at them, Hot Fudge Sundae strolled away, whistling and twirling his cane.

After he disappeared beyond the curve of the bridge, Mada heard him giggle to himself: "I'm so fast, they never saw me coming, never saw me leave!"

More giggling.

For a Guild representative, Mada rather thought Longines looked confused.

"So let me get this straight," he said eventually. "When you didn't meet the airmail pilot in person to collect the mail, that's when you believe the Atomic Clock sped up? Because you left him standing there, alone, speeding up time?"

"That's right." Mada smiled into the face of Lagoon City's own Top Gun. "The Guild masters, I think, will be relieved to know. We didn't mean to cause trouble. I'll personally petition the Prime Minister for a pardon."

Staunchly, she took a deep breath. "And I take full responsibility for this debacle. In fact, on behalf of the Head of University, from here on out, I assume full responsibility for the timely upkeep of the Atomic Clock."

"Well, I suppose," said Longines doubtfully, "if you'll come in willingly and fill out a report…"

But the troopers had already shouldered their rifles.

Ace winked at Mada. They'd been with him the whole time!

"Hold it!" Gebriele butted in, looking at her wristwatch, one finger held aloft. "Wait for it…it's 11:11 right now! Eleven is a master number. The universe is open. Anything you say right this minute means 'yes.' Well? How 'bout it?"

"Hot dog." Ace offered his manacled wrists to the rep. "How 'bout we start by removing these bracelets."

✿

One week later, as predicted by a quiet little aikido master with a sweet tooth and a penchant for sleuth work, the military had officially enacted a stand-down and evaporated back under the water, back to the mainland, back underground and inside the hills surrounding the lagoon. The University, government offices, and institutions had reopened. Business had returned to the usual mill of tradecraft by land and sea. Quiet organizations had gone back to meeting in the squares and underneath the gazeboes. Pedestrians went on their way to and fro.

Best of all? The PA system had stopped broadcasting.

"Well," Mada stood debating with Ace under the Atomic Clock at precisely twelve-noon, "if you and I have been the unwitting elements of change in the quantum mechanics of the upkeep of the Atomic Clock, due to our Bodies Electric, and, if Prof Truing, my Pa, represents the Atomic Clock itself, then what represents this all powerful 'Designer,' hum?"

This afternoon Mada had brought the baby palm with her to collect the mail, in hopes that Ace might have a solution to its growth problem. Although, she was terrified that she already knew the answer.

"Just look at what happened!" she exclaimed. "The entire city went into lockdown. We almost started a *new war*, based entirely on the *random chance* that you and I happened to miss a single meeting under the Atomic Clock!"

"I dunno, Mada," Ace replied, trading her the mail cylinder for a look at the baby palm in its new oriental blue pot. "Seems to me that the real irony here is that it takes a whole bunch more 'faith' to believe that the perfect order of the universe came about by random chance, than to believe a Designer orchestrated it all. Maybe we were both meant to off-balance things a bit."

He held up the plant for inspection, and for a moment (or maybe it was Mada's imagination playing tricks on her), it didn't appear so stunted.

"We probably woulda never figured out what's up with the baby palm, anyway," he said, setting it on the Roman Numeral IV in the Atomic Clock's face. "That's ironic too, don't you think?"

For a moment, Mada wondered if he was right. She wondered if the baby palm could live forever if she and Ace did start going steady.

"At any rate," she countered, "don't you think—"

But Ace swept her into an embrace, and as an antidote to her astonishment, he said, "Just save the argument already and kiss me, baby."

And they did, under the Atomic Clock, for the first time.

Copyright © 2021 by M. O. Muriel.

Nonsense and Other Comments:

This short story was inspired by the debate between Christian apologist William Paley in his exposition of the teleological argument for the existence of God in his work, *Natural Theology,* and evolutionary biologist Richard Dawkins's rebuttal argument for the theory of evolution by means of natural selection, in his book, *The Blind Watchmaker.*

"A Matter of Time" is also my 24-Hour Story from the Writers of the Future Contest workshop held in Hollywood, California. In this notorious writer's exercise, the twelve contest winners are provided a random object from the instructors, taken to the local library to pick a book, and are tasked with interviewing strangers on Hollywood Boulevard to glean their personal-life's tales. This strategy of using random elements is meant to inspire a short story, which must then be written within 24-hours. By pure coincidence or fate, my random object turned out to be a palm tree drink straw, my book (selected with my eyes closed, I tell no lie) *The Blind Watchmaker,* and my random stranger a Rambo Impersonator at a Wax Museum. As it happens, Mr. Rambo Impersonator at the Wax Museum is a Buddhist Monk from Argentina with this whole tragic love story. Fortunately, "A Matter of Time" doesn't actually feature Rambo. Or Buddhist monks. As for the *steampunk love story* he inspired, involving a university professor and a 1920s-inspired biplane pilot, set in a clockwork lagoon—an idea that morphed out of my very real and existing "intelligent designer" brain messing around with these random objects to compose a nicely ordered story out of chaos—I completely blame that on the Wax Museum.

Mike Resnick, along with editing the first seven years of Galaxy's Edge *magazine, was the winner of five Hugos from a record thirty-seven nominations and was, according to* Locus, *the all-time leading award winner, living or dead, for short fiction. He was the author of over eighty novels, around 300 stories, three screenplays, and the editor of over forty anthologies. He was Guest of Honor at the 2012 Worldcon.*

THE DOCTOR AND THE SPECTRE

A Doc Holliday story

by Mike Resnick

The date was November 8, 1887.

Doc Holliday lay on his deathbed in the Hotel Glenwood in Glenwood Springs, Colorado, struggling to breathe. Suddenly, he opened his eyes, and the hint of a smile crossed his lips.

"This is funny," he said, and died.

According to most of his biographers, including Ben T. Traywick, Gary L. Roberts, Sylvia D. Lynch, and E. Richard Churchill, those were the last words ever spoken by the notorious gunman, and there is no reason to doubt them.

But would you like to know *what* the dying gunfighter thought was funny?

✿

April 23, 1887. It was almost midnight. Kate Elder was down in the hotel's bar having a drink, while Doc, his body wracked by tuberculosis, lay on their bed, trying unsuccessfully to get some sleep.

Suddenly, he heard the door open, but the footsteps were too heavy to be Kate's. He reached carefully for his holster, slid his gun out, and swung his feet to the floor.

"Hold it right there!" he growled.

"Oh, damn!" said a masculine voice. "You're not her."

Holiday pulled a match out of his pocket with his free hand, struck it against the rough surface of the bed table, and lit the lamp that resided there.

And stared.

And frowned.

"Who the hell are you?" he demanded. "In fact, *what* the hell are you?"

"Isn't it obvious?" came the reply.

"Not to me," said Holliday, staring at the tall white skeleton wrapped in a black robe and carrying a wicked-looking scythe.

"I am the Spectre of Death."

"You took long enough getting here." Holliday showed little surprise. "I've been waiting years for you. Okay, how do we go about it?"

"You misunderstand," said the Spectre. "I've made a clumsy mistake."

"What the hell are you talking about?"

"You're the famous Doc Holliday," said the Spectre. "I was sure you'd be downstairs gambling." He paused, finding his words. "I have come for Kate Elder."

"Don't be silly!" snapped Holliday. "I'm a lunger who's been dying for years, and she's in perfect health."

"Nonetheless, it is she that I've come for."

"You leave her alone!" growled Holliday.

"Why?" asked the Spectre curiously. "Surely you're not going to argue that you love her. Hell, you're Doc Holliday—you've never loved anything but your gun and your cards."

"I've always had a woman," replied Holliday.

"*Had,* not *loved,*" said the Spectre. "And especially not this one."

"She takes care of me," Holliday replied, uncomfortable about even mouthing the word "love."

"Well, I'm sure you can find someone else," said the Spectre, turning toward the door. "I'll go downstairs and claim her now."

"Don't do anything foolish," warned Holliday.

"I'm just doing my job." Spectre spoke with no show of anger or malice.

"And I'm just doing mine!" Holliday aimed his pistol at the hand that held the scythe and pulled the trigger.

"Now look what you've done!" Spectre held up his hand for Holliday to see that his third and fourth skeletal fingers were completely shattered.

"Didn't seem to hurt you," noted Holliday.

"Of course not!" growled the Spectre. "But the force of the bullet, coupled with my missing fingers, knocked my scythe clear out the window."

"So pick it up on your way back to wherever the hell you came from," said Holliday sardonically. "Which had better be soon."

The Spectre shook his head rapidly. "You don't understand. If someone touches the scythe—"

Before he could finish the sentence, a horrible scream rose from the wooden sidewalk below Holliday's second-floor window.

"That was *your* fault, John Henry Holliday!" the Spectre pointed at him accusingly with his good hand. "I've got to retrieve my Scythe of Death before anyone else can lay a hand on it or trip over it in the darkness. Even the slightest contact with it is fatal."

Holliday indicated the gun still directed at the Spectre. "Our business isn't finished yet."

"This encounter was just an accident," said the Spectre. "I have no business with you."

"Yes, you do."

The Spectre frowned. "What are your suggesting?"

"Take me instead of Kate."

"Why should I? You're dying anyway."

Holliday got to his feet, walked over to the Spectre, and pointed the gun at his head. "But not necessarily alone," he said.

The skeleton stayed silent as he contemplated Doc's proposal. "You for Kate Elder?" he said at last.

Holliday nodded.

"All right." The Spectre gave Doc a resigned sigh. "It's a deal."

"Okay," said Holliday. "Give me a minute to get dressed and we can go."

The Spectre shook his head. "Not yet."

Holliday frowned. "Why not?"

"You have one more man to kill yet."

"Who?"

"I am forbidden to tell you," said the Spectre. "But you'll know him when you see him."

"And then you'll come for me?"

"As soon as I can work you into my schedule."

"It's a deal," said Holliday. The Spectre began extending its hand to cement their agreement with a handshake, noticed his shattered fingers, turned, and walked out the door.

✧

Weeks passed. Then months. November 8 arrived, and Holliday lay on his bed, from which he had not risen for almost two full days.

Kate Elder sat in a corner of the room, reading a book and waiting for the inevitable. Finally, she stood up, walked to a bucket of water, rinsed out a cool compress, and laid it across Holliday's forehead.

"It's too soon," he rasped.

"What?" she said, straining to hear him.

"I've still got to kill someone."

She sighed and shook her head sadly. "Delirious," she muttered, and walked back to her chair.

Holliday thought back on all the men he'd killed—Frank McLaury, Tom McLaury, Mike Gordon, Frank Stillwell, Jim Austin, Ed Bailey, Kid Colton, the ones with no names or faces that he could bring to his fevered mind—and decided that he'd more than held his end of the deal. But he sure as hell couldn't see how he was going to kill one more man before the Spectre came back for him.

He thought he heard a sound near the door, and tried to prop himself up on an elbow to see if it was the Spectre with a new game plan, or perhaps the man he was suppose to kill—but his strength, what little remained of it, failed him and he collapsed back onto the bed.

"Is something wrong, Doc?" asked Kate solicitously.

"No," he rasped hoarsely.

"Can I get you anything?" she continued. "Anything at all?"

He stared at her, the woman who, on different occasions, had broken him out of jail, sworn out an arrest warrant against him, supplied him with guns, and even backed him up in a fight.

"Just keep on being my Kate," he whispered.

She was about to answer him, realized that she didn't know quite how to reply to that, and settled for smiling. Nodding her assent, she went back to reading her book.

Holliday closed his eyes again, and thought back across the tapestry of his life. What would have been the odds, he wondered, when he was twenty years old and a serious dental student, that over the next decade and a half he'd be wanted for murder in four different states, or that he and the Earp brothers would take on their enemies in the single most famous gunfight in history—or that he'd wind up at age 36, unable to stand on his own power, in a bed in the middle of Colorado, which wasn't even on a lot of maps when he was a kid?

Or, he added mentally, *that I'd be lying in a hotel bed in a room with one of the more notorious women in the West, wishing that my number was up and scared that it isn't?*

Kate got to her feet and walked to the door, where she paused and turned to Holliday.

"I'll be right back," she told him, holding up an empty flask. "I'm just going down to the bar to fill this up."

"Go." Holliday mouthed the word, but nothing came out.

He closed his eyes again, then opened them a couple of minutes later when he heard footsteps walking across the floor.

"Back already?" he tried to say, but again, no words emerged.

"Good afternoon, Doc," said a masculine voice that seemed vaguely familiar. "It's been awhile."

Holliday made a supreme effort and opened his eyes. Standing at the foot of the bed was the Spectre of Death.

You're early, thought Holliday.

Actually, I'm a few days late, answered the Spectre. *I hope you haven't been in too much pain.*

I can't feel much of anything, including pain, replied Holliday.

Be grateful for small favors, said the Spectre.

I haven't killed anyone since last we met, Holliday admitted.

I know, answered the Spectre. *It was determined by the Celestial Record Keeper that you'd never be strong enough to do so. Anyway, the paperwork's all done, the permissions have all been granted, and I'm here to take you now.*

Good, said Holliday. *I've been ready for weeks. Months, even.*

You see? said the Spectre, his lipless, fleshless face contorted in a nightmare version of a smile. *Not everyone has a reason to fear me.*

I've never feared much of anything, Holliday confessed.

Just then the door opened and Kate re-entered. She walked over to the bed, laid a hand on Holliday's forehead, then went to her chair, sat down, picked up her book, and started reading.

Son of a bitch! thought Holliday. *She can't see you.*

Certainly not, answered the Spectre. *She belongs to this world.*

But I can see you.

You're more than halfway inside my domain already, explained the Spectre.

The hell I am, said Holliday. *I'm laying in a bed in a godforsaken little town in Colorado.*

Only the unimportant parts of you, said the Spectre.

Okay, said Holliday. *Let's get this show on the road.*

That's what I'm here for, said the Spectre.

Quick question, said Holliday. *Do they play poker where I'm going?*

Beats the hell out of me, answered the Spectre.

Holliday frowned. *What are you talking about?*

I'm just your guide between worlds, said the Spectre. *I live in the in-betweens.*

Some guide! snorted Holliday.

Some dentist! shot back the Spectre.

I was a damned good dentist! said Holliday angrily. *I lost my clients because I kept coughing and bleeding on 'em, not because I couldn't fix 'em.*

I know, answered the Spectre gently. *And now, are you prepared for the voyage to that Other Place?*

I've been ready a long, long time, said Holliday.

Then let's go!

Holliday tried to sit up and swing his legs over to the floor. The movement was barely discernible.

I can't do it, he announced.

I'll give you a hand, said the Spectre, reaching out for him.

Holliday looked at the Spectre's hand, missing most of its third and fourth fingers from when he had shot it in April.

Ain't you healed yet? he asked.

Not a problem, answered the Spectre. *I don't feel pain. You know that.*

He tried without much success to grab Holliday's arm and help him up to a sitting position.

Maybe you don't feel pain, said Holliday, *but you don't grip too well neither. Better use your other hand.*

I can't, said the Spectre.

Why the hell not?

The Spectre held up his other hand. It was missing the thumb, the forefinger, and had a large ugly hole in the palm.

What happened? asked Holliday.

It seems that unlike you, John Wesley Harden had no interest or desire to come with me.

Yeah, that sounds like John Wesley, agreed Holliday. He paused for a moment. *So what do we do now?*

I'll think of something, said the Spectre. *After all, it's my job. I've messed up the Holliday file enough as it is, trading you for the lady in the corner, then making a deal you couldn't keep. I'm not about to screw it up a third time.*

So like I said: What do we do now?

We sit here and wait. Something will come to me.

Holliday opened his eyes for the last time. He looked briefly at his less-than-elegant surroundings and at the woman reading in the corner, the woman who defied every assumption the world had made of her. Then Doc turned his gaze to the skeletal creature standing at the foot of the bed, awkwardly holding its Scythe in the shattered fingers of one hand, frowning as it concentrated on the seemingly insoluble problem confronting it.

A hint of a smile crossed Holliday's dry, cracked lips.

"This is funny," he whispered aloud, and died.

The date was November 8, 1887. Kate Elder lived until November 2, 1940.

Copyright © 2019 by Mike Resnick.

Andrew Dykstal lives in Arlington, Virginia, where he writes across all manner of speculative genres. In 2003, long before the associated meme, he took an arrow to the knee, which was about as much fun as it sounds. His fiction has appeared in Daily Science Fiction *and* Beneath Ceaseless Skies, *and his novelette "Thanatos Drive" won the 35th Writers of the Future contest. Find him online at andrewdykstal.com or follow him on Twitter at @Adykstal.*

A CLEAN AND LIQUID MADNESS

by Andrew Dykstal

Eli Fuller—he thought of himself as Eli Fuller even in his dreams now—leaned on the schooner's rail and tried not to worry about everything at once. He'd spent the last five years learning the language, accent, habits, and general knowledge needed to pass for a subject of the Caeline Empire. Now, about to set foot in that empire's busiest port, all he could imagine were the thousand ways he could fail. As his ship eased into its moorings and launches set out across the harbor to meet it, random bits of training and trivia kept leaping to mind:

The Caeline don't grasp the forearm to shake hands, just the palm—

Eli Fuller is from the north country, which means ignorance is less likely to be noticed than perspicacity, so don't be too clever—

Hesitation has been the bane of more ventures than treachery, bad luck, and incompetence combined—

It had been an excellent education, albeit one he'd never wanted. Five years previous, he'd tried to pickpocket the wrong man and found himself awaiting the gallows. He'd been twelve years old, an orphan, and desperate. His age, coupled with the diverse and alarming contents of his pockets, had eventually steered his course away from the noose. The authorities had given him a choice between the naval and clandestine services. Moved by an old and unholy fear of drowning, he'd found himself in the foreign intelligence service of the Gilded Ascendency.

Where, for the last six months, he'd been learning how to build ships in bottles.

The wind changed, and the reek of the city poured over the harbor. Crofthold was the largest port city in the Caeline Empire, and its capital in all but name. To Eli, it was the very heart of the enemy. *A half-dozen fire ships and the right wind*, Eli thought, *and we'd lay this city to waste.*

But those ships would never reach the harbor. In a decade of war, Caeline had not suffered a single naval defeat. It had lost a bare handful of ships while exacting a grievous toll in lives and vessels from the Gilded Ascendency. Even against impossible odds, the Caeline Fleet emerged unscathed. It was magic, the rumors ran; it had to be magic. The Caelines were a strange people, possessed of all manner of rituals and habits. A few might be more than empty forms.

And even the Caelines seemed to find the Bottlers' Guild damned peculiar.

The first launch drew up alongside. Cheerful mockery passed between the harbormen and the bluewater sailors as lines were flung down and secured, followed by a rope ladder.

Eli was so preoccupied with not falling into the harbor as he boarded the launch that he forgot his other worries until he was ashore and walking briskly through the cobbled streets. He had three days to familiarize himself with the city and lay a trail that would withstand cursory inspection. Only then would he present himself to the Bottlers' Guild and find out whether the last five years had been a waste.

Depending upon which ledgers Eli's compatriots pilfered, the Bottlers' Guild operated under the auspices of the Department of the Navy, or the Imperial Astronomical Society, or the Friends of New Science, or the not-quite-governmental Listener Trading Company. Eli's superiors had speculated that it drew funds from all four and others besides, and why not? They all had maritime interests.

Because, as everyone knew, a ship in a sealed bottle is all but impossible to sink.

So for quite literally royal sums, the Bottlers' Guild bottled ships, and by these charms or tokens or fetishes, Caeline's merchant and naval fleets were made secure. The secret of the Bottlers' craft remained a mystery, but it was assumed to lie in the perfect correspondence of each model to the ship

it warded from harm, and perhaps in the subtle incorporation of a bit of real ship into the model itself. "Likeness and contagion," the usual line went. "Alchemy, philosophy, and magic all come down to likeness and contagion."

Wary of pat answers, Eli neither accepted nor rejected the usual line. Still, he'd thrown himself wholly into his own masterwork: a replica of the *I.M.S. Sparrowhawk* the length of his hand. The project had cost him six months of labor, and his fingertips had grown rough with a crosshatch of tiny cuts and chemical burns. Even now it remained incomplete; he carried his *Sparrowhawk* in a close-folded cradle of paper within a box, an empty bottle packed beside it. As the final proof of his skill before the guild masters, he would slide the ship through the bottle's mouth, then gently draw out the threads that would free the masts to spring up and the sails to unfurl.

But now, standing in line under autumn drizzle outside the Bottlers' Guild, he studied his fellow applicants for apprenticeship and considered the possibility that the whole enterprise—the stories of magic, the art of model making, the efforts spent training him until he could pass for a Caeline native—was perfect lunacy. The denizens of the queue were a miscellany of idlers, eccentrics, and obvious fanatics. Each clutched a parcel or openly carried a ship in a bottle. Most held them close, eyes darting suspiciously. Two dozen had come today alone, and by rumor the guild took only one or two new apprentices each year.

The woman in line ahead of him was bent with age over a wooden box large enough for a mantel clock. Her fingers were white with the strength of her grip. She gave Eli a frightened look and attempted to fold herself around her parcel.

"I'm here like you," he said hesitantly, shifting the paper-wrapped bottle and ship in his hands by way of demonstration.

"That's the problem," said the next man in line—a young man, scarcely older than Eli. "If we wanted different things, there'd be aught to worry over."

Eli found himself clutching his ship closer, and he resolved to hold his tongue for the rest of the wait.

The line crept forward. The applicant nearest the doors would be ushered in, a delay of four or five minutes would follow, and the applicant would leave, sometimes empty-handed, sometimes still bearing the masterwork that had proven their inadequacy. One emerged with his hands sheeted in blood, a long splinter still jutting from his palm where he'd crushed his model. Red droplets hung like a bead curtain below his hands. The blood was clinging to a fall of tattered rigging so fine it was invisible. Spider silk, perhaps, and even this had been found wanting.

For all the coolness of the autumn day, Eli began to sweat. His little *Sparrowhawk* suddenly seemed a clumsy, amateurish thing, all too plausibly the work of a rustic with dreams above his station.

"Why," he heard himself ask, "are we even trying?"

The hunched woman turned to face him, still clutching her parcel. "To save everything," she said softly, unsmiling. For the first time, her eyes met his, and he saw burning there a clean and liquid madness, clear as an alchemist's flame. Then she vanished into the guild, and though the line stretched on behind him, Eli was alone.

She did not return.

✿

Eli was received in a parlor floored in hardwood and decorated with rich rugs. A broad, dark stain shone wetly before a massive teak desk at the far end of the room. A tall woman stood behind the desk, quill pen in hand. She wore a complex contraption of lenses and mirrors over one eye, lending her face a lopsided, inhuman look only slightly softened by her mop of flyaway gray hair. A small glass amphora and a bottle of gin stood on one corner of the desk beside a half-empty tumbler.

"Sorry," she said, gesturing toward the tumbler. "It's been a long morning, aye? Last one went and tried to off herself when we didn't take her." She made a quick flicking motion over each wrist. "I think the doctors got to her quick enough, all things considered, but it's not the getting for somebody like her; it's the keeping. She has three sons in the Fleet and was dead sure they'd all be drowned in a year if we didn't take her on. It's out the back door into a padded room in Paxgate for that one."

Unsure what to make of this greeting, Eli bowed. "Eli Fuller, at your service."

"We'll see. My name is Evangeline Cowl. You don't have anything sharp on you, do you? Pen knife? Maybe I could lock it up in a drawer while we talk…?"

Instead of answering, he set his wrapped ship and bottle on the desk, went to remove the paper, and paused. The amphora was surely the attempted suicide's work, and it held a man o' war the size of an oak leaf. It was beautiful, its sails gently bowed but not taut, and he could make out miniature figures on her decks. Metal glinted in her gunports. She canted slightly as though caught mid-turn, and he could all but hear the creaking of her timbers as she came about to run full before the wind.

It was, beyond question, superior to his own ship. It also hadn't been enough to win acceptance to the Bottlers' Guild.

"It's the *I.N.S. Devastator*," Cowl said, following his gaze. "The Fleet loves its bombastic names, doesn't it? Odd to see it looking so small, like it's ready to conquer a bathtub."

"She's a storied ship," Eli said carefully. In truth, she was obsolete, her sail plan and oarsmen long since replaced by more efficient designs. But she was a survivor and had been a holy terror to the Gilded Ascendency: a slow-sailing juggernaut of a ship, and unaccountably unsinkable. Strange, then, that Cowl spoke as though she'd never seen it reduced to a model.

"Know your naval history, then?" she said. "I've never met a naval historian too young to shave." She doffed her complex eyepiece and studied him from a pair of cool gray eyes. "I see two kinds of applicants. Those afraid to lose someone, and those who already have. Who did you lose?"

"My father was in the merchant marine. He was on the *Sparrowhawk*. The Ascendancy sank her six years ago."

She gestured impatiently at his wrapped model. "Let's see it, then."

He hesitated, caught between his months of labor and a sudden, biting suspicion rooted in the perfect ship in the amphora and in the ruined lines worked in spider silk. Delicately, he held up his ship, unfolded the paper, and took a deep breath. Then he snapped the keel. "You don't care about the models," he said, laying aside the splintered mess that had been the *Sparrowhawk*. He felt like his heart was trying to claw its way up his throat, but he held his voice steady. "The lady before me—hers was better than mine. It's…beautiful. But it's not what you want."

"Hm," she said, face betraying nothing but mild interest. She prodded the broken ship. "Just how were you planning on getting that into the bottle? Hinged masts?"

"Yes, ma'am."

"We don't do that," she said. "We build the entire model inside the bottle." Another pause as she scratched at the miniature mainmast with a fingernail. "I'm right in thinking you're from the north country?"

He nodded. The accent had taken months to learn. Even now, he had to be cautious not to overemphasize it.

"Nothing but hard times to be had up there, from all I hear. So. Your father died at the hands of the Gilded Navy, you've come of age with no prospects, and here you are, knocking at a door you have to know won't open…tell me, why didn't you join the Fleet?"

It was a question he'd prepared for. A young man in his circumstances *not* joining the Fleet would be considered odd if not outright suspicious. His planned reply involved a passionate speech about how much more good he might do in the Bottlers' Guild than as a mere sailor. His mentors had shaped every word of it, calculating an appeal to the vanity that had to define an institution as vital as the guild.

Watching Cowl delicately crack open his *Sparrowhawk* to study the transverse frames, he knew with a sudden, dead certainty that she wouldn't believe a word of it. There was no lie that wouldn't make him pretentious, daft, or coldhearted. So he told the truth: "We had some hard times when I was young. I tried to steal a few scraps from a butcher, and he didn't take it kindly. There was a rainwater barrel behind his shop. He damn near drowned me in it." Memory tugged at him. Water like fire in his lungs. Darkness closing around the edges of his vision. The sucking desperation that twisted inside him even after the butcher had let him go. The sound of water spattering over the cobbles as he retched. "Ever since…I can't say I like the idea of life at sea. So I've found myself here instead."

"The fear of drowning," Cowl murmured. She selected a mast and snapped it in two, then carefully arranged the halves beside the rest of the wreck. "I know it well. Still, it was a rash choice, coming to the city with no letter of introduction or patron. Do you have enough in your purse to see you home again?"

It wasn't a dismissal. Not quite. "A purse that heavy would see me dead in an alley, ma'am. Besides, there's only so much you can do with one foot on the dock."

Cowl was silent for a long moment. Then she broke into a smile. "You're wrong, naturally. The models matter. They matter very much. We also must be unafraid to break things. You've created, at the last moment, a…plausible case for your suitability. We don't make ships in bottles, Master Fuller. We bottle shipwrecks." She extended a hand. "Welcome to the guild."

In his mind's eye, the *Devastator* lay keelbroke in ocean mud, her tattered sails stirring with the current while all around her dead men sank into the muck…and then the moment was gone, sealed away in a bottle, and she sailed again, unscathed. *We bottle shipwrecks.* His was a wild supposition, based on nothing more than a jarring phrase and an unrecognized model, but he knew with sudden certainty that he had the truth of it. The great question was how.

He stepped around the bloodied swath of carpet and accepted Cowl's hand.

In the following weeks, Eli unlearned almost all he'd taught himself of model making, losing himself in the tools and techniques of the guild. Every week brought a new instrument: fine, hinged saws manipulable through the mouth of a bottle; delicately curved applicators for adhesives; miniature scaffolds to support each wreck until faux sea floor could be poured in around it. The masters taught patterns of breakage and tested him over tomes describing every structural harm that might befall a ship.

He began, with slow care and under constant supervision, construction of his first shipwrecks. There were no other apprentices and few enough masters.

None of it smelled even faintly of magic, not until he found himself remembering old newspapers and tavern scuttlebutt detailing Caeline naval defeats. Conflicting pasts writhed in his head: the

Guilded Ascendency breaking the Caeline Fleet in a dozen different ways, a dozen subsequent negotiated peaces. His own past fluctuated with them: he might have remained a thief, or become a smith's apprentice, or died on the gallows. The memories were distorted, dreamlike, and slid away whenever he tried to bring one into focus.

Two months into his apprenticeship, word came that the *Devastator* had been sunk off the Gilded Port of Pillars. The masters laid aside all other work to model the wreck. Eli saw only the preparations for construction—sketches of a half-burned man o' war careened on the ocean floor; precise notes detailing interior damage and counts of which men had died under cannon fire and which had drowned; selections of wood, paper, and fine thread.

The morning came not long after when he woke to realize the *Devastator* had never sunk. Contradictory worlds hung inside him, delicately balanced. The moment of the *Devastator*'s destruction had been sealed away, but it lingered in his memory. A conviction broke over him that the moment was alive, horribly aware, like a parasite growing fat in the back of his mind.

He clung ever tighter to the invented history of Eli Fuller, which was fiction and therefore constant.

When he told Cowl that he could remember at least two different histories, she smiled, and a flicker of what might have been relief passed over her face. "Come," she said. "It's time to show you our collection."

As they descended into the deepest of the guild's basements, she spoke of ghostly memories of maritime disasters and naval defeats that had been but were no longer. "We're down in the flux of it," she said, touching one of the wall timbers. The floors were cold stone, and the corridor ended in a small, chapel-like room containing an elaborately carved trough of water. She steered him away from it and toward a heavy iron door. "They say that everything comes back from the sea. That is a lie. Nothing comes back from the sea, not wholly, nor unchanged. There are always shadows in the world, cast by the might-have-been. Some—not all—are in this room."

She unlocked the door and ushered him into the gallery of shipwrecks.

His first thought was of a wine cellar. The same endless racks of bottles, the same fixation on order, the same peculiar air of purposeful disuse. But as Cowl lit lanterns and hung them high, the resemblance faded. These bottles were of myriad shapes and sizes, and each radiated a faint unquiet. Little stirs of motion caught his eye, and he bent over a bottle holding a wrecked galley listing on a coral outcrop. The wreck rocked gently, and debris swirled freely within the bottle. Water, he realized. Each bottle was full of water.

"Seawater," Cowl said, unasked. "Ideally from near the site of the wreck. But seawater is seawater, more or less."

He stooped closer, peering at the bits of flotsam that shivered on the edge of neutral buoyancy. One or two seemed almost to be moving—

He jerked back. Bodies. Dozens lay strewn about the wreck. Others contorted in the clear water above it as though still struggling to swim.

"You…make sailors too?" he asked.

"In a way. Master Gault says you've been making progress on the wreck of the *I.M.S. Left of Fortune*."

"It's taking a while," Eli said, still staring into the bottle. "Nobody will tell me what the wreck is supposed to look like, and seeing as she went down four months ago…."

"*It*," Cowl said patiently. "Ships are not people."

"It, then. But I don't know how I'm supposed to make a perfect model if I can't even see what I'm copying."

"Fair point. You'll have to be shown." She did not elaborate. She handed him the key to the door and left him alone in the room of shipwrecks, where he lingered for hours, watching men the size of ants caught forever on the cusp of drowning.

✿

Eli's one connection to home was a man he'd never met. With a chalk *x* on a specific brick wall, he signaled the need for a meeting. It was premature—he still didn't know how the Bottlers' Guild altered past events—but he had access to a room full of divergent histories and no notion of what to do with it. A single question ate into his sleep and bent his attention: *What happens if I break a bottle?*

Sitting in a tavern and waiting for his contact, he could imagine only that the world would change.

The possibility hovered before him like an exotic, dangerous insect. Would he find himself rewriting great swaths of history? Erasing the grounds for his own mission?

His contact, identified by the wilting flower in his buttonhole and a hat five years out of style, slid into the chair opposite him. He was middle aged, bland faced, and spoke with an accountant's air of bone-dry, absolute focus. When he said his name was Tom, he did not trouble with sincerity.

"I know what they do," Eli said. "Just not how they do it." He outlined what he'd seen and inferred, keeping his tone conversational. Whispers would draw attention.

Tom listened intently, then grimaced. "Time is running short. Have you been reading the papers? The Caeline Fleet has taken to shelling the ports of Lore and the Pillars. The shore batteries have been useless."

"Not useless," Eli said softly. "They sank the *Devastator*."

Tom ignored him. "If we lose those ports, we've lost the war. Find the secret. Relay it to me. Follow your escape plan. We have a few months—perhaps less—to complete our own program."

Eli pictured a room of Gilded Navy shipwrecks, each surrounded by the dead and dying. "We can't *use* it," he said. "Don't you see? They're all still drowning. Hundreds of them—thousands—"

A weary look answered him. "Immaterial. None of it would be *real*."

"There's another option. I could destroy their shipwreck collection. I could make a bomb, or just spend about ten minutes in there with a hammer—"

"No," Tom said flatly. "Our aim is to end this war, not eradicate decades of history. If we can emulate the Bottlers' Guild, we can force a stalemate. Don't contact me again until you have their method. Then, and only then, will we revisit the question of whether to change any recent events through our Crofthold operations."

Only recent events? Eli thought. Then: *Of course. The current leadership exists because of attrition, because their predecessors are all dead or disgraced. They can't undo the whole war without losing their stations.*

He didn't know whether to laugh, cry, or defect. So he acknowledged his orders and left, wishing that he could disappear wholly into Eli Fuller, who never would have gone willingly to the Bottlers' Guild, and whose pains and choices were nothing more or less than real.

Stalemate. The word echoed as he set out into the night streets of Crofthold, evoking a vision of two endlessly expanding storehouses of shipwrecks and bottled suffering. It was madness, and his feet led him not back to the guild but to Paxgate. The asylum was alive with noises: nonsense noises, cries, perfectly cogent pleas that everyone else just *be quiet*.

His meagre purse bought him a name and access to the half-lit cell where Mrs. Lena Rogers drowsed in a laudanum haze. The cuts on her wrists were scarring up beautifully. When her gaze slid across him, he judged her madness undiminished. It was merely hidden, a monstrosity veiled, for now, in a sea of fog.

"How did you know?" he asked. "How did you know you had to save your sons?"

She smiled vaguely. "I saw," she mumbled. "I saw it all so clear…their ship on fire…a long fall into the dark…."

He believed her. And yet the guild had rejected her. He could guess why: had she known the truth, she never would have bottled her sons' ship, not even to see them again in the changed timeline. "Goodmother Rogers," he said softly, addressing her in the Gilded style, "I am so very sorry."

Her face was a lamp in the semidarkness. "There's nothing worse than drowning. There was a lagoon, and when I was a girl…."

"It was a damned barrel for me," he heard himself murmur. "You're right. There's nothing worse than drowning." He kissed her hands. "Whatever it costs, I'll see that your sons suffer it no more than once."

✧

That night, he dreamed as Eli Fuller. He saw the *Sparrowhawk* and his invented father and mother embracing by the gangplank. The smells of brine and animal pens and hot tar filled the air. Blue skies overhead, and tears, and prayers for safe return. The small part of him still anchored in the waking world wondered if this was how Lena Rogers dreamed: a tangle of possible pasts and futures, all shaped by a handful of craftsmen with their clever little tools and damned bottles. No wonder she'd gone mad.

He woke when the masters seized him and dragged him from his bed.

The assault was swift, precise, scientific. By the time his body remembered how to move, he'd been bound. The sensations were disconnected, surreal, moving through his mind and body without reference to one another. A glint of Cowl's gray eyes, now the color of old ice. The warm smell of Master Gault's pipe tobacco. Pressure on his arms and legs. Rapid, irregular motion. The ceiling of a descending stair.

"…knew you for one of us," Cowl was saying, "knew that you belonged to the kinship of death by water. There's a god of drowning, Eli." Her hand brushed his cheek. "There's *something* down there, anyway. An awareness, an intelligence living at the edges: the lines between sea and land, life and death, the possible and the real. By it, we remake the world. All it requires is sacrifice."

An open trough of water, ornate, carved surfaces shining wetly. They were in the basement. *It's like an altar shagged a bathtub*, he thought. The mad urge to laugh subsided when they bore him down and forced his head underwater.

Time fled. Pain and heat in his chest. Salt in his mouth.

Then he was walking the ocean floor, seeing without light. A figurehead loomed before him: the stylized, wolf-mouthed woman of the *I.M.S. Left of Fortune*. Her hull was intact but she'd been dismasted. High above, men writhed slowly, easing toward the relaxation of death. Higher still, a storm beat the sea into white froth. Alien pleasure quivered inside him, mingling hunger and satiation.

A heavy blow to his back shattered the vision, and he lay beside the altar, retching. Strong hands supported him as he vomited bile and seawater. Metal brushed his arm as someone cut his bonds. He choked, retched again. When he could speak, he sought out Cowl. "How?" he rasped. "How could I see?"

She shrugged, not unkindly. "You're one of his— one of the drowned. Now you know it. You're in the flux, at the point where changes happen."

"And the sacrifices? I'm still alive. I think I'm still alive."

Her eyes cut toward the room of shipwrecks. "What did you think we were building?" Her voice took on a faraway quality. "We drown for him, and he gives us back our lives. The bottles are frozen moments, aye. They're temples too. Sites of worship and of sacrifice. Each one is an edge and therefore a place for our god to dwell."

He thought back on his dream of the *Sparrowhawk*, on the desperate madness of Lena Rogers, on the possibility of another collection of shipwrecks accumulating in some hidden nook in the Gilded Ascendency. A war of overwritten pasts, all preserved in glass, all built upon the perpetually drowning.

Perhaps Cowl was as mad as any poor soul in Paxgate. Perhaps she'd gone horribly sane. The alien pleasure of standing in the wreck of the *Left of Fortune* shuddered in the deeps of his mind, stirring with wordless, shapeless thoughts.

And he was sure that, whatever being or mechanism lay at the heart of the Bottlers' Guild and in the oceans' hunger, he would not stand by and see it fed.

"I know how to build the *Left of Fortune*," he said. "I can see."

Cowl pressed his shoulder. "Then make it so."

☼

He set up a bench in his quarters and worked alone in quiet frenzy. The masters left him to his task, trusting rapture to guide him. But for every hour he spent on the *Left of Fortune*, he spent two on his old *Sparrowhawk*. Slowly, he repaired the damage he'd done: gluing the hull back together, replacing snapped spars, recreating the rigging from scratch.

Every night, he dreamed of the *Sparrowhawk* and the past he'd imagined for Eli Fuller.

When he finished, he slipped the ship into a bottle, raised the masts, and teased open the sails. He poured in enough seawater to float the model and sealed the bottle. In the right light, he could have sworn he saw tiny figures at work upon the deck as the sails billowed to catch the wind. The bottle held a moment of reality: the *Sparrowhawk* he'd imagined, and with it a whole past that might have been.

I'm in the flux of it all, he told himself as he began to pick through the guild's shelves of sealants, solvents, and paints to use as explosive precursors. *I'm where things can change.*

☼

The papers reported the final defeat of the Gilded Navy. Criers repeated the news up and down the streets of Crofthold. Cowl seemed uninterested. "The work goes on," she said. "There will always be reefs and storms. And there are rumors that Verule is expanding its navy and issuing letters of marque in the hopes of becoming more than a regional power."

Tom left one final message at a dead-drop: *Relay methods to superiors. We will raise our fleet or be overrun.*

And we'll have two empires again, Eli thought as he burned the message. *Each built over a secret mausoleum. An endless repetition of shipwrecks, all to feed a god nobody's even heard of.*

Already, the world around him felt unreal. He was almost finished constructing his satchel charge, and the *Sparrowhawk* sailed beneath his cot and in his dreams.

☼

When he went to plant the charge in the room of shipwrecks, he found Cowl already there. She was damp, and her voice was rough. He wondered whether she'd just half-drowned herself at the altar.

"Eli," she said. There was gin on her breath. She nodded to the cloth bundle in his hands. "What might that be? It smells like ammonia."

She won't be real, he thought. *Not after I change everything. I won't have hurt her.* He carefully set the charge on the highest shelf in the middle of the room and began to unwind the fuse.

"Eli," she said sharply. Then: "Ah. Not Eli, I suppose. It's a wonder the Ascendency took this long." Her voice stayed level. "I suspect it won't matter. I've long wondered whether ours was the only Bottlers' Guild. Perhaps in a few months some clever craftsman will finish a model of our collapsed building in the heart of Crofthold, and all will be as it was. Stranger things have happened. The oldest among us have recollections, so very faint, of a fire that devastated Crofthold itself…and yet here the city stands. What a labor that must have been, aye? Building the ruin of an entire city under glass…Eli? You have to know this will fail, Eli. Ah, but that isn't your name. What shall I call you?"

He couldn't leave her with the satchel. All she would have to do was extinguish the fuse. "Eli," he said. "My name is Eli." He drew a knife. "It will be, anyway. None of this will have been real."

She smiled and took down a bottle, tilting it gently to catch the lamplight. "As real as anything in this room…."

All around him, sharp as the knife in his hand, came the silent screams of the drowning. "Exactly," he said, and he moved.

☼

He set a long fuse, one that gave him enough time to reach Paxgate. He sat quietly with Lena Rogers, who greeted him with unfocused courtesy and began to tell him about her sons, who were good Navy boys. He listened, waiting for the distant explosion and the fire bells that would follow. The bottled *Sparrowhawk* lay cradled in his hands. He'd left bloodied fingerprints on the glass.

"That's fine work…very pretty…."

He smiled at her. "Thank you. Yours was better. It's just as well Cowl didn't choose you. You'd never have paid her prices. *Its* prices. I don't know what your life will be like—will have been like—after this is all done. I hope it will be better. I hope this war will have been too expensive for Caeline to keep fighting. I can't know."

A sound like distorted thunder. Distant screams and bells. A twist in his memory, a sudden flurry of competing recollections as contradictory pasts erupted from shattered glass and sped back through history. The world seemed to bend around him, to hesitate as though unsure what it was meant to become.

And you, he thought to the nameless thing in the depths. *I hope you starve.*

He gripped the bottled *Sparrowhawk*, focused on the past that might have been his, the small family in a quiet corner of a nation no longer able to afford its empire. One last time, he recalled the name under which he'd grown up. It didn't feel like his own.

Eli Fuller drew a deep breath, raised the bottle, and flung it down, releasing all that might have been into the world.

Copyright © 2021 by Andrew Dykstal.

New York Times *bestselling author Todd Johnson McCaffrey wrote his first science-fiction story when he was twelve. Since then he has published over two dozen novels and nearly twenty shorter works. He lives in Las Vegas. You can learn more about him at http://www.toddmccaffrey.org.*

GOLDEN

by Todd McCaffrey

"How does this sound? 'It can never be stressed sufficiently: to anger a dragon is to die. To steal a dragon's gold is to die, to covet a dragon's mate is to die. Death by dragon is swift but not painless, usually involving flames which can melt steel.'"

"I think you could have stopped with the first sentence, Daddy," Golden said. "The rest are merely illustrations of how to anger a dragon."

"And you forgot to mention challenging a dragon to a joust," Elveth said.

"If I mention that then you'll get fewer jousts and less gold," Simon replied. "I thought the idea was to create more challenges."

"The *idea* is to get more gold," Elveth corrected testily. She smiled at her daughter, adding, "Golden isn't getting younger and she'll need a horde of her own." Her smile faded as she added pointedly, "You're certainly not getting any of mine."

"Of course, Mother," Golden said demurely. When Elveth wasn't looking, she shot a pleading look toward her father who shrugged sympathetically.

"Your mother left you quite a nice pile, if I remember," Simon said.

"That's because I killed her," Elveth reminded him waspishly. She flicked a finger at her daughter. "You're not to get any ideas, little miss gold scales."

"Yes, Mother," Golden replied, dipping her head and avoiding eye contact. Elveth was the sort of mother who would *literally* rip your head off if she got too angry. Golden had seen it once and needed no reminders—in this she was like her mortal and human father.

In most other things she was the exact replica of her mother. Only where Elveth was a mottled copper color when a dragon, Golden was pure gold—hence her name. Even when born, she had a beautiful head of fine golden hair and there was no contention over her name.

"She is Golden because she is my gold child," Elveth had said, and Simon had wisely kept silent, particularly as, according to his studies, he was the first human dragon-mate to survive through the rigors of a childbirth with a head still upon his shoulders.

Simon and Elveth had often conversed on their daughter's coloring: Simon was convinced that it was protective in nature while Elveth held to the old dragon lore that color predicted flame.

"A pure gold like that will mark the hottest of fires," Elveth had declared with much warranted maternal pride.

At the time, Golden had yet to have her first molt and was still clinging to the forlorn hope that she was not a dragon but, rather, a normal human child. She loved her father as fiercely as all girls—perhaps a bit more so because of her draconish heritage. Simon, because he loved his daughter, hoped that her wish would come true but deep down he was convinced—and secretly relieved—that she would molt and turn into a dragon when she was of age.

There were tears all around when that day finally came and Golden found herself molted into the slim body of a young dragon princess.

"Oh, my dear, you are so beautiful!" Elveth had cried with tears of joy.

"I'm a dragon!" Golden had cried with tears of despair.

"You shall live forever," Simon had said with tears of relief.

"As a dragon!" Golden had wailed. "I don't want to be a dragon!"

"Well, you are," Elveth had snapped, her copper-color eyes warming dangerously.

"Ixnay on the agon-dray," Simon had muttered warningly to his daughter.

"But it's true!" Golden cried, flouncing out of their small house and accidentally destroying the staircase, the good dining table, and three large iron pots.

When they had found her later, she was lying on her mother's horde in the deep cavern that was hidden behind their house.

Elveth growled and looked ready to change but Simon put an arm on hers. "She must have a terrible headache."

"Golden, how do you feel?" Elveth asked, primed by her mate.

"My head feels like it's going to explode!" Golden had cried.

"Oh, dear! It's all the magic going around," Elveth had said sympathetically. She turned to Simon. "I should go out and kill more mages to ease the pain of my poor little girl."

"Now, dear, we've had this conversation before," Simon told her soothingly. "The evidence is that magic flows from the sun. The mages merely tame and use it. Ridding yourself of them leaves more magic to pain you."

"At least I've got my gold," Elveth said, moving to join her dragon daughter in the huge pile that spilled from its mound in the center of the cavern. She turned back to smile at her mate. "And I've got you to thank for it."

Simon blushed but said nothing.

"How's that, Mother?" Golden asked, her talons digging deep into the pile and spilling it over her like a torrent of pebbles—although these pebbles were mostly gold doubloons mixed with the occasional broken crown or necklace.

"Well, it was your father who realized that knights and princes would wager much to fight against a dragon," Elveth said, glancing slyly at her mate. "And so he arranged it and I've been successfully ridding the countryside of useless knights and worthless princes."

"But I thought Daddy was—"

"Your father, a knight?" Elveth asked with a laugh. She eyed Simon thoughtfully. "Well, he *is* of the nobility or he would not be a suitable consort for one such as myself, but he was a squire when we met and much more scholarly than most." She smiled at him. "The bashful boy was completely taken with me after I'd scorched that useless knight of his into mere ash."

"Sir Girwhed was noble and brave," Simon said in defense of his long-lost knight, "but he would not listen to my counsel."

"And that was?" Golden prompted, lifting her snout through a pile of treasure and letting it spill to either side.

"I told him if he fought the dragon, she'd burn him to a crisp," Simon said with a shrug.

"See!" Elveth cried, giving her mate a look of adoration. "He's one of the smartest humans I'd ever met."

"Of course, it took a while for our courtship to mature," Simon reminded her.

Elveth laughed long and brassily. "Yes, I recall telling you every night that while I enjoyed our conversations, I was never going to be foolish to transform into a woman just so you could kill me."

"Actually," Simon said, "I seem to recall endless nights of your telling me how quick and painful my demise would be."

"Only after you beat me at chess!" Elveth said, her expression slipping.

"And then she changed into human form," Simon said with a smile that bordered on a leer. To Elveth, he added, "I always knew that you'd be the most beautiful of women."

"Flatterer!" Elveth chuckled. "And, of course, well, Golden dear, you came along."

"And now I'm a dragon!" Golden cried. "And I'll horde gold and flame useless knights to ash just to build my horde!"

"And it had never get bigger than mine, missy," Elveth added warningly.

"Of course, Momma," Golden replied shyly.

"How's your headache?" Simon asked.

"Better."

"Then maybe you can change back," Simon suggested.

"Change back?" Golden repeated in wonder. "How do I do that?"

"Close your eyes," Elveth told her. "Close your eyes and think your wings away. Think your pretty scales gone and your beautiful slitted eyes turned back into small golden round orbs. Feel your hair on your shoulders and your body shrink as you become a mere human shape."

It took more coaxing but in twenty minutes, Golden was once again in human form.

"Later, dear, we'll teach you how to build clothes," Elveth promised as Simon lent his daughter the jacket he'd worn just for the occasion.

✧

That had been the beginning of dark days all around.

"Well, I'm learning a lot," Simon had quipped when challenged to find the good in the emotional stew that was two dragon-queens in the same house—one daughter of the other.

Golden would wail about her mother, Elveth would shriek about her daughter, and Simon would spend most of his time trying to perfect his flame-proof armor and—naturally—work on creative ways to keep one or the other from escalating things into a firestorm.

"The house is made of wood!" Simon had cried hopelessly at the beginning of their first mother-daughter, dragon-dragon spat.

Not long after, the ruins were made of ash.

A year later, Simon was saying, "I didn't know your flame was hot enough to melt brick."

It had been Golden's flame which had reduced their second home to glowing glass slag—much to the surprise of all.

Simon had taken to spending much time in the village tavern—they knew nothing of his home life, thinking him merely a farmer with a wife and daughter but to no avail. It had ended the night Golden had run into the inn crying, and a copper dragon had flamed off the roof.

Simon had, at least, earned much respect from the villagers when he'd stood up to the copper dragon and had sent it packing.

Of course, as he knew, the whole family was shortly packing to find some new dwelling—not just because of Elveth's flame tantrum but also because the villagers decided that they were better off without the services of a farmer who spoke to dragons.

They settled many hundreds of miles away in an entirely new kingdom far in the south where, after not too much time, Simon had begun convincing princes in other lands that their greatest glory lay in challenging a flaming dragon in a duel to the death.

Simon also learned much of the ways of daughters and mothers from those willing to share their knowledge—and there were many—and grew more and more despairing for the survival of not just his dwelling or his hide but of his family.

It seemed like it would all end when Golden, just barely fifteen and far too young for a dragon to go a-roaming, fled the house in a flaming huff which set the far mountains alight.

With the flames marking a clear path back to their home, Simon knew that he and Elveth would also have to move or face uncomfortable questions and other such things—like pitchforks.

"Pitchforks won't hurt me!" Elveth had exclaimed when Simon brought them up.

"I, on the other hand, am not so sturdy," Simon reminded her. She had not been so distracted by the loss of her daughter as to consider the impending loss of her husband unworthy of her concern and so, as Simon had urged, they fled for healthier parts.

Fortunately, Simon was a wise man and had their destination long-planned—when living with two strong-minded dragons, it was practically inevitable that one way or the other they would find themselves relocating—so, even though her family fled in her wake, Simon had the comfort of knowing that Golden would know where to find them.

They were settled into the cold, wet north that was safely far away from their other homes for over two years before Elveth started pining for her missing daughter.

"She's old enough to take care of herself, dear," Simon had staunchly assured her, trying to believe the words that he'd been telling himself for the past twenty-four months.

"A dragon isn't mature until her fiftieth year!" Elveth cried.

"You were forty-five when you ate your mother," Simon reminded her.

"Exactly!" Elveth said. "I'm glad you take my side in this, Simon. If only you had been quicker, she would still be with us."

Simon wisely kept silent. The only result of his reminding his dragon-wife of her part in their daughter's departure would be to have her grieving over the ashes of her husband…and, doubtless, complaining that *that* was her daughter's fault.

When Elveth had finally dissolved into a flood of heart-broken tears, Simon said, "There, dear, we'll find her. She'll be back, you'll see."

"She'd better," Elveth hiccuped, pushing herself away from her husband, her eyes slitting as she speared him with her gaze. "After all, it's all *your* fault."

"Yes, dear," Simon had said wisely. He then excused himself on the grounds that he needed to get some water. He did not say that he intended to douse himself in it for protection. He was away long enough that Elveth was asleep when he returned, her human body slumped in her chair, head on the table. With a sigh, Simon gently pulled the chair back, lifted her up, and carried her to their bed.

He was still drying himself off, having covered her in their blankets, when he heard wings rustling. He dropped the towel and tore out the front door.

Out of the darkness a golden-haired girl emerged hesitantly.

"Daddy?" Golden asked in a small quiet voice.

Simon raced to her, grabbed her and twirled with her in his arms, his head pressed firmly against her shoulder, his tears flowing unabashed. "Baby!"

They stood, entwined, for the moment that was forever. Then, because even eternity must end, Simon pulled away from her.

"Are you staying?" he said, glancing back to their newest home and wondering how to manage the reunion and its aftermath.

Golden shook her head, and her fine blonde hair shimmered around her like a gold waterfall. "I can't."

Simon heard another noise rustle in the darkness and quickly pushed her behind him, ready to defend her with his life.

A small, dark-haired, green-eyed woman shrank back from his motions.

"This is Erayshin," Golden said, grabbing his arm and pulling him to a halt. She beckoned with her other hand for the girl to approach.

"Is she—?" Simon asked, his eyes wide in fear.

Golden shook her head.

"Does she—?"

"Yes," Golden said. She gestured again for the girl to join them. The girl stepped forward. She was smaller than Simon, short, and lithe. Her eyes were on his daughter. They flicked to him with worry and then back to Golden with determination. Golden's voice hardened as she said, "They wanted her to marry a prince and she didn't."

"She saved me," Erayshin said, her voice fluid with words learned far away.

"He brought a dowry," Golden said, her voice filled with the sharpness and longing that Simon had first heard so many years before from his dragon wife— the voice of dragon lust.

"There have been twelve more," Erayshin said. An impish look crossed her green eyes and gave Simon the distinct impression that the foreign girl was just as devilish as his daughter.

"I've got a rather nice horde," Golden agreed.

"I asked to come here," Erayshin said, giving Simon a frank, and somewhat terrified look.

Simon had rarely seen that look but he knew all the muscles that caused it. He waved to his daughter. "Why don't you let me talk with your friend for a bit, Golden?"

"I need to stretch my wings," Golden said agreeably.

"There are some nice places to the north—the far north," Simon suggested.

"Thirty minutes?" Golden asked.

"That would be plenty," Simon agreed. His daughter smiled at him, waved at her friend and walked off into the dark. Not long after, a beautiful gold dragon erupted into the skies above them and raced away northward.

"She's been gone two years," Simon said in the silence.

"I met her about six months after," Erayshin said, moving closer to him so that she could look up into his eyes in the gloomy dark.

"My wife—her mother—is inside, sleeping," Simon said, waving toward the house. "I'd invite you in but…well, Elveth is jealous."

Erayshin smiled. "So is your daughter."

"She learned it from the best of teachers," Simon told her with an answering smile. A moment later he said, "Will there be a prince who claims your heart?"

"Will there be a woman who claims yours?" Erayshin responded. When Simon shook his head, she nodded. "I came to ask you how you managed."

"It will be easier for you," Simon told her. "Without a daughter to argue with, all you'll have to—"

"There will be a child," Erayshin said, her hand going to her belly. "I wanted to know—"

"A child?" Simon interrupted in amazement. "How?"

"Golden told me: 'Where there is a heart, there is a way,'" Erayshin said. "It took her many months but we found a way."

"The child is *hers*?" Simon cried.

"Ours," Erayshin said. Her smiled turned inward for a moment. "Just once, she became a male."

"I must write of this," Simon said, preparing to run back to the house for pen and paper.

"Please," Erayshin said, reaching forward and touching his arm for the first time. "I must know—how, what, how—?"

Simon put his other hand over hers. "You have to say yes if you say anything," he said, glad to have this one chance to share his hard-won knowledge with someone. "You must be silent when you want to scream, be obeisant when you want to fight—"

"I can do that," Erayshin said, trying to sound certain.

"You should be ready to move often," Simon warned.

"She has a horde, we know where to go," Erayshin affirmed.

"And you must never stop loving the both of them," Simon said finally.

"How do you do that?" Erayshin said as they heard wings in the distance flapping back toward them. "She's been gone all this time—how did you—"

"And you have to love them more than life itself, love them enough to let them go when they need, love who they want," Simon told her. He moved and brought her close against him, wrapping her into a tight embrace.

Erayshin looked up at him, her eyes wet with tears. "Will you forgive me? For taking her love from you?"

Simon shook his head, his lips quilting upward. "You could never do that. I will honor you."

"For what?"

"For having the courage to love her."

The wings hovered near the forest, stopped, and Simon turned them to face the darkness.

Golden rushed out into the light, paused fearfully, and then rushed into their open arms.

✿

Twenty minutes later, Simon returned to his home, pausing just long enough to watch the gold dragon and her rider wheel overhead and then disappear into the dark night.

He sighed and quietly entered the house, went to the bedroom and crawled into bed with his wife.

Elveth nuzzled against him and murmured sleepily in a combination accusation and comfort with a plain meaning: Where have you been? I missed you.

"Golden came back," Simon told her softly. She tensed against him. "She has a partner, a horde, and a home."

Copper-colored eyes opened and peered up at him.

"They are with child," Simon said, choosing his words as carefully as always. "You're going to be a grandmother."

Elveth was silent for a long while, her eyes closed tightly. When she opened them again, tears streaked from them. "There has never been a dragon who knew her grandchild!"

Simon leaned forward and kissed her tears away. "I know."

Elveth was silent for a moment, then snuggled herself against Simon.

"She's a good child," Elveth murmured before turning to face him directly. "Let's make another."

Simon, wisely, said nothing.

Copyright © 2014 by Todd McCaffrey.

Walter Jon Williams is the author of over thirty volumes of fiction, in addition to works in film, television, comics, and the gaming field. He's won awards, appeared on the bestseller lists of the Times *and the* New York Times, *and he's a world traveler, scuba diver, and a black belt in Kenpo Karate.*

INCARNATION DAY

by Walter Jon Williams

It's your understanding and wisdom that makes me want to talk to you, Doctor Sam. About how Fritz met the Blue Lady, and what happened with Janis, and why her mother decided to kill her, and what became of all that. I need to get it sorted out, and for that I need a real friend. Which is you.

Janis is always making fun of me because I talk to an imaginary person. She makes even more fun of me because my imaginary friend is an English guy who died hundreds of years ago.

"You're wrong," I pointed out to her, "Doctor Samuel Johnson was a real person, so he's not imaginary. It's just my *conversations* with him that are imaginary."

I don't think Janis understands the distinction I'm trying to make.

But I know that *you* understand, Doctor Sam. You've understood me ever since we met in that Age of Reason class, and I realized that you not only said and did things that made you immortal, but that you said and did them while you were hanging around in taverns with actors and poets.

Which is about the perfect life, if you ask me.

In my opinion Janis could do with a Doctor Sam to talk to. She might be a lot less frustrated as an individual.

I mean, when I am totally stressed trying to comprehend the equations for electron paramagnetic resonance or something, so I just can't stand cramming another ounce of knowledge into my brain, I can always imagine my doctor Sam—a big fat man (though I think the word they used back then was "corpulent")—a fat man with a silly wig on his head, who makes a magnificent gesture with one hand and says, with perfect wisdom and gravity, *All intellectual improvement, Miss Alison, arises from leisure.*

Who could put it better than that? Who else could be as sensible and wise? Who could understand me as well?

Certainly nobody *I* know.

(And have I mentioned how much I like the way you call me *Miss Alison?*)

We might as well begin with Fahd's Incarnation Day on Titan. It was the first incarnation among the Cadre of Glorious Destiny, so of course we were all present.

The celebration had been carefully planned to showcase the delights of Saturn's largest moon. First we were to be downloaded onto *Cassini Ranger*, the ship parked in Saturn orbit to service all the settlements on the various moons. Then we would be packed into individual descent pods and dropped into Titan's thick atmosphere. We'd be able to stunt through the air, dodging in and out of methane clouds as we chased each other across Titan's cloudy, photochemical sky. After that would be skiing on the Tomasko glacier, Fahd's dinner, and then skating on frozen methane ice.

We would all be wearing bodies suitable for Titan's low gravity and high-pressure atmosphere—sturdy, low to the ground, and furry, with six legs and a domelike head stuck onto the front between a pair of arms.

But my body would be one borrowed for the occasion, a body the resort kept for tourists. For Fahd it would be different. He would spend the next five or six years in orbit around Saturn, after which he would have the opportunity to move on to something else.

The six-legged body he inhabited would be his own, his first. He would be incarnated—a legal adult, and legally human despite his six legs and furry body. He would have his own money and possessions, a job, and a full set of human rights.

Unlike the rest of us.

After the dinner, where Fahd would be formally invested with adulthood and his citizenship, we would all go out for skating on the methane lake below the glacier. Then we'd be uploaded and head for home.

All of us but Fahd, who would begin his new life. The Cadre of Glorious Destiny would have given its first member to interplanetary civilization.

I envied Fahd his incarnation—his furry six-legged body, his independence, and even his job, which wasn't all that stellar if you ask me. After fourteen years of being a bunch of electrons buzzing around in a quantum matrix, I wanted a real life even if it meant having twelve dozen legs.

I suppose I should explain, because you were born in an era when electricity came from kites, that at the time of Fahd's Incarnation Day party I was not exactly a human being. Not legally, and especially not physically.

Back in the old days—back when people were establishing the first settlements beyond Mars, in the asteroid belt and on the moons of Jupiter and then Saturn—resources were scarce. Basics such as water and air had to be shipped in from other places, and that was very expensive. And of course the environment was extremely hazardous—the death rate in those early years was phenomenal.

It's lucky that people are basically stupid, otherwise no one would have gone.

Yet the settlements had to grow. They had to achieve self-sufficiency from the home worlds of Earth and Luna and Mars, which sooner or later were going to get tired of shipping resources to them, not to mention shipping replacements for all the people who died in stupid accidents. And a part of independence involved establishing growing, or at least stable, populations, and that meant having children.

But children suck up a lot of resources, which like I said were scarce. So the early settlers had to make do with virtual children.

It was probably hard in the beginning. If you were a parent you had to put on a headset and gloves and a body suit in order to cuddle your infant, whose objective existence consisted of about a skazillion lines of computer code anyway…well, let's just say you had to want that kid *really badly*.

Especially since you couldn't touch him in the flesh till he was grown up, when he would be downloaded into a body grown in a vat just for him. The theory being that there was no point in having anyone on your settlement who couldn't contribute to the economy and help pay for those scarce resources, so you'd only incarnate your offspring when he was already grown up and could get a job and help to pay for all that oxygen.

You might figure from this that it was a hard life out there on the frontier.

Now it's a lot easier. People can move in and out of virtual worlds with nothing more than a click of a mental switch. You get detailed sensory input through various nanoscale computers implanted in your brain, so you don't have to put on oven mitts to feel your kid. You can dandle your offspring, and play with him, and teach him to talk, and feed him even. Life in the virtual realms claims to be one hundred percent realistic, though in my opinion it's more like ninety-five percent, and only in the realms that *intend* to mimic reality, since some of them don't.

Certain elements of reality were left out, and there are advantages—at least if you're a parent. No drool, no messy diapers, no vomit. When the child trips and falls down, he'll feel pain—you *do* want to teach him not to fall down, or to bang his head on things—but on the other hand there won't be any concussions or broken bones. There won't be any fatal accidents involving fuel spills or vacuum.

There are other accidents that the parents have made certain we won't have to deal with. Accidental pregnancy, accidental drunkenness, accidental drug use.

Accidental gambling. Accidental vandalism. Accidental suicide. Accidentally acquiring someone else's property. Accidentally stealing someone's extra-vehicular unit and going for a joy ride among the asteroids.

Accidentally having fun. Because believe me, the way the adults arrange it here, all the fun is *planned ahead of time*.

Yep, Doctor Sam, life is pretty good if you're a grownup. Your kids are healthy and smart and extremely well educated. They live in a safe, organized world filled with exciting educational opportunities, healthy team sports, family entertainment, and games that reward group effort, cooperation, and good citizenship.

It all makes me want to puke. If I *could* puke, that is, because I can't. (Did I mention there was no accidental bulimia, either?)

Thy body is all vice, Miss Alison, and thy mind all virtue.

Exactly, Doctor Sam. And it's the vice I'm hoping to find out about. Once I get a body, that is.

We knew that we weren't going to enjoy much vice on Fahd's Incarnation Day, but still everyone in the Cadre of Glorious Destiny was excited, and maybe a little jealous, about his finally getting to be an adult, and incarnating into the real world and having some real-world fun for a change. Never mind that he'd got stuck in a dismal job as an electrical engineer on a frozen moon.

All jobs are pretty dismal from what I can tell, so he isn't any worse off than anyone else really.

For days before the party I had been sort of avoiding Fritz. Since we're electronic we can avoid each other easily, simply by not letting yourself be visible to the other person, and not answering any queries he sends to you, but I didn't want to be rude.

Fritz was cadre, after all.

So I tried to make sure I was too busy to deal with Fritz—too busy at school, or with my job for Dane, or working with one of the other cadre members on a project. But a few hours before our departure for Titan, when I was in a conference room with Bartolomeo and Parminder working on an assignment for our Artificial Intelligence class, Fritz knocked on our door, and Bartolomeo granted him access before Parminder and I could signal him not to.

So in comes Fritz. Since we're electronic we can appear to one another as whatever we like, for instance Mary Queen of Scots or a bunch of snowflakes or even *you*, Doctor Sam. We all experiment with what we look like. Right now I mostly use an avatar of a sort-of Picasso woman—he used to distort people in his paintings so that you had a kind of 360-degree view of them, or parts of them, and I think that's kind of interesting, because my whole aspect changes depending on what angle of me you're viewing.

For an avatar, Fritz's used the image of a second-rate action star named Norman Isfahan. Who looks okay, at least if you can forget his lame videos, except that Fritz added an individual touch in the form of a balloon-shaped red hat. Which he thought made him look cool, but which only seemed ludicrous and a little sad.

Fritz stared at me for a moment, with a big goofy grin on his face, and Parminder sends me a little private electronic note of sympathy. In the last few months Fritz has become my pet, and he followed me around whenever he gets the chance. Sometimes he'd be with me for hours without saying a word, sometimes he'd talk the entire time and not let me get a single word in.

I did my best with him, but I had a life to lead too. And friends. And family. And I didn't want this person with me every minute, because even though I was sorry for him he was also very frustrating to be around.

Friendship is not always the sequel of obligation.
Alas, Doctor J., too true.

Fritz was the one member of our cadre who came out, well, wrong. They build us—us software—by reasoning backward from reality, from our parents' DNA. They find a good mix of our parents' genes, and that implies certain things about *us*, and the sociologists get their say about what sort of person might be needful in the next generation, and everything's thrown together by a really smart artificial intelligence, and in the end you get a virtual child.

But sometimes despite all the intelligence of everyone and everything involved, mistakes are made. Fritz was one of these. He wasn't stupid exactly—he was as smart as anyone—but his mental reflexes just weren't in the right plane. When he was very young he would spend hours without talking or interacting with any of us. Fritz's parents, Jack and Hans, were both software engineers, and they were convinced the problem was fixable. So they complained and they or the AIs or somebody came up with a software patch, one that was supposed to fix his problem—and suddenly Fritz was active and angry, and he'd get into fights with people and sometimes he'd just scream for no reason at all and go on screaming for hours.

So Hans and Jack went to work with the code again, and there was a new software patch, and now Fritz was stealing things, except you can't really steal anything in sims, because the owner can find any virtual object just by sending it a little electronic ping.

That ended with Fritz getting fixed yet *again*, and this went on for years. So while it was true that none of us were exactly a person, Fritz was less a person than any of us.

We all did our best to help. We were cadre, after all, and cadres look after their own. But there was a limit to what any of us could do. We heard about unanticipated feedback loops and subsystem crashes and weird quantum transfers leading to fugue states. I think that the experts had no real idea what was going on. Neither did we.

There was a lot of question as to what would happen when Fritz incarnated. If his problems were all software glitches, would they disappear once he was meat and no longer software? Or would they short-circuit his brain?

A check on the histories of those with similar problems did not produce encouraging answers to these questions.

And then Fritz became *my* problem because he got really attached to me, and he followed me around.

"Hi, Alison," he said.

"Hi, Fritz."

I tried to look very busy with what I was doing, which is difficult to do if you're being Picasso Woman and rather abstract-looking to begin with.

"We're going to Titan in a little while," Fritz said.

"Uh huh," I said.

"Would you like to play the shadowing game with me?" he asked.

Right then I was glad I was Picasso Woman and not incarnated, because I knew that if I had a real body I'd be blushing.

"Sure," I said. "If our capsules are anywhere near each other when we hit the atmosphere. We might be separated, though."

"I've been practicing in the simulations," Fritz said. "And I'm getting pretty good at the shadowing game."

"Fritz," Parminder said. "We're working on our AI project now, okay? Can we talk to you later, on Titan?"

"Sure."

And I sent a note of gratitude to Parminder, who was in on the scheme with me and Janis, and who knew that Fritz couldn't be a part of it.

Shortly thereafter my electronic being was transmitted from Ceres by high-powered communications lasers and downloaded into an actual body, even if it was a body that had six legs and didn't belong to me. The body was already in its vacuum suit, which was packed into the descent capsule—I mean nobody wanted us floating around in the *Cassini Ranger* in zero gravity in bodies we weren't used to— so there wasn't a lot I could do for entertainment.

Which was fine. It was the first time I'd been in a body, and I was absorbed in trying to work out all the little differences between reality and the sims I'd grown up in.

In reality, I thought, things seem a little quieter. In simulations there are always things competing for your attention, but right now there was nothing to do but listen to myself breathe.

And then there was a bang and a big shove, easily absorbed by foam padding, and I was launched into space, aimed at the orange ball that was Titan, and behind it the giant pale sphere of Saturn.

The view was sort of disappointing. Normally you see Saturn as an image with the colors electronically altered so as to heighten the subtle differences in detail. The reality of Saturn was more of a pasty blob, with faint brown stripes and a little red jagged scrawl of a storm in the southern hemisphere.

Unfortunately I couldn't get a very good view of the rings, because they were edge-on, like a straight silver knife-slash right across a painted canvas.

Besides Titan I could see at least a couple dozen moons. I could recognize Dione and Rhea, and Enceladus because it was so bright. Iapetus was obvious because it was half light and half dark. There were a lot of tiny lights that could have been Atlas or Pan or Prometheus or Pandora or maybe a score of others.

I didn't have enough time to puzzle out the identity of the other moons, because Titan kept getting bigger and bigger. It was a dull orange color, except on the very edge where the haze scatters blue light. Other than that arc of blue, Titan is orange the same way Mars is red, which is to say that it's orange all the way down, and when you get to the bottom there's still more orange.

It seemed like a pretty boring place for Fahd to spend his first years of adulthood.

I realized that if I were doing this trip in a sim, I'd fast-forward through this part. It would be just my luck if all reality turned out to be this dull.

Things livened up in a hurry when the capsule hit the atmosphere. There was a lot of noise, and the capsule rattled and jounced, and bright flames of ionizing radiation shot up past the view port. I could feel my heart speeding up, and my breath going fast. It was *my* body that was being bounced around, with *my* nerve impulses running along *my* spine. *This* was much more interesting. *This* was the difference between reality and a sim, even though I couldn't explain exactly what the difference was.

It is the distinction, Miss Alison, between the undomesticated awe which one might feel at the sight of a noble wild prospect discovered in nature; and that which is produced by a vain tragedian on the stage, puffing and blowing in a transport of dismal fury as he tries to describe the same vision.

Thank you, Doctor Sam.

We that live to please must please to live.

I could see nothing but fire for a while, and then there was a jolt and a *crash bang* as the braking chute deployed, and I was left swaying frantically in the sudden silence, my heart beating fast as high-atmosphere winds fought for possession of the capsule. Far above I could just see the ionized streaks of some of the other cadre members heading my way.

It was then, after all I could see was the orange fog, that I remembered that I'd been so overwhelmed by the awe of what I'd been seeing that I forgot to *observe*. So I began to kick myself over that.

It isn't enough to stare when you want to be a visual artist, which is what I want more than anything. A noble wild prospect (as you'd call it, Doctor Sam) isn't simply a gorgeous scene, it's also a series of technical problems. Ratios, colors, textures. Media. Ideas. Frames. *Decisions.* I hadn't thought about any of that when I had the chance, and now it was too late.

I decided to start paying better attention, but there was nothing happening outside but acetylene sleet cooking off the hot exterior of the capsule. I checked my tracking display and my onboard map of Titan's surface. So I was prepared when a private message came from Janis.

"Alison. You ready to roll?"

"Sure. You bet."

"This is going to be *brilliant.*"

I hoped so. But somewhere in my mind I kept hearing Doctor Sam's voice:

Remember that all tricks are either knavish or childish.

The trick I played on Fritz was both.

I had been doing some outside work for Dane, who was a communications tech, because outside work paid in real money, not the Citizenship Points we get paid in the sims. And Dane let me do some of the work on Fahd's Incarnation Day, so I was able to arrange which capsules everyone was going to be put into.

I put Fritz into the last capsule to be fired at Titan. And those of us involved in Janis' scheme—Janis, Parminder, Andy, and I—were fired first.

This basically meant that we were going to be on Titan five or six minutes ahead of Fritz, which meant it was unlikely that he'd be able to catch up to us. He would be someone else's problem for a while.

I promised myself that I'd be extra nice to him later, but it didn't stop me from feeling knavish and childish.

After we crashed into Titan's atmosphere, and after a certain amount of spinning and swaying, we came to a break in the cloud, and I could finally look down at Titan's broken surface. Stark mountains, drifts of methane snow, shiny orange ethane lakes, the occasional crater. In the far distance, in the valley between a pair of lumpy mountains, was the smooth toboggan slide of the Tomasko Glacier. And over to one side, on a plateau, were the blinking lights that marked our landing area.

And directly below was an ethane cloud, into which the capsule soon vanished. It was there that the chute let go, and there was a stomach-lurching drop before the airfoils deployed. I was not used to having my stomach lurch—recall if you will my earlier remarks on puking—so it was a few seconds before I was able to recover and take control of what was now a large and agile glider.

No, I hadn't piloted a glider before. But I'd spent the last several weeks working with simulations, and the technology was fail-safe anyway. Both I and the onboard computer would have to screw up royally before I could damage myself or anyone else. I took command of the pod and headed for Janis' secret rendezvous.

There are various sorts of games you can play with the pods as they're dropping through the atmosphere. You can stack your airfoils in appealing and intricate formations. (I think this one's really stupid if you're trying to do it in the middle of thick clouds.) There's the game called "shadowing," the one that Fritz wanted to play with me, where you try to get right on top of another pod, above the airfoils where they can't see you, and you have to match every maneuver of the pod that's below you, which is both trying to evade you and to maneuver so as to get above you. There are races, where you try to reach some theoretical point in the sky ahead of the other person. And there's just swooping and dashing around the sky, which is probably as fun as anything.

But Janis had other plans. And Parminder and Andy and I, who were Janis's usual companions in her adventures, had elected to be a part of her scheme, as was our wont. (Do you like my use of the word "wont," Doctor Sam?) And a couple other members of the cadre, Mei and Bartolomeo, joined our group without knowing our secret purpose.

We disguised our plan as a game of shadowing, which I turned out to be very good at. It's not simply a game of flying, it's a game of spatial relationships, and that's what visual artists have to be good at understanding. I spent more time on top of one or more of the players than anyone else.

Though perhaps the others weren't concentrating on the game. Because although we were performing the intricate spiraling maneuvers of shadowing as a part of our cover, we were also paying very close attention to the way the winds were blowing at different altitudes—we had cloud-penetrating lasers for that, in addition to a constant meteorological data from the ground—and we were using available winds as well as our maneuvers to slowly edge away from our assigned landing field, and toward our destined target.

I kept expecting to hear from Fritz, wanting to join our game. But I didn't. I supposed he had found his fun somewhere else.

All the while we were stunting around, Janis was sending us course and altitude corrections, and thanks to her navigation we caught the edge of a low-pressure area that boosted us toward our objective at nearly two hundred kilometers per hour. It was then that Mei swung her capsule around and began a descent toward the landing field.

"I just got the warning that we're on the edge of our flight zone," she reported.

"Roger," I said.

"Yeah," said Janis. "We know."

Mei swooped away, followed by Bartolomeo. The rest of us continued soaring along in the furious wind. We made little pretense by this point that we were still playing shadow, but instead tried for distance.

Ground Control on the landing area took longer to try to contact us than we'd expected.

"Capsules six, twenty-one, thirty," said a ground controller. She had one of those smooth, controlled voices that people use when trying to coax small children away from the candy and toward the spinach.

"You have exceeded the safe range from the landing zone. Turn at once to follow the landing beacon."

I waited for Janis to answer.

"It's easier to reach Tomasko from where we are," she said. "We'll just head for the glacier and meet the rest of you there."

"The flight plan prescribes a landing on Lake Southwood," the voice said. "Please lock on the landing beacon at once and engage your autopilots."

Janis's voice rose with impatience. "Check the flight plan I'm sending you! It's easier and quicker to reach Tomasko! We've got a wind shoving us along at a hundred eighty clicks!"

There was another two or three minutes of silence. When the voice came back, it was grudging.

"Permission granted to change flight plan."

I sagged with relief in my vac suit, because now I was spared a moral crisis. We had all sworn that we'd follow Janis's flight plan whether or not we got permission from Ground Control, but that didn't necessarily mean that we would have. Janis would have gone, of course, but I for one might have had second thoughts. I would have had an excuse if Fritz had been along, because I could have taken him to the assigned landing field—we didn't want him with us, because he might not have been able to handle the landing if it wasn't on an absolutely flat area.

I'd like to think I would have followed Janis, though. It isn't as if I hadn't before.

And honestly, that was about it. If this had been one of the adult-approved video dramas we grew up watching, something would have gone terribly wrong and there would have been a horrible crash. Parminder would have died, and Andy and I would have been trapped in a crevasse or buried under tons of methane ice, and Janis would have had to go to incredible, heroic efforts in order to rescue us. At the end Janis would have Learned an Important Life Lesson, about how following the Guidance of our

Wise, Experienced Elders is preferable to staging wild, disobedient stunts.

By comparison, what actually happened was fairly uneventful. We let the front push us along till we were nearly at the glacier, and then we dove down into calmer weather. We spiraled to a soft landing in clean snow at the top of Tomasko Glader. The airfoils neatly folded themselves, atmospheric pressure inside the capsules equalized with that of the moon, and the hatches opened so we could walk in our vac suits onto the top of Titan.

I was flushed with joy. I had never set an actual foot on an actual world before, and as I bounded in sheer delight through the snow I rejoiced in all the little details I felt all around me.

The crunch of the frozen methane under my boots. The way the wind picked up long streamers of snow that made little spattering noises when they hit my windscreen. The suit heaters that failed to heat my body evenly so that some parts were cool and others uncomfortably warm.

None of it had the immediacy of the simulations, but I didn't remember this level of detail either. Even the polyamide scent of the suit seals was sharper than the generic stuffy suit smell they put in the sim.

This was all real, and it was wonderful, and even if my body was borrowed I was already having the best time I'd ever had in my life.

I scuttled over to Janis on my six legs and crashed into her with affectionate joy. (Hugging wasn't easy with the vac suits on.) Then Parminder ran over and crashed into her from the other side.

"We're finally out of Plato's Cave!" she said, which is the sort of obscure reference you always get out of Parminder. (I looked it up, though, and she had a good point.)

The outfitters at the top of the glacier hadn't been expecting us for some time, so we had some free time to indulge in a snowball fight. I suppose snowball fights aren't that exciting if you're wearing full-body pressure suits, but this was the first real snowball fight any of us had ever had, so it was fun on that account anyway.

By the time we got our skis on, the shuttle holding the rest of the cadre and their pods was just arriving. We could see them looking at us from the yellow windows of the shuttle, and we just gave

them a wave and zoomed off down the glacier, along with a grownup who decided to accompany us in case we tried anything else that wasn't in the regulation playbook.

Skiing isn't a terribly hazardous sport if you've got six legs on a body slung low to the ground. The skis are short, not much longer than skates, so they don't get tangled; and it's really hard to fall over—the worst that happens is that you go into a spin that might take some time to get out of. And we'd all been practicing on the simulators and nothing bad happened.

The most interesting part was the jumps that had been molded at intervals onto the glacier. Titan's low gravity meant that when you went off a jump, you went very high and you stayed in the air for a long time. And Titan's heavy atmosphere meant that if you spread your limbs apart like a skydiver, you could catch enough of that thick air almost to hover, particularly if the wind was cooperating and blowing uphill. That was wild and thrilling, hanging in the air with the wind whistling around the joints of your suit, the glossy orange snow coming up to meet you, and the sound of your own joyful whoops echoing in your ears.

I am a great friend to public amusements, because they keep people from vice.

Well. Maybe. We'll see.

The best part of the skiing was that this time I didn't get so carried away that I forgot to *observe*. I thought about ways to render the dull orange sheen of the glacier, the wild scrawls made in the snow by six skis spinning out of control beneath a single squat body, the little crusty waves on the surface generated by the constant wind.

Neither the glacier nor the lake is always solid. Sometimes Titan generates a warm front that liquifies the topmost layer of the glacier, and the liquid methane pours down the mountain to form the lake. When that happens, the modular resort breaks apart and creeps away on its treads. But sooner or later everything freezes over again, and the resort returns.

We were able to ski through a broad orange glassy chute right onto the lake, and from there we could see the lights of the resort in the distance. We skied into a big ballooning pressurized hangar made out of some kind of durable fabric, where the crew removed our pressure suits and gave us little felt booties to wear. I'd had an exhilarating time, but hours had passed and I was tired. The Incarnation Day banquet was just what I needed.

Babbling and laughing, we clustered around the snack tables, tasting a good many things I'd never got in a simulation. (They make us eat in the sims, to get us used to the idea so we don't accidentally starve ourselves once we're incarnated, and to teach us table manners, but the tastes tend to be a bit monotonous.)

"Great stuff!" Janis said, gobbling some kind of crunchy vat-grown treat that I'd sampled earlier and found disgusting. She held the bowl out to the rest of us. "Try this! You'll like it!"

I declined.

"Well," Janis said, "if you're afraid of new things…"

That was Janis for you—she insisted on sharing her existence with everyone around her, and got angry if you didn't find her life as exciting as she did.

About that time Andy and Parminder began to gag on the stuff Janis had made them eat, and Janis laughed again.

The other members of the cadre trailed in about an hour later, and the feast proper began. I looked around the long table—the forty-odd members of the Cadre of Glorious Destiny, all with their little heads on their furry multipede bodies, all crowded around the table cramming in the first real food they've tasted in their lives. In the old days, this would have been a scene from some kind of horror movie. Now it's just a slice of post-humanity, Earth's descendants partying on some frozen rock far from home.

But since all but Fahd were in borrowed bodies I'd never seen before, I couldn't tell one from the other. I had to ping a query off their implant communications units just to find out who I was talking to.

Fahd sat at the place of honor at the head of the table. The hair on his furry body was ash-blond, and he had a sort of widow's peak that gave his head a kind of geometrical look.

I liked Fahd. He was the one I had sex with, that time that Janis persuaded me to steal a sex sim from Dane, the guy I do outside programming for. (I should point out, Doctor Sam, that our simulated bodies have all the appropriate organs, it's just

that the adults have made sure we can't actually use them for sex.)

I think there was something wrong with the simulation. What Fahd and I did wasn't wonderful, it wasn't ecstatic, it was just…strange. After a while we gave up and found something else to do.

Janis, of course, insisted she'd had a glorious time. She was our leader, and everything she did had to be totally fabulous. It was just like that horrid vat-grown snack food product she'd tried—not only was it the best food she'd ever tasted, it was the best food *ever*, and we all had to share it with her.

I hope Janis actually *did* enjoy the sex sim, because she was the one caught with the program in her buffer—and after I *told* her to erase it. Sometimes I think she just wants to be found out.

During dinner, those whose parents permitted it were allowed two measured doses of liquor to toast Fahd—something called Ring Ice, brewed locally. I think it gave my esophagus blisters.

After the Ring Ice, things got louder and more lively. There was a lot more noise and hilarity when the resort crew discovered that several of the cadre had slipped off to a back room to find out what sex was like, now they had real bodies. It was when I was laughing over this that I looked at Janis and saw that she was quiet, her body motionless. She's normally louder and more demonstrative than anyone else, so I knew something was badly wrong. I sent her a private query through my implant. She sent a single-word reply.

Mom…

I sent her a glyph of sympathy while I wondered how Janis's mom had found out about our little adventure so quickly. There was barely time for a light-speed signal to bounce to Ceres and back.

Ground Control must have really been annoyed. Or maybe she and Janis's mom were Constant Soldiers in the Five Principles Movement and were busy spying on everyone else—all for the greater good, of course.

Whatever the message was, Janis bounced back pretty quickly. Next thing I knew she was sidling up to me saying, "Look, you can loan me your vac suit, right?"

Something about the glint in her huge platter eyes made me cautious.

"Why would I want to do that?" I asked.

"Mom says I'm grounded. I'm not allowed to go skating with the rest of you. But nobody can tell these bodies apart—I figured if we switched places we could show her who's boss."

"And leave me stuck here by myself?"

"You'll be with the waiters—and some of them are kinda cute, if you like them hairy." Her tone turned serious. "It's solidarity time, Alison. We can't let Mom win this one."

I thought about it for a moment, then said, "Maybe you'd better ask someone else."

Anger flashed in her huge eyes. "I knew you'd say that! You've always been afraid to stand up to the grownups!"

"Janis," I sighed. "Think about it. Do you think your mom was the only one who got a signal from Ground Control? My parents are going to be looking into the records of this event *very closely*. So I think you should talk someone else into your scheme—and not Parminder or Andy, either."

Her whole hairy body sulked. I almost laughed.

"I guess you're right," she conceded.

"You know your mom is going to give you a big lecture when we get back."

"Oh yeah. I'm sure she's writing her speech right now, making sure she doesn't miss a single point."

"Maybe you'd better let me eavesdrop," I said. "Make sure you don't lose your cool."

She looked even more sulky. "Maybe you'd better."

We do this because we're cadre. Back in the old days, when the first poor kids were being raised in virtual, a lot of them cracked up once they got incarnated. They went crazy, or developed a lot of weird obsessions, or tried to kill themselves, or turned out to have a kind of autism where they could only relate to things through a computer interface.

So now parents don't raise their children by themselves. Most kids still have two parents, because it takes two to pay the citizenship points and taxes it takes to raise a kid, and sometimes if there aren't enough points to go around there are three parents, or four or five. Once the points are paid the poor moms and dads have to wait until there are enough applicants to fill a cadre. A whole bunch of virtual children are raised in one group, sharing their upbringing with their parents and creche staff. Older cadres often join their juniors and take part in their education, also.

The main point of the cadre is for us all to keep an eye on each other. Nobody's allowed to withdraw into their own little world. If anyone shows sign of going around the bend, we unite in our efforts to retrieve them.

Our parents created the little hell that we live in. It's our job to help each other survive it.

A person used to vicissitudes is not easily dejected.

Certainly Janis isn't, though despite cadre solidarity she never managed to talk anyone else into changing places with her. I felt only moderately sorry for her—she'd already had her triumph, after all—and I forgot all about her problems once I got back into my pressure suit and out onto the ice.

Skating isn't as thrilling as skiing, I suppose, but we still had fun. Playing crack-the-whip in the light gravity, the person on the end of the line could be fired a couple kilometers over the smooth methane ice.

After which it was time to return to the resort. We all showered while the resort crew cleaned and did maintenance on our suits, and then we got back in the suits so that the next set of tourists would find their rental bodies already armored up and ready for sport.

We popped open our helmets so that the scanners could be put on our heads. Quantum superconducting devices tickled our brain cells and recovered everything they found, and then our brains—our essences—were dumped into a buffer, then fired by communication laser back to Ceres and the sim in which we all lived.

The simulation seemed inadequate compared to the reality of Titan. But I didn't have time to work out the degree of difference, because I had to save Janis's butt.

That's us. That's the cadre. All for one and one for all.

And besides, Janis has been my best friend for practically ever.

Anna-Lee, Janis's mom, was of course waiting for her, sitting in the little common room outside Janis's bedroom. (Did I mention that we sleep, Doctor Sam? We don't sleep as long as incarnated people do, just a few hours, but our parents want us to get used to the idea so that when we're incarnated we know to sleep when we get tired instead of ignoring it and then passing out while doing something dangerous or important.

(The only difference between our dreams and yours is that we don't dream. I mean, what's the point, we're stuck in our parents' dream anyway.)

So I've no sooner arrived in my own simulated body in my own simulated bedroom when Janis is screaming on the private channel.

"Mom is here! I need you *now!*"

So I press a few switches in my brain and there I am, right in Janis's head, getting much of the same sensor feed that she's receiving herself. And I looked at her and I say, "Hey, you can't talk to Anna-Lee looking like *this.*"

Janis is wearing her current avatar, which is something like a crazy person might draw with crayons. Stick-figure body, huge yellow shoes, round bobble head with crinkly red hair like wires.

"Get your quadbod on!" I tell her. "Now!"

So she switches, and now her avatar has four arms, two in the shoulders, two in the hip sockets. The hair is still bright red. Whatever her avatar looks like, Janis always keeps the red hair.

"Good," I say. "That's normal."

Which it is, for Ceres. Which is an asteroid without much gravity, so there really isn't a lot of point in having legs. In microgravity, legs just drag around behind you and bump into things and get bruises and cuts. Whereas everyone can use an extra pair of arms, right? So most people who live in low- or zero-gravity environments use quadbods, which are much more practical than the two-legged model.

So Janis pushes off with her left set of arms and floats through the door into the lounge where her mom awaits. Anna-Lee wears a quadbod too, except that hers isn't an avatar, but a three-dimensional holographic scan of her real body. And you can tell that she's really pissed—she's got tight lips and tight eyelids and a tight face, and both sets of arms are folded across her midsection with her fingers digging into her forearms as if she's repressing the urge to grab Janis and shake her.

"Hi, Mom," Janis said.

"You not only endangered yourself," Anna-Lee said, "but you chose to endanger others too."

"Sit down before you answer," I murmured in Janis's inward ear. "Take your time."

I was faintly surprised that Janis actually followed my advice. She drifted into a chair, used her lower limbs to settle herself into it, and then spoke.

"Nobody was endangered," she said, quite reasonably. Anna-Lee's nostrils narrowed.

"You diverted from the flight plan that was devised for your safety," she said.

"I made a new flight plan," Janis pointed out. "Ground Control accepted it. If it was dangerous, she wouldn't have done that."

Anna-Lee's voice got that flat quality that it gets when she's following her own internal logic. Sometimes I think she's the program, not us.

"You are not authorized to file flight plans!" she snapped.

"Ground Control accepted it," Janis repeated. Her voice had grown a little sharp, and I whispered at her to keep cool.

"And Ground Control immediately informed *me!* They were right on the edge of calling out a rescue shuttle!"

"But they didn't, because there was no problem!" Janis snapped out, and then there was a pause while I told her to lower her voice.

"Ground Control accepted my revised plan," she said. "I landed according to the plan, and nobody was hurt."

"You planned this from the beginning!" All in that flat voice of hers. "This was a deliberate act of defiance!"

Which was true, of course.

"What harm did I do?" Janis asked.

("Look," I told Janis. "Just tell her that she's right and you were wrong and you'll never do it again.")

("I'm not going to lie!" Janis sent back on our private channel. "Whatever Mom does, she's never going to make me lie!")

All this while Anna-Lee was saying, "We must all work together for the greater good! Your act of defiance did nothing but divert people from their proper tasks! Titan Ground Control has better things to do than worry about you!"

There was no holding Janis back now. "You *wanted* me to learn navigation! So I learned it—because *you* wanted it! And now that I've proved that I can use it, you're angry about it!" She was waving her arms so furiously that she bounced up from her chair and began to sort of jerk around the room.

"And do you know why that is, Mom?" she demanded.

"*For God's sake shut up!*" I shouted at her. I knew where this was leading, but Janis was too far gone in her rage to listen to me now.

"It's because you're second-rate!" Janis shouted at her mother. "Dad went off to Barnard's Star, but *you* didn't make the cut! And I can do all the things you wanted to do, and do them better, and *you can't stand it*!"

"*Will you be quiet!*" I tell Janis. "Remember that *she owns you*!"

"I accepted the decision of the committee!" Anna-Lee was shouting. "I am a Constant Soldier and I live a productive life, and I will *not* be responsible for producing a child who is a *burden* and a *drain on resources*!"

"Who says I'm going to be a burden?" Janis demanded. "*You're* the only person who says that! If I incarnated tomorrow I could get a good job in ten minutes!"

"Not if you get a reputation for disobedience and anarchy!"

By this point it was clear that since Janis wasn't listening to me, and Anna-Lee *couldn't* listen, there was no longer any point in my involving myself in what had become a very predictable argument. So I closed the link and prepared my own excuses for my own inevitable meeting with my parents.

END PART I OF II

Copyright © 2006 by Walter Jon Williams.

Richard Chwedyk sold his first story in 1990, won a Nebula in 2002, and has been active in the field for the past thirty-one years.

RECOMMENDED BOOKS

by Richard Chwedyk

THE [WIDGET], THE [WADGET], AND BOOKS

To relieve any suspense, the title is a reference to a well-known (I hope) novella by Theodore Sturgeon (about a pair of aliens who run a rooming house in order to study humans; find it, it's a great story), "The [Widget], the [Wadget], and Boff." Relevant because it may have been my first exposure to the word "widget," though not in the way it is currently used.

It's like this:

You can always tell book reviewers because they always have stacks and boxes of books about, many of them ARCs (advanced readers' copies). The books collect in all sorts of places—in closets, on back stair landings, in neat (or not-so neat) stacks by the kitchen door. For reviewers like me, clutter is part of the business (not that my world wasn't cluttered with books before). It comes with the territory.

But publishing is changing with the times.

Now, publishers send emails to reviewers with links to *widgets* that allow the reviewers to read the latest releases digitally. No more stacks. No more clutter. No more paper, or ink, or binding. No more feel of the paper as you turn the pages. And no smell of that same paper, and the ink, and all the other materials that go into the making of a book. And for publishers, no more shipping costs, and any other costs they incur by producing these concrete objects that so often (well, often enough) enchant and captivate us.

The times change, and so must we.

One problem: widgets don't like me.

I log into the digital galley site, create an account, click on a widget, and am assailed by a selection of apps I can (theoretically) use to access the digital text. I have none of them. I choose one to load into my system, click on "install" and wait. After a few minutes I get the "installed" message and try the text again. Apparently, I can do all sorts of things except one: I can't *open the darn book*.

My column deadline is coming up fast. As Snuffy Smith used to say in the comics, "Time's a wastin'!"

What do you do when the widgets fail you?

Me, I put on my mask, pop a bottle of sanitizer into my jacket, and drive to the nearest bookstore.

Instead of reading promotional material and press releases for the books I'm trying to access (or the ones the publishers want me to access), I just wander through the stacks and shelves, real ones, and look for what's new and interesting to me.

I call this, for no good reason, "using my wadget."

Winter's Orbit
by Everina Maxwell
Tor
February 2021
ISBN: 978-1-250-75883-5

Architects of Memory
by Karen Osborne
Tor
September 2020
ISBN: 978-1-250-21547-5

The Rush's Edge
by Ginger Smith
Angry Robot
November 2020
ISBN: 978-0-85766-864-6

Space opera is here to stay. On that you can rely. They've become as ubiquitous as westerns were in the last century. Every other widget I couldn't open seemed to be one. They've become another kind of "portal fantasy" these days (see my column last issue re: portal fantasies). And, with many, but for the technological accoutrements, they stop feeling like science fiction after a while. They become some recognizably familiar story structures dressed up in spacesuits.

These three novels (all first novels too), however, distinguish themselves from the norm in different ways that make them satisfying reads no matter how you feel about form's conventions.

Pay no regard to the high-power blurbs that accompany Everina Maxwell's *Winter's Orbit*. Well-intentioned authors keep trying to find media-related comparisons that do the novel no justice. I won't try, though I'll tell you that I *did* feel, while reading, I'd been here before—not a bad place, but familiar. It then occurred to me that this novel is a hybrid of Regency romance, Ruritanian intrigue and murder mystery, cast with a diverse and open-minded set of sexual identities. It's well-structured and written with exemplary competence. Typically, I groan at any interplanetary adventure that contains emperors and aristocracies, but what most impressed me as "science-fictional" here is that its LGBTQ emphasis is presented neither self-consciously nor ostentatiously. Theodore Sturgeon, and other writers who pioneered topics of sexuality in SF, would have been impressed.

Karen Osborne's *Architects of Memory* does all the things space opera readers might want it to do. Its female protagonist, Ash Jackson, is a salvage pilot tied to a big, faceless, corporate concern. If you can't have evil emperors, you go for evil corporations. Ash, however, has a terminal illness, and if there's any hope of her finding a cure she must first sever the bonds to that servitude. The novel deals honestly with these critical entanglements, with a satisfyingly intricate plot. What impressed me most—and maybe I shouldn't say this because it might scare you away—is its implicit meditation on mortality. Space operas can rack up vast body counts, and most of its protagonists face death at some point or another (at least once), but Ash's inner struggle with the certainties (and uncertainties) of facing death is the kind of thing one rarely finds among the space opera widgets.

There are struggles aplenty in Ginger Ash's *The Rush's Edge*. A pair of ex-military salvagers, Tyce and Hal, are at the core of our story. Hal was genetically altered for his service, and his situation echoes the alienation many ex-military people feel once they get out—conditioned for a job they can no longer do, at least legally. But Tyce is there to provide Hal a little balance. Things get interesting once the two pick up, in their salvaging, a sphere that is really, *really* alien. Ash has a deceptively dry, direct approach to her prose that's not unlike the better practitioners of noir writing from the 1950s, and effectively balances passion and heart as well as Tyce and Hal balance each other. The story is compelling and Ash is a promising new voice to watch for.

Spin
by Robert Charles Wilson
Tor Essentials
November 2020
ISBN: 978-1-250-23751-4

It first struck me as odd that Robert Charles Wilson's brilliantly original novel would be chosen by Tor for its "Essentials" series, but then I looked at the first publication date: fifteen years ago. From there, my wonder was reserved only for why this extraordinary work had been out of print for quite a while (though the trilogy of which this forms the first volume is available as an e-book). Reading it again only confirms my surprise that this hasn't been a perennial "classic" from the get-go.

With much of the current science fiction I've been reading, I'm fortunate to run into a couple of new concepts or perspectives per volume. Wilson's novel is teeming with them. From the very first chapter, when the stars "disappear" as Jason, Diane and our narrator, Tyler Dupree, watch. Of course, the stars haven't really gone out, but a "spin membrane" surrounds our planet, blocking our view of the heavens. Earth is cut off in more ways than we first imagine, and things only get stranger from there. We get time paradoxes, Martians, terraforming, nanotechnology married with genetic engineering, and things even stranger.

What keeps this from being a wild OCIAA (acronym based upon John Masefield's novel *ODTAA*, which stands for "One Damn Thing After Another" —so here, "One Crazy Idea After Another"), are the trio of characters we begin with, and through which we experience a world not exactly turned upside down but run through an obstacle course of what at first seem insurmountable challenges that turn out to have a panoply of anomalous solutions. His characters are vivid and passionate (in their own specific ways), their immediate surroundings always vivid and detailed. And in spite of all the weirdnesses being thrown at us seemingly with every page, the novel maintains a pace that neither races us past the "gosh-wow" things we get (and want) to see, nor drags us at a funeral march to pore over every square and squiggle of minutia.

I rarely make note of introductions to editions such as this, since so few provide much of interest to say that can't be found better said elsewhere, but John Scalzi outdoes himself in making some pertinent points about what distinguished this novel from so much else published in the last decade and a half. Also, in doing so, he mentions he is writing this introduction at the start of his sixth week in quarantine from the COVID-19 pandemic. That he makes this point at all, along with making it painfully clear how relevant it is to our reading of *Spin*, makes this introduction a welcome addition to this boldly innovative novel.

◆ ◆ ◆

Surrender
by Ray Loriga, translated by Carolina De Robertis
Mariner
February 2020
ISBN: 978-1-328-52852-0

One of my unofficial mentors (all my mentors are/ were unofficial) in my undergraduate days was John Schultz, who taught at Columbia College in Chica-go and developed the Story Workshop approach to the teaching of writing. He used to tell us whenever the subject of "story" came up, "A story is something and something else." He never explained what he meant, but I spent a few decades thinking it over. What he meant, I think, is that a good story is never the thing it's nominally "about," not completely. "Man bites dog" may be a story in its plainest sense, but we really need to know, whether we want to or not, *why* the man bit the dog. Necessity? Compulsion? A whim? Behind the apparent reason for the story, there's a "real" reason. It's the thing we didn't know we wanted until we get it.

And it's the real engine of Ray Loriga's brief, powerful *Surrender*. It can be placed in the category of dystopian literature, and it will do so comfortably. A war has been going on for a decade. We never discover a reason for the war. A couple, farmers, have not seen their sons in years, but they're presumed to be still alive, fighting somewhere. There's no shortage of ambiguous messages from the government, and plenty of orders, but everything else is in short supply, until the couple is ordered to relocate to "the transparent city."

> The city seemed larger from a distance, but it was actually even larger. And though at first it looked like a round dome, from up close we could clearly see that it was made of diamond-shaped slabs of glass or crystal affixed to the ground and placed one on top of the other to form a gigantic transparent half-sphere protecting the whole city. How something like that was built is beyond me, but it seemed— and to her [his wife], too, well read as she is— the most fabulous construction we'd ever seen or imagined, and not even in the capital, with its grand buildings and skyscrapers, had we ever known anything like it. It's hard to describe its magnitude and beauty to someone who hasn't seen it, let alone the complexity of everything beneath that dome, as it housed endless highways and blocks full of buildings and trains and tracks and markets, all of them made of glass or some other transparent material. I don't think it could really be glass or crystal, since either would have broken under

all the weight, and yet, without knowing the first thing about architecture or the science behind this vast, gleaming city, I can't find a better way to describe it.

For an old science fiction fan like me, this conjures up an image of one of illustrator Paul Lehr's surrealistic cityscapes. The important element, practically and symbolically, is the transparency of the city. Nothing is "private." In this respect, the government's assault on its own citizens has proved more effective than its war on the unnamed enemy.

Before they're moved to the transparent city, the couple is ordered to burn down their own house.

I'm in charge of burning the house because I don't want her [the wife] to hurt herself, not for anything in the world. I'll do it the way they told us to and use the gasoline cans we were given. I don't understand why so much gasoline is being wasted in times like these, when you think about it I could burn the house with just a bit of alcohol and cardboard and wool, but the order arrived on officially embossed paper and it's always best to obey these types of papers without complaints or questions, since not doing so could raise suspicions, especially when there's a war going on and enemies will take advantage of anything that could harm morale.

Jaded American readers of dystopian fiction may shrug and say there's nothing new here. True, the landscape may be the same, but the focus is different. *Surrender* is not about the causes of the authoritarian system, but its effects, and not the external effects of a government robbing its citizens of its humanity, but the deeper, internal effects.

The active question here is not, "Does the system rob people of their humanity?" That we see plainly enough. The real question is, "In robbing people of their humanity, what are they really being robbed of?" The answer isn't as simple as we might first surmise. It's the thing we didn't know we wanted until we get it.

I'm very glad to see this novel, by Spanish writer and filmmaker Ray Loriga, translated into English (and very ably so, as far as I can tell, by Carolina

De Robertis). Not only that, but to find this novel shelved with science fiction, where it belongs. The discussion never dies, though the landscape often shifts, concerning the "shape of science fiction"— who should be writing it, what it should be written about. Expand the horizons. Include more voices in the conversation. We need to include voices from other countries, other languages, looking at the same subjects from different angles. We really need to add more translated novels to our consumption of science fiction and fantasy here in the States. We're missing something important.

◆ ◆ ◆

Lame Fate | Ugly Swans
by Arkady and Boris Strugatsky, translated by Maya Vinokour
Chicago Review Press
August 2020
ISBN: 978-1-64160-071-2

There are those who will think this novel is a stunt. Others will think this novel—or the phrase the publishers use, "nested novels"—stunning. To relieve your suspense, I fall into the latter category. If you have read other works by the Strugatsky brothers, like *Roadside Picnic* or *Hard to Be a God*, you won't be surprised. Scratch that. You will still be surprised at how surprising the Strugatsky brothers could be, even in their later years.

Once upon a time, just after the Second World War, there were things called "fixup novels." The term was coined by A. E. van Vogt, who would put together a few novellas of related material and call it a novel. The practice reflected the changing publishing market, where pulp and digest magazines were being replaced by paperbacks. Publishers wanted novels for their new lines, and science fiction writers found they could package their older works by bundling related stories together. In a way, *The Martian Chronicles* is also a fixup novel. Asimov's Foundation trilogy are all fixups. Why sell a story once when you can sell it at least twice?

What the Strugatskys did here is a little more complex than that. *Lame Fate* is a novel about an aging science fiction writer, Felix Sorokin, asked by the Soviet Writers Union to submit one of his novels as a sample to a new computer program designed to determine any book's "objective value." Who needs editors when you can rely on algorithms?

Think of it as a publisher's "widget."

The novel submitted to the program is *Ugly Swans* (actually written by the Strugatskys years earlier), about a disgraced author, Victor Banev, who returns to his hometown where he finds these strange, masked people, outsiders with alleged supernatural powers, called "clammies," who have insinuated themselves into the social structure. The adults in town are highly suspicious of the clammies where they're not out-and-out afraid of them, but the children, including Banev's daughter, find them fascinating.

Literary scholars like to say that all of literature is a conversation—among books, among authors, among readers and readings (and *I'm* fond of saying that if literature is a conversation, science fiction is a barroom brawl, but that's another matter). What the Strugatskys have managed here, through the interweaving of these two novels, is to apply this conversation to itself, through Felix Sorokin and Victor Banev, the latter a fictional character but as "valid" as the "real" Sorokin. The science fictional germ of *Lame Fate* unexpectedly interacts with the mysterious clammies of *Ugly Swans* in unanticipated ways, along with laying bare how the process of making what we call science fiction, or speculative fiction if you will, is in itself a kind of "science fiction." The two storylines, each in their way, intermingle and contrast in ways that suggest that "process" and "result" can sometimes be indistinguishable. Even for readers with wider literary reading experience—not unlike the "objective value" software—the answers you find will not be the ones you expected to find.

All of this set in a background generously provided by the twilight years of the Soviet Union, collapsing in on itself while promising its citizens a utopian future—once we get past these few rough edges. Another of the science-fictional revelations in store for readers of this book is that the failed workers' paradise is looking more and more like the world surrounding us at the moment: another reason why it's vital we English-speaking SF readers familiarize ourselves with voices from other cultures, even through translation.

The only other thing I'll add to anyone who may be a bit timorous about taking on a threaded tale set in the grim, late-Soviet sphere of omnipresent authoritarianism buttressed by incompetence and neglect, this book is *funny*. I mean, you'll be amazed at how often you find yourself laughing out loud. Sometimes it's the only way to survive the inexplicable cosmic weirdness we call reality.

That, and my wadget.

Gregory Benford is a professor of physics at the University of California, Irvine and the author of Timescape, *among other novels.*

A SCIENTIST'S NOTEBOOK

by Gregory Benford

THEOLOGY AND SCIENCE FICTION: FAITH AND REASON

In the early 2000s The Matrix series of three films set new box office records. It got few notices in the religious press. Yet it is the story of a quest for the true world hidden behind what we think of as the real one—and, of course, it's science fiction.

This collusion and collision of theology and science fiction is not new. The Matrix movies are elaborated views of a world dominated by artificial intelligences, which keep most of us in pods, feeding us an illusory world—this one you're sitting in—through spinal taps. Our lives are piped into our brains, complete sensory experiential Muzak.

Rebels living underground in Zion (yes) are led by a mysterious guerrilla figure (Morpheus, given to stentorian pronouncements in a butterscotch voice). They unplug from the Matrix illusion a man whose hacker name is Neo. Their mission and message is to *free your mind* (remember the '60s!) and, by the way, achieve an apocalyptic end to the artificial intelligences' enslavement of humanity.

Morpheus plays John the Baptist to Neo's Jesus. They battle inside the Matrix against the Agents, using ultraviolence shown in spectacular slow-motion special effects. This is no messiah who redeems by suffering. Rather, as ancient Jewish texts expected, Neo is a fighting liberator. Neo has a literal calling—he reaches Morpheus first by answering a cell phone, delivered by a messenger who says, "Hallelujah! You're my savior, man. My own personal Jesus Christ!"

To overcome the laminated malignancy of the Agents, Neo must learn to use his spiritual powers and focus his mind. His training is a cyber-techno take on meditation, the traditional path to enlightenment. Visiting the Oracle, he asks if he is the One, and she says coyly, "Maybe next life," setting the stage.

His learned skills let him deliver dazzling martial arts blows to the Agents, but he, well, lacks something: enlightenment. We get the drift when in a bold sally, Neo swoops down to save a nearly comatose Morpheus, saying "Morpheus! Get up!" echoing Jesus's "Lazarus, come out!"

Neo then enters the center of Matrix power, like Jesus cleansing the Temple, fights and is shot dead. His girl friend Trinity (yes) holds the lifeless Neo, as Mary Magdalene did Jesus—and Neo comes back to life. He has saved himself, reaching deep inside—transcendent knowledge, self-enlightenment.

After this self-resurrection, Neo has an unmistakable radiance. His aura dominates the film's frames. He manifests what St. John termed the after-resurrection "spiritual body" of Jesus. Stopping bullets with a raised hand, entering an Agent's body and exploding it, flying into the sky like Superman—all simple, now that he has been enlightened to his true nature.

The Matrix itself is not some external evil, but rather an outcome of our own error, our karmic payoff of past actions.

Both Matrix films carry forward this spiritual, eschatological story, of the new One who will return and win the last grand battle, bringing peace. A rebel named Cypher plays Judas, they ride in a battleship called *Nebuchadnezzar* ("we're on a mission from God") in defense of the transcendent last stronghold of humanity, Zion.

This blend of high tech and time-defying science fictional special effects seems to be a good example of our culture calling forth what the postmodernists term "floating signifiers"—ideas like exile from reality, and restoration of a radical newness, adrift on the *Zeitgeist* and ready to be used. Science fiction grounds this in the future and thus in hope; teenagers (the Matrix core audience) will not sit still for a big-budget Biblical epic.

Virtual reality you can't tell from life, downloaded worlds, malign machines—these are customary landscapes of the young, who are probably destined to live among them. The Matrix is one way for this audience to think about a future they see more clearly than we elders do—an essential reason that science fiction has been a young, brassy culture since the 1930s.

Indeed, computers have shown us the 2D poverty of digital deserts, the postmodernist "desert of the real" (quoted in the films). A techno-take on radical philosophical doubt is very hip these days. It works especially if we can see the grunge look of Zion versus the all-black look of cool dusters and plenty of leather.

In SF, basic doubts featured prominently in the worlds of Philip K. Dick. I knew Phil for twenty-five years, and he was always questioning me, a scientist. He was a great fan of quantum uncertainty, epistemology in science, the lot. Whether in science fiction or academic philosophy, we lately seem bemused by the notion that our reality may be a swindle. Computers in their flat-screen worlds help along a sensation of irreality, a liking not merely for the plausibly weird, but for the weirdly plausible. Already several Dick tales of fake realities have made it into major movies: *Blade Runner*, *Total Recall*, *Minority Report*.

Which way would *you* vote, given a choice of a secure life in a pod illusion, or a tricky, dangerous reality? Plugged or unplugged? For worker-drones living in corporate lattices satirized in the hugely popular comic strip Drabble, the choice is obvious.

✿

As Freeman Dyson noted, "Between science and theology there is a genre of literature which I like to call theofiction. Theofiction adapts the style and conventions of science fiction to tell stories that have more to do with theology than with science."

His examples include novels of Octavia Butler (a MacArthur Grant winner), C.S. Lewis, Madeleine L'Engle, and principally, Olaf Stapledon. Their works, and the burgeoning interest in films, point to the continuing evolution of this form of philosophical fiction, with strong ties to science fiction.

Wild thinking about religion and theology abounds in perhaps the most unlikely quarter, modern science fiction.

Though many think of science fiction (SF) as atheistic, Walter Miller, Jr.'s *A Canticle for Leibowitz* is just one of the genre's classics that spring equally from scientific/technological and theological concerns. This balance is typical, refuting the customary materialistic chasm between belief and knowledge.

The theofiction tradition was truly set forth in Olaf Stapledon's novels such as *Star Maker* (1937), which portrays God the Scientist as an agency forever shaping his Creation to attain higher expressions of his vision. Stapledon incorporated both biological evolution and the grander evolution of the cosmos into a sort of pantheistic pantheon, with a hovering Godlike presence, the Star Maker.

Still, Stapledon stood out for two reasons. His style ignored conventional character and plot, focusing upon ideas and scope. And he spoke about the largest issues without a hint of conventional theology. He stood alone in his time.

After World War II, though, religious SF flourished. That grand conflict apparently forced the emerging scientific/technological culture to grasp its roots. To grapple with the implications of interplanetary flight, Ray Bradbury in "The Man" (1949) envisioned Jesus carrying salvation to other worlds. In "The Quest for Saint Aquinas" by Anthony Boucher a robot emulates St. Thomas Aquinas by logically deducing God's existence, justifying its (and Boucher's) Catholic faith. The story has a sad, reverential tone.

In James Blish's novel *A Case of Conscience* (1958), a Jesuit infers from his faith's axioms that a planet is the work of the Devil, and so the Manichean worldview is right; he decides it must be destroyed. In Lester del Rye's 1954 short story, "For I Am a Jealous People," God sides with alien invaders against us, because He has given up on us as the Chosen People, and moved on.

Reversing this, in Arthur C. Clarke's 1955 "The Star" interstellar astronauts find a world whose star has exploded, obliterating a civilization more noble than ours. Working out the dating, they discover that it was the star of Bethlehem.

Similarly insouciant, Clarke's 1953 *Childhood's End* depicts aliens who look like the Devil, and concludes with an apotheosis in which humanity ascends to a higher state of being at the hands of the same aliens. (This idea he reworked considerably into the looming black monoliths and Technicolor conceptual blowout ending of the later film *2001: A Space Odyssey*.) Such imagery comes from the heretic Jesuit Pierre Teilhard de Chardin (1881–1955), who saw scientific knowledge as key to God's plan, an upward march to transcendence.

This postwar flowering of interest climaxed in Walter M. Miller Jr.'s *A Canticle for Leibowitz* (1960), in which the Catholic church once again conveys an ancient, high cultureoursto one that slowly emerges after a nuclear war.

Many thought this postwar effervescence came from a crisis of faith in the face of nuclear weaponry. The film *The Day the Earth Stood Still* best exemplifies the idea, with a mild, Christ-like alien who dies and is resurrected by his faithful robot, finally delivering an odd message: make peace among your nations or we will burn your world to a crisp.

This effervescence crowned a sea change in science fiction's attitude toward alien religions as well. Before World War II, stories satirized or mocked alien faiths. After it, they took a reverent view, even crediting them with truthful aspects. This may reflect the sudden encounter of Americans with other cultures, particularly those of Asia. Many, like Katherine Maclean's 1958 "Unhuman Sacrifice," showed human missionaries finding that the "superstitions" harbored by aliens could turn out to be true, or at least ambiguous. Poul Anderson's *The Problem of Pain* contrasts human vs. alien values of sacrifice, without giving either the edge.

Robert A. Heinlein's pivotal 1961 *Stranger in a Strange Land* powerfully made the case for new ideas in theology by portraying "a Martian named Smith"a human stranded there since birth, who brings to Earth Martian ideas, founding a new faith that grows quickly, with many Christ-like echoes, including a scene where Michael Valentine Smith's followers literally eat of his body. The new Messiah disposes of his enemies by shifting them into some other realm. The novel prefigured many of the "free love" ideas of the late 1960s, and much else; Heinlein was always ahead of the cultural curve.

It also satirizes a fictional Earthly religion that seems a combination of Mormonism and L. Ron Hubbard's vastly successful Scientology (itself a faith constructed by a science fiction writer, starting with a series of articles in a science fiction magazine, *Astounding*, in the late 1940s).

I wrote with Gordon Eklund an exploration of alien theology in *If the Stars Are Gods*, treating an astronaut who encounters several life forms in the solar system, all with theological implications. The central image is aliens who journey here not to meet us, but to visit our star, which they believe is a God. The astronaut is able to share their way of perception, and so glimpses a wholly different worldview.

This concern to share differing insights animates much of science fiction's reaching for the "other side"—up to and including Godlike states. *Star Trek* in its earliest form ("classic Trek") often gave us aliens or deranged humans who thought they were Gods because they had vast powers; inevitably, a fall followed.

Hubris seldom bodes well in SF. Roger Zelazny's *Lord of Light* depicted people who, cast into a primitive off-world society, used their high-tech gifts to present themselves as members of the Hindu pantheon. Such overblown confidence inevitably fails, of course, but it has a lot of fun along the way.

Some approaches try to revisit great religious events, not conceptually but literally. Time travel to the crucifixion is a staple. Robert Silverberg's time traveler in *Up the Line* matter-of-factly finds that no matter how many tourists he escorts to the scene, the crowd never gets larger. Is this an ingenious inversion of Christ's miracle of the fishes? The story wisely doesn't say.

Richard Matheson's 1954 "The Traveler" visits Calvary to find faith. In Michael Moorcock's 1969 *Behold the Man* and Barry Malzberg's 1982 *Cross of Fire* protagonists find the opposite—there is no Christ, so they feel compelled to become Him, suffering the crucifixion as a path for their own personal redemptions. Though on the surface antireligious, their emotional currents run oppositely, creating a vortex effect.

Not everybody was so reverential. Ian Watson in *God's World* (1979) and Ted Reynolds in *The Tides of God* (1989) suppose that God is not supernatural, but in fact a truly powerful alien presence. After much vexing, the only reasonable solution is to oppose and destroy Him.

The persistent science fictional posture of confronting categories of Godhood, and of revelation, is typical of the culture that made modern science fiction. The genre is, more than anything else, about *change*. Religions change too, the writers remind us.

We incorporate into our mind's eye of God our current knowledge. This is inevitable, and fundamentally positive.

Today science fiction has many currents. Popular writers like Orson Scott Card depict future societies much like Mormon ones, but suffused in a utopian glow. Other writers excoriate fundamentalist faiths, and satirize theocracy. The genre is a useful antidote to certainty. It promotes a more experimental, and historically sophisticated, view of the whole range of theological thought. It especially is unafraid of spiritual insights and methods like Zen Buddhism, and often contrasts nature-centered Asian faiths with the more axiomatic and rigid Western ones.

The point of speculative ideas and science fictional treatments is not to foster propaganda (though many do so, usually too obviously and unsuccessfully), but to make us think. As a literature of change driven by technology, SF presents religion to a part of the reading public that probably seldom goes to church.

Movies are another matter. *The Matrix* sometimes seems like the New Testament on steroids. But beyond the cool violence and dazzling special effects, the prominently Matrix world points both toward our future and to basic theological mythologies, to spiritual meta-narratives that can appear backlit by modern science.

In this sense science fiction is an ambassador between the two most widely separated tribes of modern thought, the scientific and the religious.

Negotiations should prove profitable, but only if they are imaginative.

L. Penelope is the award-winning author of the Earthsinger Chronicles. The first book in the series, Song of Blood & Stone, *was chosen as one of* Time *magazine's 100 Best Fantasy Books of All Time. Equally left and right-brained, she studied filmmaking and computer science in college and sometimes dreams in HTML. She lives in Maryland with her husband and furry dependents. Visit her at: http://www.lpenelope.com.*

LONGHAND

by L. Penelope

READY TO RESEARCH?

At a local monthly meeting for writers, one writer would always introduce herself the same way. She'd give her name and then say she wrote fantasy because she didn't like doing research and she'd rather make stuff up. It would always get a chuckle, and while I understand the sentiment, I've found that at least with fantasy writing, there's actually quite a lot of research involved. Making stuff up is the dream and goal of most fiction writers, but that doesn't mean that our flights of fancy aren't based in very deliberate and sometimes strenuous research.

Why Research?

Everything in our world is a system. I would venture to say everything on *any* world is a system of one kind or another. By system, I simply mean a set of rules that bounds behavior or to quote Merriam-Webster, "a regularly interacting or interdependent group of items forming a unified whole." When we're writing about a lost prince who needs to overthrow and evil, despotic king, then we're telling the story of the system of a monarchy and that system has rules. As the author, we can set the rules we follow and can choose to have them align with existing monarchies or deviate in significant and creative ways. But even when we're breaking the rules, we need to know them first. (Sage advice for breaking any sort of rule.)

So even if we're creating a second world fantasy with a culture and society that bears little resemblance to our own, if we're not at least glancingly familiar with the mechanics that make up the individual systems of our society, culture, and world, then it is extremely difficult to create a brand-new one that resonates with readers.

All the myriad aspects of worldbuilding, from geography and climate to economics and politics, transportation, fashion, religion, culture, and beyond require research in order to craft believable systems that hold together well.

Careful readers of our finished work will often point out the plot holes and inconsistencies in a world and aside from producing unpleasant emails or poor reviews, inattention to certain details could introduce story problems as well. To some extent, speculative fiction writers need to keep entire worlds in our heads and be able to understand how that world's systems interact and the potentials of for conflict within them. This is the fertile ground from which engaging stories grow. Which begs the question…

What to Research?

Potentially everything could be researched. (More on why this is a bad idea in a bit.) But look up any worldbuilding tutorial of your choice and delve into a topic. You could go down rabbit holes for days or weeks (or longer if you're not careful) on an endless array of topics. I myself have been seduced by such topics as the intricacies of desert culture furniture making or the science of how thermodynamic engines work or the migration of the boll weevil across 19th century America. Of course since it's both impossible and inadvisable to research everything, you'll want to dive deep into subjects that enhance the story.

Knowing your subject matter inside and out before sitting down to write is a great way to create something unique and fresh. For her Broken Earth trilogy, novelist N. K. Jemisin has spoken about researching geology and seismology and taking a research trip to Hawaii to visit volcanoes. The world she created in those novels has undergone drastic shifts over the millennia to the point where the culture is heavily based around a new system of "sea-sons." Magic and science blend for those in the series with the power of orogeny which allows them to control tectonic activity.

In such a way, research can occur before any writing or even plotting begins as a way to "find the story." Or it can occur simultaneously to story development, drafting, or revising. My current work-in-progress is an alternate history, so I had to steep myself in the time period before I could even figure out the plot. However, with my epic fantasy series, often I've found myself deep in the weeds of a manuscript only to discover some detail that must be fleshed out before I can move forward.

Perhaps you have an idea for a world covered in ice or water. Doing research will give you fantastic ideas for how culture develops. Examples of existing cultures that have developed on isolated islands or mountains or deserts are a great place to start creating a tale with a sense of verisimilitude that can be felt through the page. Alternatively, if you want to eschew the types of cultures that emerged on earth, you'll know where there was a deviation and how your world/culture/society is different.

How to Incorporate Your Research

It's important that research not overwhelm the prose. Many writers give into the temptation to "show their hand," and prove how much they know about a topic by including detailed information that does nothing to push the story forward or reveal character.

It's up to each writer to use their best judgment about these issues; however, it's important to keep in mind that the world should serve the story and not the other way around. Likewise with character details like professions. If you're writing about a law enforcement agent and spent a week doing ride-alongs with your local police department, then you may well be tempted to stuff your fictional character with your personal experiences. Or, if you are or were a police officer with twenty years of experience, you need to take care not to dump in details for the sake of proving how much you know. Readers will be able to spot the excess and may not thank you for it.

There is also a high chance of getting caught in the procrastination that research provides. Diving into fascinating aspects of science, technology, or history can keep you busy for long periods of time. Time when you are not writing. How do you know when enough is enough? It's not always clear, but having deadlines, even self-imposed ones, can help you reel yourself in. For instance, if you've spent more than three days researching and have gotten no writing done, you may have a problem.

Connecting it to Theme

At the end of the day, the theme is the thing that the reader will take away from your story. When craftily weaved with emotion, you can give a reader some tasty mental food to chew on. One good way of determining if your research has strayed or if you're including details that don't matter is to reconnect what you're writing to your theme.

Director Francis Ford Coppola stated in a recent interview with NPR's Terry Gross that he always gives his films a one-word theme. Then, if he has a question about some production or story detail, whether it's wardrobe or dialogue or something else, he reconnects the question back to the theme and chooses whatever reinforces that theme. This is a handy tip and one I've found helpful as well.

Research can do much to help us ground our worlds, characters, and stories and flesh out the systems that keep them aloft. It aids in our lofty task of making things up but makes the imaginary and invented sing with realism. If you create a system that's believable, then you can sell your audience on just about anything. Likewise, if your system is faulty, then readers will poke holes into the diaphanous material that it's made of.

Like the writer in my local group, I'm a big fan of making things up as well. That's one of the many reasons I write fantasy. But I'm just as interested as inventing a world that feels real and inhabited, and research is how I'm able to achieve that.

Copyright © 2021 by L. Penelope.

OVER THE WINE-DARK SEA

HARRY TURTLEDOVE

ORIGINALLY WRITING AS H. N. TURTELTAUB

Harry Turtledove writes alternate history, science fiction, fantasy and historical fiction and has won a Hugo Award, two Sidewise Awards for alternate history, and the Hal Clement Award for YA science fiction. With more than a hundred books, a couple of hundred pieces of short fiction, as well as a translation of a Byzantine chronicle and four academic articles published throughout his career, Turtledove also ended up with a doctorate in Byzantine history from UCLA. He wrote his dissertation alongside the first novel he sold. Along with teaching at UCLA, Cal State Fullerton, and Cal State Los Angeles, he worked as a technical writer for the Los Angeles County Office of Education before resigning from that job to freelance in 1991. He is married to Laura Frankos, herself a writer. They have three daughters (one also a published author) and two granddaughters. Two cats, Boris and Hotspur, run the household with iron, clawed fists.

OVER THE WINE-DARK SEA

by Harry Turtledove

III

"Rhyppa*pai*! Rhyppa*pai*!" Diokles used the oarmaster's chant along with the rhythm of mallet on bronze. As Menedemos had thought it would, the wind blew straight out of the north, straight into his face, as the merchant galley he commanded made for Kos. A sailing ship bound for Kos from Knidos would have had to stay in port; it could have made no headway against the contrary breeze. He just left the sail brailed up tight, so that the akatos proceeded on oars alone.

Waves driven by the headwind splashed against the *Aphrodite*'s ram and pointed cutwater. Striking the ship head-on, they gave her an unpleasant pitching motion. Menedemos, who stood on the raised poop deck handling the steering oars, didn't mind it so much, but he'd spent the night aboard ship. Some of the rowers who were rather the worse for wear leaned out over the gunwales and fed the fish of the Aegean.

"Keep an eye peeled," Menedemos called to the lookout at the bow. "The mainland of Asia belongs to Antigonos." He took his right hand off the steering-oar tiller to wave toward the misty mainland. "Kos, though, Kos is under Ptolemaios' thumb. And if the treaty the generals signed last summer is just a broken pot, the way it seems, they're liable to go at each other any time."

He kept a wary eye out for warships and pirate galleys himself. All he saw, though, were a few little fishing boats bobbing in the chop. A couple of them spread their sails and scooted away from him as fast as they could go. He laughed at that: the akatos looked too much like a piratical pentekonter for them to want to let it get close.

"You're the one who's been hearing most of the news lately, cousin," he said to Sostratos. "Do you have any idea what sort of fleet Ptolemaios has at Kos?"

But Sostratos tossed his head. "Sorry—haven't heard that. It had better be a good-sized one, though, because Antigonos has a lot of ports on the mainland and the islands farther north." He grimaced. "The same holds for Rhodes, you know."

"We *have* got a good-sized fleet, and a good thing, too," Menedemos said. "Antigonos knows better than to quarrel with us, the same as a dog knows better than to bite a hedgehog. Now, where have you got those perfumes stowed?"

"To port, a little aft of amidships," Sostratos answered. "Are you thinking of trading them for silk?"

"That's just what I'm thinking," Menedemos told him. "The Hellenes in Italy can make their own perfume. You can't get silk anywhere but Kos."

"If we can make a good bargain with the silk merchants, that's fine," Sostratos said. "If not..." He shrugged. "If not, we'd do better spending silver on silk and saving the perfumes for a market where they'll bring us more."

"You'll be the judge of that," Menedemos said. "That's why you're along."

"Nice to know you think I have some use," Sostratos said dryly.

"Some," Menedemos agreed, to make his cousin squirm. He pointed. "And you'd better keep an eye on that peahen, too, before she goes into the drink."

As one had done on the first day it was let out of its cage, a peahen had hopped up onto a vacant rower's bench and was peering over the side. Menedemos didn't know if the bird would try to fly off and fall into the sea, but he didn't want to find out the hard way, either. Sostratos was of like mind. He netted the bird before it could do anything the young men who'd bought it would regret.

The peahen pecked Sostratos through the mesh of the net. "Down to the house of Hades with you, you accursed, abominable thing!" he shouted, rubbing at his ribs through his chiton. He turned to Menedemos. "If it weren't for what we paid for them, I'd *like* to watch them drown."

"So would I," Menedemos said. "I'd hold them under myself, in fact."

"I never imagined sailing with a valuable cargo I hated," Sostratos said, releasing the peafowl by the socket that fixed the mast to the keel. He pointed a warning finger at the bird. "Stay down here where you belong, Furies take you!" To Menedemos, he added, "I don't much care for cargo that won't stay where I stow it, either."

"The birds would, if you left them in their cages," Menedemos said.

His cousin tossed his head. "We've been over that. I think they'll be better for getting out, though they may drive *me* mad by the time we make Italy."

Menedemos laughed. Sostratos rolled his eyes. That made Menedemos laugh more. But before he could twit his cousin any further, the watchman on the foredeck sang out: "Sail ho, off the starboard bow!" A moment later he amended that: "Sails ho! She's got a foresail, captain!"

"A big one," Menedemos muttered, peering in the direction the lookout's pointing finger gave. He had sharp eyes; he needed only a moment to spot the ship. When he did, he cursed. He'd hoped to see a big merchantman, bound perhaps for Rhodes and then Alexandria. No such luck: that low, lean shape could belong only to a war galley.

"He's seen us, too," the lookout called. "He's turning this way."

His voice held alarm. Menedemos didn't blame him. He was alarmed, too. "What do we do, skipper?" Diokles asked.

"Hold course," Menedemos answered. "Best thing we can do is put up a bold front. If we were in a pentekonter or a hemiolia, we might have hoped to turn and outrun him downwind, but we haven't got a prayer of that in this akatos—she's too beamy. We have every right to be here, and a proper warship won't give us any trouble, because nobody wants any trouble with Rhodes."

I hope. He'd spoken brashly to hearten his men—and to hearten himself, too. But brashness didn't come easy, not as the galley approached, now under sails and oars. "Eagles on the sails," the lookout called.

"He's one of Ptolemaios', then," Sostratos said.

Menedemos dipped his head in agreement. "Patrolling out of Kos, I suppose."

"Too big and broad to be a trireme," his cousin observed. "A four or a five."

"A five," Menedemos answered. "Three banks of rowers, see? One man on each thalamite oar down low, two on each zygite, and two on each thranite oar on top. If it were a four, it'd be two-banked, with two men on each oar."

"You're right of course." Sostratos thumped his forehead with the heel of his hand, as he often did when he thought he'd been foolish. "Whatever it is, it's big enough to eat us for opson and still be hungry for sitos afterwards."

"And isn't that the truth?" Menedemos said unhappily. "Got to be a hundred cubits long, if it's even a digit." For a merchant galley, the forty-cubit *Aphrodite* was of respectable size. Compared to the war galley, it was a sprat set beside a shark. The five was fully decked, too; armored marines with spears and bows strode this way and that, their red cloaks blowing in the breeze. The outrigger through which the thranite oarsmen rowed was enclosed with timber, too, making the ship all but invulnerable to archery.

"Catapult at the bow," Sostratos remarked. "From what Father says, they were just starting to mount them on ships when we were little."

"Yes, I've heard my father say the same thing," Menedemos agreed. He hadn't been paying the dart-thrower any mind; he'd been looking at the eyes painted on either side of the five's prow. The *Aphrodite* had them, too, as did almost every ship in the Middle Sea, but these seemed particularly fierce and menacing—not least because, at the moment, they were glaring straight at his ship.

One of the men on the war galley's deck cupped his hands in front of his mouth and shouted: "Heave to!"

"What do we do, skipper?" Diokles asked again.

"What he says," Menedemos answered, watching seawater foam white over the topmost fin of the five's ram. The green bronze fins had to be a cubit wide; they could smash a hole in the *Aphrodite*'s side that would fill her with water faster than he cared to think about. Even if he were mad enough to try to use his much smaller ram against her timbers, she had extra planking at the waterline to ward against such attacks.

"*Oöp!*" the keleustes shouted, and the akatos' rowers rested at their oars.

Up came the five to lie alongside the *Aphrodite*. Men brailed up the sails to keep the great ship from gliding away to the south. The war galley's deck rose six or seven cubits out of the water; the archers there could shoot down into the akatos' waist, while Menedemos' men could do next to nothing to reply.

A fellow in a scarlet-dyed tunic looked the *Aphrodite* over. By the way he put his hands on his hips, what he saw didn't much impress him. "What ship is this?" he demanded.

"The *Aphrodite*, out of Rhodes," Menedemos said. And then, deliberately mocking, he gave the galley the same sort of once-over her officer had given the akatos. It wasn't so easy for him, because he had to crane his neck upwards to do a proper job of it, but he managed. And, looking up his nose because he couldn't look down it, he asked, "And what ship are *you*?"

Perhaps taken by surprise, the war galley's officer replied, "The *Eutykhes*, General Ptolemaios' ship, out of Kos." Then he glared at Menedemos, who smiled back. He snapped, "I don't have to answer your questions, and you do have to answer mine. If you're lucky"—he played on the meaning of his ship's name—"you'll be able to."

"Ask away," Menedemos said cheerfully. Out of the corner of his eye, he saw Sostratos looking worried. Sostratos would never have baited the *Eutykhes'* officer. Because he was rational and sensible, he thought everybody else was, too. Menedemos had a different opinion. Insulting an arrogant ass was often the only way to get him to acknowledge you.

Of course, it also had its risks. With a scowl, the officer said, "You look like a gods-detested pirate to me, is what you look like. Rhodes? Tell me another one. Give me the name of the man you serve and give me your cargo and do it fast, or you'll never get the chance to do anything else."

"I serve two men: my father Philodemos and Lysistratos, his younger brother," Menedemos answered, all business now. "If you don't know of them, ask your crew: someone will."

And, to his relief, one of the marines aboard the *Eutykhes* came up to the officer. Menedemos couldn't make out what the fellow said, but the sour look on the officer's face argued that the other man did know of Philodemos and Lysistratos. A snap in his voice, the officer said, "Any rogue may hear a name or two, and put them in his own mouth when he finds them handy. I am not convinced you are what you claim to be. Your cargo, and be quick about it."

"Quick as you please," Menedemos answered. "We carry ink and papyrus and crimson dye and fine perfumes and…" He grinned slyly. "Five peahens and a peacock."

As he'd hoped, that rocked the *Eutykhes'* officer back on his heels. "A peacock?" he growled. "I don't believe you. If you had a peacock on board, I'd see it. And if you're lying to me, you'll be sorry."

"Sostratos!" Menedemos called. His cousin waved. "Show the gentleman the peacock, if you please."

"Right." Sostratos hurried up to the foredeck. He undid the latches on the peacock's cage and opened the door. The bird, which would have bolted out screeching at any other time, stayed where it was and kept quiet. Menedemos flicked a glance to the officer aboard Ptolemaios' five. The man stood on the deck with his arms folded across his chest. He wasn't about to believe anything Menedemos said, not till he saw it with his own eyes.

There had been times when Menedemos faulted Sostratos for dithering when he should have been doing. This wasn't one of those times. When the peacock refused to come out of its cage, Sostratos picked up the cage and dumped the bird out onto the foredeck. It squawked then, squawked and ran down into the waist of the *Aphrodite*.

"A peacock," Menedemos said smugly. "Tied up at anchor, we'd charge you a khalkos or two to see it, but here on the sea I give you the sight for nothing."

He was, perhaps, lucky: the *Eutykhes'* officer paid no attention to his patter. The fellow stared down at the bird and its magnificent tail. Marines and other officers hurried over to have a look, too. So many men rushing to starboard might have capsized the *Aphrodite*, but they only gave the far bigger war galley a slight list.

"A peacock," Menedemos repeated softly.

"A peacock," the officer agreed. Because the *Aphrodite*'s sailors weren't watching the bird so closely as they might have been, it pecked a rower in the leg. He sprang up from his bench, howling curses. The men on the *Eutykhes* howled laughter.

"May we cage it up again now?" Menedemos asked. "It's pretty, no doubt about it, but it's a cursed nuisance."

"Go ahead." The *Eutykhes'* officer absently dipped his head in assent. His eyes remained fixed on the bird. He had to gather himself before finding a question of his own: "You'll be putting in at Kos today?"

"That's right," Menedemos answered. "We're bound for Italy, and we'll want to take some silk with us if we can get a decent price."

"Good trading, then," the officer said. He turned away from Menedemos and shouted orders to his own crew. The five's mainsail and foresail descended from their yards. The keleustes clanged on something louder and less melodious than the bronze Diokles used. The oars began to work. Eyeing the *Eutykhes*, Menedemos judged the crew had been together for a while: their rowing was very smooth. The war galley resumed its southbound course, picking up speed quickly despite its massive bulk.

Once it had got out of arrow range, Menedemos allowed himself the luxury of a long sigh of relief. Diokles dipped his head to show he understood why. "That could have been sticky," the oarmaster said.

"That *was* sticky," Menedemos said. "But you're right. It could have been even stickier. He might not have stopped to ask questions. He might have just lowered his masts and charged right at us." He paused, imagining the *Eutykhes*' ram bearing down on the *Aphrodite*, driven toward her by three hundred rowers pulling like madmen. The mental picture was vivid enough to make him shudder. He tried to drive it from his mind: "Maybe we could have dodged."

"Maybe," Diokles said. "Once, maybe." He didn't sound as if he believed even that. And Menedemos didn't argue with him, because he didn't believe it, either.

Having wrestled the peacock into its cage once more, Sostratos made his way back to the stern. "Ptolemaios' men must be jumpy now that they're fighting Antigonos again," he said, and waved toward the mainland of Asia off to starboard. "Plenty of towns where old One-Eye could put a fleet together for the invasion of Kos. And the channel between the island and the mainland can't be more than twenty-five stadia wide. You can almost spit across it."

"You're right, and I'm an idiot," Menedemos said. Sostratos gaped at him, not used to hearing such things: Menedemos was more likely to call *him* an idiot. Not now, though. Menedemos went on, "I didn't see the connection between Kilikia and here

till you rubbed my nose in it. I probably wouldn't have, either."

"All the pieces fit together," his cousin answered seriously. "That's what history is all about—showing how the pieces fit together, I mean."

"Well, maybe it's good for something after all, then," Menedemos said. "Maybe." He didn't quite know it, but he sounded as dubious as Diokles had when talking about the *Aphrodite*'s chances of escaping the *Eutykhes* had the five chosen to attack. He didn't worry about that, though. He had more important things to worry about: "On to Kos, and let's see if we can get some silk."

☼

Kos, the main city on the island of Kos, was a new town, even newer than Rhodes. The Spartans, Sostratos knew, had sacked Meropis, the former center, during the Peloponnesian War after an earthquake left it half wrecked. Meropis had stood in southwestern Kos, looking back toward Hellas. The new city of Kos was at the northeastern end of the island, and looked across the narrow strait to Halikarnassos on the Asian mainland.

Like Rhodes', the new city's harbor boasted all the modern improvements: moles to moderate the force of the waves, and stone quays at which merchantmen and war galleys could tie up (though the galleys usually stayed out of the water in shipsheds to keep their timbers from getting heavy and waterlogged). "It's a pretty sight, isn't it?" Sostratos said as the *Aphrodite* eased up to a quay. "The red tile roofs of the city against the green of the hills farther inland, I mean."

"When I get a chance to look, I'll tell you," Menedemos answered, making a minute turn with the port steering oar. All his attention was on the quay, none on the scenery. He turned to Diokles. "I think that will do it. Bring us to a stop just as we come alongside here."

"Right you are, skipper." The keleustes raised his voice: "Back oars!" A couple of strokes killed the akatos' forward motion. "Oöp!" Diokles shouted, and the men rested at the oars with the *Aphrodite* motionless in the water only a short jump from the quay.

Sailors tossed lines to men on the quay, who made the akatos fast. "Who are you?" one of the

Koans asked. "Where are you from?" another asked. "What's your news?" a third said.

Sostratos wasn't surprised that they already knew about the murders of Alexandros and Roxane, and of course they knew Ptolemaios had gone back to war with Antigonos. They hadn't heard that Antigonos' nephew had gone over to Kassandros, and one of them clapped his hands when Menedemos mentioned it. "Anything that keeps the Cyclops busy somewhere else is good for us here," the fellow said, and his friends chimed in with loud agreement.

"Remind me how I get to the shop of Xenophanes the silk merchant," Sostratos said.

"It's simple, sir," one of the harbor workers answered, and then paused expectantly. With a mental sigh, Sostratos tossed him an obolos. He popped it into his mouth, saying, "Many thanks, best one. Go up three streets"—he pointed—"then turn right and go over two. You can't miss it: there's a bawdy house full of pretty boys across the street."

"That's right." Sostratos dipped his head and turned to Menedemos. "Remember the fellows who were brawling in the street over that one boy when we were here last spring?"

"I certainly do," his cousin said. "That little chap with the gray hair was going for his knife when a couple of people sat on him."

"Foolishness," Sostratos said. "A brothel boy's not worth quarreling over. He wouldn't have cared a fig for either one of them, except for what he could squeeze out of them. Hetairai are the same way, most of the time: more trouble than they're worth, and more expensive, too."

"You sound like my father." By the way Menedemos said that, he didn't mean it as a compliment. He raised an eyebrow. "Besides, what do you know about hetairai?"

Ears burning, Sostratos hurried up the gangplank to the quay. Menedemos stayed aboard the *Aphrodite* for a little while, setting up a watch schedule that would keep enough men on the ship at all times to deter robbers. The delay let Sostratos recover his composure. Unlike Menedemos—unlike most young men of his wealth—he wasn't in the habit of keeping a mistress. His cousin made it sound as if there were something wrong with him.

But I've never met a hetaira who made me believe she cared about me more than she cared about my silver. He didn't bother saying it aloud. Letting it drop seemed better than enduring whatever snide comeback his cousin would surely find.

Menedemos pranced up the gangplank, almost as if he were about to start dancing the kordax. He had one of the little pots of perfume in his left hand. "Let's go," he said cheerfully, and slapped Sostratos on the shoulder. He'd already forgotten he'd been teasing his cousin. Sostratos hadn't. Menedemos continued, "With any luck at all, we'll be able to make a deal before sundown and get back to the ship without having to hire torchbearers."

"Now who's fretting about every khalkos?" Sostratos said, and savored the dirty look Menedemos gave him.

Being a new city, Kos was laid out in a grid, as Rhodes was. Once they got directions, Sostratos and Menedemos had no trouble finding Xenophanes' establishment. A man came out of the establishment across the street with his tunic rumpled and a lazy smile on his face. Other than that, the bawdy house seemed as peaceful as if the proprietor sold wool.

A plump Karian slave bowed when Sostratos and Menedemos walked into Xenophanes' shop. "The gentlemen from Rhodes!" he said in excellent Greek.

"Hail, Pixodaros," Sostratos said.

"My master will be as pleased to see you as I am, best ones," Pixodaros said. "Let me go get him." He bowed again, beamed at Sostratos, and hurried into a back room.

"How did you remember his name?" Menedemos whispered. "You could set a vulture tearing at my liver, the way Zeus did with Prometheus, and I couldn't have come up with it."

"Isn't that why you bring me along?" Sostratos answered. "To keep track of details, I mean?"

"He's just a slave," Menedemos said, as if Pixodaros weren't important enough to be even a detail.

But Sostratos tossed his head. "He's more than *just* a slave. He's Xenophanes' right-hand man. If he's happy with us, his master will be, too. That can't hurt, and it might help."

Pixodaros returned, Xenophanes following him and leaning on a stick like the last part of the answer to the riddle of the Sphinx. The silk merchant's white beard spilled down over half his chest. A cataract clouded his right eye, but the left remained clear. He shifted the stick to his left hand and held out his right. "Good day, gents," he said, his Doric drawl almost as severe as the language in which Hippokrates—also a Koan—had written his medical treatises.

Menedemos and Sostratos clasped his hand in turn. His grip was still warm and firm. "Hail," Menedemos said.

"What's that?" Xenophanes cupped a hand behind his ear. "Speak up, young fellow. My hearing isn't quite what it used to be."

It hadn't been good the year before, Sostratos remembered. Now, evidently, it was worse. "Hail," Menedemos repeated, louder this time.

Xenophanes dipped his head. "Of course I'm hale. If a man my age ain't hale, he's dead." He laughed at his own wit. So did his slave. And so, dutifully, did Sostratos and Menedemos. Xenophanes turned to Pixodaros. "Fetch us some stools from the back, why don't you? And a jar of wine, too. I reckon we'll chat for a spell before we commence to dickering."

Pixodaros made two trips, one for the stool, the other for the wine, some cool water to mix with it, and cups. He served Xenophanes and the two Rhodians.

"Thanks," the silk merchant said. He waved toward the stools. "Set a spell," he told Sostratos and Menedemos as he perched on the one Pixodaros had brought for him. The Karian had also brought one for himself, and sat down beside his master.

They sipped wine and swapped news. Like the rest of the Koans, Xenophanes hadn't heard about Polemaios' defection from Antigonos. "The nephew will have seen that the sons are rising men," Pixodaros remarked.

"My thought exactly," Sostratos agreed.

Xenophanes ran a hand through his beard. "I'd be just about of an age with One-Eye," he said. "Still a few old mulberry trees the wind hasn't blown down."

"Mulberry trees?" Sostratos said: he hadn't heard that figure of speech before.

"Mulberry trees," Xenophanes repeated, and dipped his head for emphasis. "Call it a silk-seller's joke if you care to, sir." He took another pull from his cup and declined to explain further.

After a while—a little sooner than Sostratos would have—Menedemos said, "I've got some fine perfumes with me, made from the best Rhodian roses."

Xenophanes' smile showed teeth worn down nearly to the gums. "My friend, no matter how fine your perfumes are—and I'm sure they're very fine; your father and I have been doing business longer than you've lived, and I know he handles the best—I doubt the maidens would beat a path to my door if I wore them."

"But they might beat a path to your door if you sold them," Menedemos said. "For that matter, the pretty boys across the street might, too."

That made the silk merchant laugh, but he tossed his head even so. "Making silk, selling silk—those I know. Selling perfumes? I reckon I'm too old to start picking up things I didn't learn when I was younger."

Pixodaros leaned forward on his stool. "Master, perhaps I could—"

"No," Xenophanes broke in. "I said it once, and I'll say it twice. You don't know a single thing more about perfume than I do. As long as I'm breathing, we'll do it my way."

Being a slave, the Karian had no choice but to accept that. Sostratos thought of the character types Theophrastos had discussed at the Academy in Athens. One of them was the later learner: the old man who was always trying something new and making a botch of it. Xenophanes was not an old man of that sort; he clung like a limpet to what he understood.

Then Sostratos had another thought. He snapped his fingers and said, "We've also got crimson dye from Byblos. If you like, we can trade you that for silk. Dye, sir, I'm sure you do know."

He and Menedemos would have got more for the dye in Italy, far from Phoenicia, than they could hope to here. But they would get still more for silk. He was sure of that. Menedemos murmured, "See? It comes in handy even if you didn't know about it till the last moment."

Sostratos only half heard him; his attention was aimed at Xenophanes. The old man's good eye lit up. "Dye? I should hope I know dye," he said. "Tyre, now, Tyre made the best crimson, back in the days before Alexander sacked it. It hasn't been the same since; the men who knew the most got killed or sold for slaves. Arados, I reckon, turns out the best nowadays, with Byblos down a notch."

"I wouldn't say that." Sostratos knew a negotiating ploy when he heard one. "Arados makes more dye than Byblos, true. But better? I don't think so, and I don't think you'll find many who do."

"Which of us dyes silk?" Xenophanes returned.

"Which of us sells dye all around the Inner Sea?" Sostratos asked. They smiled at each other. Their moves were as formal, as stylized, as those of a dance.

Pixodaros said, "My master is right." That was an inevitable response, too. He went on, "The crimson of Byblos may be brighter, but that of Arados holds its color better." Sostratos tossed his head to show he disagreed.

Again, Menedemos moved faster than Sostratos would have, saying, "Each jar of dye holds about a kotyle. That may not be very much wine, but it's a whole great whacking lot of boiled-down murex juice. How much silk might you trade for a jar?"

"And of what quality?" Sostratos added. "There's dye and then there's dye, and there's silk and then there's silk."

They haggled till the light in Xenophanes' shop faded. Pixodaros lit lamps that nibbled at the edges of oncoming night without really pushing it back. The familiar smell of burning olive oil filled the air. Xenophanes began to yawn. "I'm an old man," he said. "I need my sleep. Shall we go on come morning? We're pretty close, I reckon."

"Is there an inn close by?" Sostratos asked. "My cousin and I slept on the poop deck last night. We'd sooner have something a little softer tonight."

"That there is, just a couple of blocks over," Xenophanes answered. "I'll have a couple of slaves get torches and light your way there. And I'll give you some bread to eat for your suppers—Skylax will sell you wine till you're too drunk to walk, but you have to bring in your own food. He will cook meat or fish if you pay him."

The slaves were a couple of fair-haired Thracians. They chattered in their incomprehensible language while guiding Sostratos and Menedemos to the inn. Their torches didn't shed much light; Sostratos stepped in something nasty, and kept trying to scrape it off his foot till he got to Skylax's place. He and Menedemos each gave Xenophanes' slaves a couple of khalkoi. The torchbearers hurried back toward the silk merchant's house.

More torches blazed inside the inn. Not all the smoke escaped through the hole in the roof; a lot of it hung in the main room in a choking cloud. The odor of hot oil fought with it: Skylax kept a vat bubbling over a fire. By the smell, Xenophanes lit his home with better oil than the innkeeper used for cooking.

His wine wasn't bad, though, and he didn't seem put out to see Sostratos and Menedemos eating bread and not giving him anything to throw into that bubbling vat. When Sostratos asked about his rooms, he said, "Two oboloi for the pair of you." He wouldn't haggle. When Sostratos tried, he just tossed his head. "If you don't like it, strangers, go somewhere else."

The two Rhodians couldn't very well do that, not in a strange city after dark. Sostratos thought he could have found his way back to the *Aphrodite*, but he didn't want to sleep on planking again. After a glance at his cousin, he paid Skylax the little silver coins. A slave carrying a lamp guided Sostratos and Menedemos to the room. It held only one bed. The slave set down the lamp and dragged in another one from across the hall. Then he departed, taking the lamp with him and plunging the room into stygian darkness.

With a sigh, Sostratos said, "We might as well go to sleep. Nothing else we could possibly do in here."

"Oh, there's one other thing," Menedemos said. "If you were a cute little flutegirl…"

"Me?" Sostratos said. "What about you?" They both laughed. Sostratos groped his way to a bed, took off his tunic, and draped it over himself. He wished he'd thought to bring his mantle, too; that would have made a better blanket. But the little room was too cramped and stuffy to get very cold. He twisted, trying to make himself comfortable. Creaks from the other bed said Menedemos was doing the same. Just as he heard the first snore from Menedemos, he fell asleep, too.

His cousin shook him awake. A little gray light was sneaking through the closed shutters over the narrow window. "You sound like a saw working through hard wood," Menedemos said.

"I'm not the only one," Sostratos answered. "Did they bother giving us a chamber pot? If they didn't, I'm going to piss in the corner." He looked under the bed. To his relief, both metaphorical and literal, he found one.

After buying more wine from Skylax to open their eyes, the Rhodians went back to Xenophanes'. "Good day, my masters," Pixodaros told them. "My master still sleeps. He told me to bring you food if you came before he rose." With a bow, the Karian slave went into the back of the house. He returned with bread and cheese.

"Thank you," Sostratos said, and then, "This business will be yours one of these days, won't it?"

"It could be." Pixodaros' voice was carefully neutral. "The gods gave my master no children who lived, so it could be."

Even if Xenophanes liberated Pixodaros on his deathbed, the Karian would never be a full citizen of Kos. His children might, though, depending on whom he married. *Life is a changeable business*, Sostratos thought: not original, but true.

He and Menedemos and Pixodaros made small talk till Xenophanes came out about half an hour later. "I still say you're asking too much for a jar of dye," the silk merchant began without preamble.

Menedemos put on his most winning smile. "But, my dear fellow…" he said. He could charm birds out of trees and wives into bed when he worked at it.

But he couldn't charm Xenophanes, who said, "No. It's too much, I tell you. I spent a deal of time thinking on it last night in bed, and my mind's made up."

"All right, then," Sostratos said before Menedemos could speak. Sostratos was the one who used bluntness, not charm, as his main weapon. He got to his feet. "I guess we'll go see Theagenes"—Xenophanes' chief rival—"if you won't see reason. And if Theagenes is stubborn, too, I guarantee we can get a better price for the dye in Taras or one of the other Italian cities than we can here."

That was likely true, though silk would bring more profit still. Mentioning Theagenes' name had the desired effect. Xenophanes looked as if he'd taken a big bite of bad fish. "He'll cheat you," he spluttered. "His silk is full of slubs. It's not nearly so thin and transparent as mine."

"No doubt you're right, O best one." Sostratos didn't sit down. "But he usually knows better than to price himself out of a bargain, and at least we'll have something to show the Italiotes. Come on, cousin." Menedemos rose, too. They both started for the door, though Sostratos was anything but eager to throw away most of a day's haggling.

"Wait." That wasn't Xenophanes—it was Pixodaros. He put his head together with his master. Sostratos stayed where he was. Menedemos started to get closer to try to hear what they were saying, but checked himself at Sostratos' small gesture.

"It's robbery, that's what it is!" Xenophanes spoke loud enough for the whole neighborhood to hear. Pixodaros didn't. The slave—the slave who might be a master himself one day—kept his voice low, but he kept talking, too. At last, Xenophanes threw his hands in the air and dipped his head to Sostratos and Menedemos. "All right," he said grudgingly. "A bargain. The Karian is right—we do need the dye. A hundred jars, for the bolts of silk you proposed last night."

Slaves carried the silk to the *Aphrodite* and took the dye back to Xenophanes' shop. Watching them go with the last of the jars, Menedemos said, "Gods be praised, our fathers don't have to worry about passing on what they've spent a lifetime building up to a barbarian slave."

"And here's hoping we never have to worry about it ourselves," Sostratos said, at which his cousin gave him a very peculiar look.

☼

Menedemos decided not to stop in Halikarnassos, even though it lay close by Kos. For one thing, he wanted to press north to Khios, to get some of the island's famous wine to take west. And, for another, he'd left an outraged husband behind on his last visit to the former capital of Karia, and he didn't care to appear there before things had more of a chance to settle down.

Instead, traveling under oars into the breeze, the *Aphrodite* went up the channel between the mainland and the island of Kalymnos, and beached itself for the night on Leros, the next island farther north. Sostratos quoted a fragment of verse:

"*The Lerians are wicked—not just one, but every one*

Except Proklees—and Proklees is a Lerian, too.'"

"Who said that?" Menedemos asked.

"Phokylides," his cousin answered. "Is it true?"

"I hope not," Menedemos told him. "Leros and Kalymnos are supposed to be the Kalydian isles Homer speaks of in the *Iliad*."

"If they are, they've changed hands since," Sostratos said, "for the Lerians nowadays are Ionians, colonists from Miletos on the Asian mainland."

The peacock started screeching. Menedemos winced. "You don't know how sick I am of that polluted bird," he said.

"Oh, I think I may," Sostratos replied. "I may even be sicker of it than you are, because you get to stay back at the steering oars most of the day, while I have to play peacockherd."

Before Menedemos could point out that his staying at the steering oars did have a certain importance to the journey, someone hailed them from the brush beyond the beach: "'Ere, what's making that 'orrible noise?"

"Ionians, you see," Sostratos said smugly. "No rough breathings."

He didn't say it very loud. In similarly soft tones, Menedemos answered, "Oh, shut up." He raised his voice and called, "Come and see for yourself," to the stranger.

"You'll not seize me for a slave and 'aul me off to foreign parts?" the Lerian asked anxiously.

"No, by the gods," Menedemos promised. "We're traders from Rhodes, not pirates." In another soft aside to Sostratos, he added, "Some withered old herdsman wouldn't be worth our while grabbing, anyhow."

"True enough," Sostratos said. "And it wouldn't be sporting, not after you've promised to leave him alone."

Menedemos cared little for what was sporting and what wasn't. But the rustic who emerged from the scrubby brush was middle-aged and scrawny. He wore only a goatskin tunic, hairy side out. That by itself made Menedemos' lip curl; country bumpkins were the only ones who preferred leather to cloth. And, when the Lerian got closer, Menedemos' nostrils curled, too: the fellow hadn't bathed in a long time, if ever.

"All right," he said. "'Ere I am. What was that screeching like it was being turned into a eunuch?"

"A peacock," Menedemos answered. "For a khalkos, you can go aboard and see it for yourself." He didn't think he would be able to get two bronze coins out of the local; even one might be pushing it.

As things were, the fellow in goatskins made no move to produce a khalkos. He just stared at Menedemos. "A what?" he said. "You're 'aving me on. You think because I live on a little no-account island you can tell me anything and I'll swallow it. Can't fool me, though. I know there's no such beasts, not for true. Next thing is, you'll be telling me you've got 'Ades' three-'eaded dog Kerberos on your ship, or else a tree nymph out of 'er tree. Well, you must think I'm out of mine, and I'm 'ere to tell you I ain't." He stomped off, his nose in the air.

"No, you can't fool him," Sostratos said gravely. As if to prove the Lerian couldn't be fooled, the peacock let out another screech.

"Sure can't," Menedemos agreed. "He knows what's what, and he's not about to let anybody tell him anything different."

"He would have voted to make Sokrates drink the hemlock," Sostratos said.

"How does that follow?" Menedemos asked.

"You said it yourself," his cousin answered. "He already knows everything he wants to know. That means anyone who tries to tell him anything else must be wrong—and must be dangerous, too, for wanting to tell him wrong things."

"I suppose so," Menedemos said with a shrug. "Sounds like philosophy to me, though."

"Maybe you don't want to know anything more, either," Sostratos said, which left Menedemos feeling obscurely punctured.

When the sun rose the next morning, he shouted his men awake. "Let's get the *Aphrodite* back into the sea," he called. "If we push hard, we make Samos tonight. Wouldn't you sooner do that than sleep on the sand again?"

"After that Koan inn, I think I'd just as soon stay on the beach," Sostratos said. "Fewer bugs."

"Don't think about bugs," Menedemos said. "Think about wineshops. Think about pretty girls." He lowered his voice. "Think about making the men want to work hard, not about giving them reasons to take it easy."

"Oh." Sostratos had the grace to sound abashed. "I'm sorry." He made a splendid toikharkhos. He always knew where everything was and what everything was worth. He'd done well in the dicker with Xenophanes. When the old coot got mulish, he'd picked the right time to get mulish in return. But ask him to be a man among men, to understand how an ordinary fellow thought…Menedemos tossed his head. His cousin didn't have it in him, any more than a team of donkeys had it in them to win the chariot race at Olympos.

With men in the boat pulling and men on land pushing, the *Aphrodite* went back into the Aegean more readily than she had after beaching on Syme. Menedemos steered the akatos north and a little east, toward Samos. He wished the wind would swing round and come out of the south so he could lower the sail, but it didn't. Through most of the sailing season, winds in the Aegean would stay boreal.

"Rhyppa*pai*! Rhyppa*pai*!" Diokles called, amplifying the stroke he gave with mallet and bronze. Menedemos had ten men on the oars on each side of the galley. He planned on shifting rowers when the sun swung past noon, and on putting the whole crew on the oars if he was close to making Samos in the late afternoon. If not…

Sostratos asked, "What will you do if we come up short?"

"We have choices," Menedemos replied. "We could head for Priene, on the mainland. Or we could beach ourselves again. Or I might spend a night at sea, just to remind the men there will be times when they need to work hard."

"You didn't want to do that before," Sostratos remarked.

Patiently, Menedemos explained, "Before, it would have just annoyed them. If I can turn it into a lesson, though, that would be worthwhile."

"Ah," his cousin said, and stepped over to the rail: not to ease himself, but to think about what Menedemos had told him. Sostratos was anything but stupid; Menedemos knew that. But he had a lot less feel for what made people work than Menedemos did. Once things were set out before him, though, as if at the highfalutin Academy at Athens, he could grasp them and figure out how to use them.

After a bit, Menedemos interrupted his musing, saying, "Why don't you give the peafowl some exercise?"

"Oh." Sostratos blinked his way out of contemplation and back to the real world. "I'll do that. I'm sorry. I forgot."

"The ship won't sink," Menedemos said as his cousin headed for the bow. *And you'll be too busy to do any philosophizing for a while.*

Except when Sostratos' antics were funny or his curses got frantic, Menedemos put him out of his mind for a while. He took in the *Aphrodite*'s motion through the soles of his feet and through the steering-oar tillers in the palms of his hands. It was almost as if he were peering out through the eyes painted at the merchant galley's bow, so much did he feel himself a part of the ship.

More ships were on the sea than had been true even when the *Aphrodite* set out from Rhodes a few days before. Fishing boats bobbed in the light chop. Some were hardly bigger than the akatos' boat. Others, with many more men dangling lines over the side or trailing nets behind them, were almost half the size of the *Aphrodite* herself. Menedemos saw most of them at a rapidly increasing distance, as he had the day before. The merchant galley really was beamier and slower than any proper pirate ship, but few skippers conning fishing boats cared to wait around till such details grew obvious.

Larger merchantmen—merchantmen big enough to dwarf the akatos—also spread their sails and scudded away, sometimes fast enough to kick up a creamy white wake at the bow. Their captains commanded bigger ships than Menedemos did, but he had more men aboard his. Like the men in charge of the more numerous fishing boats, they weren't inclined to take chances.

And then, not long before midday, Menedemos felt like scurrying aside himself when he spotted a five majestically making its way south under sails and oars. Instead of Ptolemaios' eagle, this war galley bore the Macedonian royal sunburst on foresail and mainsail both. "Ptolemaios and Antigonos are liable to start going nose to nose here along with their squabbles in Kilikia," Menedemos said.

"I wouldn't be surprised," Diokles answered. "And what can a free polis like Rhodes do if they start?"

"Duck," Menedemos said, which startled a laugh out of the keleustes.

Unlike the *Eutykhes*, Antigonos' five didn't change course to look over the *Aphrodite*. Menedemos watched the big ship glide over the waves in the direction of Kos with nothing but relief. Ptolemaios' crew hadn't turned robber. Maybe Antigonos' wouldn't have, either. Maybe. Menedemos was just as well pleased not to have to find out.

Little by little, the mountains of Samos and of Ikaria slightly to the southwest rose up out of the sea. Those of Samos, especially Mount Kerkis in the western part of the island, were taller than their Ikarian neighbors. Menedemos had noticed that every time he approached Samos—Ikaria, inhabited mostly by herdsmen, was hardly worth visiting—but hadn't wondered about it till now.

Diokles just gave him a blank look when he mentioned it. "Why, skipper?" the oarmaster said. "Because that's how the gods made 'em, that's why."

He might well have been right. Right or not, though, the answer wasn't interesting. Menedemos waited till Sostratos came up onto the poop deck and asked the question again. He might joke about philosophy, but it did sometimes lead to lively conversation.

"They are, aren't they?" Sostratos said, looking from the peaks of Samos over to those of Ikaria and back again. Then he did something Menedemos hadn't done: he looked to the Asian mainland east of Samos. "There's Mount Latmos, back of Miletos, and I'd say it's taller than anything on Samos."

"I…think you're right," Menedemos said; Mount Latmos was also farther away, which made its height hard to judge. "Even if you are, though, so what?"

"I don't know for certain, but it looks to me as if the islands carry the mountains of the mainland out into the sea," his cousin answered. "If that's so, it would stand to reason that the peaks would get lower the farther out into the sea the islands went. After a while, no more peaks—and no more islands, either."

Menedemos considered, dipped his head, and sent Sostratos an admiring glance. "That would make sense, wouldn't it?"

"It seems to me that it would," Sostratos answered. "I don't know whether it's true, mind you—that isn't the same as being logical."

"Close enough for me," Menedemos said. His cousin raised an eyebrow, but didn't rise to the bait.

Samos rose ever higher out of the sea, while the sun sank ever closer to the water. "Looks to me like we'll make it, skipper," Diokles said.

"We will if the boys put their backs into it," Menedemos replied. Actually, he was pretty sure the keleustes was right, but he wanted to get the rowers worked in as a team. "Call everyone to the oars and give them a sprint, why don't you? Let's pretend we've got a hemiolia full of Tyrrhenians on our tail."

Diokles stroked the ring with the image of Herakles Alexikakos on it to turn aside the evil omen. "That could happen, you know, even here in the Aegean. Those polluted whoresons don't stay in the Adriatic any more. They're like cockroaches or mice—they're all over the stinking place."

Like any merchant sailor, Menedemos knew that entirely too well. He dipped his head, but said, "They've got more teeth than mice, worse luck. Come on—get the men to the oars and up the stroke. We'll see what kind of crew we've got."

"Right you are." The oarmaster shouted the whole crew to their benches and kept right on shouting once they were in their places: "We're going to push it to get to port before sundown—and so we know what we can do if pirates come after us. Give it everything you've got, boys. Rhyppa*pai*! Rhyppa*pai*!"

Mallet met bronze in an ever-quicker rhythm. Diokles hit the bronze harder, too, so each clang seemed more urgent. The rowers didn't spare themselves. Panting, their bodies glistening with oil and sweat, their muscular arms working as if belonging to Hephaistos' automata from the *Iliad*, they worked like men possessed.

And the *Aphrodite* fairly seemed to leap ahead. She arrowed through the deep-blue water; a creamy wake streamed from her bow. After a very short time, Menedemos grew sure they would make Samos.

Diokles held the oarsmen to the sprint as long as he could, and eased off as slowly as he could. "Not too bad, captain," he said. "No, not too bad at all. And the rowing's smooth as that silk you bought. We knew we had some good men here, and this proves it."

"You're right," Menedemos answered. "I wouldn't quarrel with a single word you said. But tell me: would we have got away from a pirate ship?"

"Well…" The keleustes looked unhappy. "We'd've needed some luck, wouldn't we? They did get her up as fast as she'll go."

"I know they did," Menedemos said. "The trouble is, she won't quite go fast enough." The *Aphrodite* carried cargo, not just rowers who doubled as fighting men. She was beamier than a hemiolia or a pentekonter, too, which meant there was more of her to resist the sea than held true for their lean, deadly shapes. And she rode deeper in the water, because of her cargo and because her timbers were more waterlogged and heavier than those of pampered pirate ships, which dried out on the beach every night. Because of all that, odds were a ship full of pirates could overhaul them from behind.

"We're all right if we've got a friendly port we can run for," Diokles said.

"Of course we are. But if we don't, we're going to have to fight." Menedemos drummed his fingers on the steering-oar tiller. "I'd sooner do it ship against ship, not man against man. They'll have bigger crews than we do."

"Pirate crews mostly aren't disciplined," the keleustes observed. "They don't want to fight unless they have to. They're out to rob and kidnap, either for ransom or for slaves."

"We've got a lot of men who've put in time aboard war galleys," Menedemos said. "Once we sail west from Khios—maybe even sooner—we will work hard."

"Good," Diokles replied.

Though the sun was not far from setting when the *Aphrodite* glided into Samos' harbor, Menedemos had enough light to reach the quays and tie up without any trouble. A temple dedicated to Hera lay to the left, where the Imbrasos River ran down into the sea from the mountains in the island's interior. To the right was a shrine for Poseidon that looked across a seven-stadia strait to the mainland.

As longshoremen made the akatos fast to the wharf, the rowers rested at their oars, still worn with the effort they'd put forth in the sprint. One of them said the worst thing he could think of: "I'm liable to be too tired to want to go into town and screw."

"Well, if you are, I hear there are girls up in Khios, too," Menedemos said.

"Likely there are," the sailor agreed, "but I hate to waste a chance." Since Menedemos hated to waste a chance, too, he just laughed and dipped his head.

✧

As Kos lay under Ptolemaios' thumb, so Samos belonged to Antigonos. Sostratos wasn't surprised when a couple of officers in gleaming armor tramped up to the quay to inquire about the *Aphrodite* and where she'd been before coming to Samos. He *was* surprised when they started asking their questions: he could hardly follow a word they said.

"What *is* that gibberish?" Menedemos asked out of the side of his mouth.

"Macedonian dialect, thick enough to slice," Sostratos replied, also in a whisper. He raised his voice: "Please speak slowly, O best ones. I will gladly answer all I can understand." That might have been a lie, but the Macedonians didn't have to know it.

"Who…art tha?" one of them asked, his brow furrowed in concentration, his accent both rustic and archaic. *Homer might have spoken like that, had he been an ignorant peasant and not a poet*, Sostratos thought. The Macedonian went on, "Whence…art tha from?"

"This is the *Aphrodite*, owned by Philodemos and Lysistratos of Rhodes," Sostratos said. The officer dipped his head; he could follow good Greek even if he couldn't speak it himself. Sostratos continued, "We're for Khios, and we've stopped at Syme, at Knidos, and at Kos."

"Did you have to tell him that?" Menedemos murmured.

"I think so," Sostratos said. "Someone else may come in who saw us in port or rowing up from the island."

Mentioning Kos got the Macedonians' attention. "What be there?" demanded the one who could make a stab at real Greek. "Ships? Ptolemaios' ships? How many of Ptolemaios' ships?"

"How gross?" the other one added, and then corrected himself: "How big?"

"I wasn't watching all that closely," Sostratos answered, and proceeded to exaggerate what he had seen. No one gave him the lie; though Rhodes' shipwrights had built war galleys for Antigonos, the island inclined more toward Ptolemaios. Rhodes shipped a lot of Egyptian grain all over the Hellenic world.

Sostratos didn't exaggerate enough to make the Macedonians serving Antigonos suspect him—only enough to give them long faces. They spoke back and forth between themselves; he understood not a word. Then, to his relief, they left.

Beside him, Menedemos let out a glad sigh to match his own. "I thought they were going to jump out of their corselets when you started talking about Ptolemaios' sixes and sevens at Kos," Sostratos' cousin said.

"So did I," Sostratos said. "I wanted to give them something to think about—something that wasn't quite true, but sounded as if it could be."

"Well, you hit the nail on the head," Menedemos told him. "If that doesn't set Antigonos' carpenters building like maniacs, to the crows with me if I know what would."

"I wouldn't mind—but where will it stop?" Sostratos wondered. "If you can build sevens, are nines better? What about thirteens, or maybe seventeens?"

Menedemos shrugged. "Not my worry. Not Rhodes' worry, either, I shouldn't think. How many rowers would you need in a seventeen?" He held up a warning hand. "No, don't go trying to figure it out, by the gods. I don't want to know, not exactly. However many it is, Rhodes might be able to man one or two of them. No more, I'm sure."

He was stretching things, but not by that much. He did persuade Sostratos not to finish the calculation he had indeed started. Instead, Sostratos asked, "You don't intend to do much in the way of trading here, do you?"

His cousin tossed his head. "Not much point to it: ordinary wine and plain pottery. I mostly wanted the anchorage." Menedemos hesitated. "If we could get our hands on those statues in Hera's temple, though, they'd bring a pretty price in Italy, don't you think?"

"Myron's Zeus and Athena and Herakles?" Sostratos laughed. "I'm sure they would. But remember, Ikaria's close by, and it got its name because Ikaros fell to earth there after flying too close to the sun. You'd fall and fail if you tried to get those statues, too."

Menedemos laughed. "I know. Had you worried there, didn't I?" Before Sostratos could answer, the peacock screeched. Menedemos snapped his fingers. "That reminds me—time to make ourselves a little money. Do you want to show people the peafowl?"

"I'm dying to," Sostratos replied.

He might as well have saved his breath; Menedemos paid no attention to him. Menedemos paid attention to him only when that suited his purposes. Sostratos' cousin hurried up the gangplank to the wharf and started singing the praises of peafowl. In short order, he started collecting khalkoi. Nobody got to look at the birds without handing over a couple of the little bronze coins. Sostratos showed off the peafowl till it got too dark for spectators to see them.

"What's the take today?" he asked when Menedemos gave up on luring any more spectators aboard the *Aphrodite*.

Khalkoi clinked as Menedemos built them into shaky piles. "Half an obolos, an obolos, an obolos and a half…" When he was through reckoning piles, he said, "A drakhma, four oboloi, six khalkoi. Nothing that'll make us rich, but not bad, either."

"Sixty-three people," Sostratos said after a moment's thought. "No, that isn't bad at all. Peafowl are interesting birds—it'll be interesting to see if we can get them to Italy without tossing them overboard, for instance."

For once, his cousin didn't rise to the bait of the joke. Instead, Menedemos gave him an odd look. "Without a counting board, I couldn't have figured out how many people saw the birds to save my life."

"It wasn't hard." Sostratos changed the subject: "Will you look for an inn?"

Menedemos tossed his head. "Too late now. I'll just sleep on the deck. I've done it before. I can do it again." He waved a hand. "If you want to go into town, though, don't let me stop you. Plenty of sailors heading in for a good time."

"No, thanks," Sostratos said. His cousin was the one who was fond of luxury. If Menedemos could stand another night wrapped in his himation on the poop deck, Sostratos could, too. A man of philosophical bent was supposed to be indifferent to bodily pleasures…wasn't he?

Sostratos wondered about that as he lay with his chiton bundled up under his head for a pillow. Even though he was wrapped in his mantle, he couldn't get comfortable on the planks. He'd had an easier time drifting off on the beach on Leros.

As Menedemos had said, some of the rowers went into Samos to roister. The rest dozed on their benches. Some of them snored. Others, probably even more uncomfortable than Sostratos, talked in low voices so as not to disturb their shipmates. Sostratos tried to eavesdrop on them till he finally fell asleep.

He woke once in the middle of the night, pissed into the water of the harbor, and fell asleep again almost at once. The next time he woke, it was daybreak. Menedemos was already sitting up, an almost wolfishly intent look on his face. He dipped his head to Sostratos. "A lot to do today," he said. "We won't make Khios in one day from here, not rowing all the way. A good two-day pull. Since we didn't pass the night at sea coming to Samos, I intend to do that, to give the men a taste of what it's like."

"Whatever seems good to you," Sostratos agreed. "Our fathers trust you to command the ship. I haven't seen anything that makes me think they're wrong." Saying that didn't come easy to him; Menedemos often wore on his nerves. But his cousin did know what to do with the *Aphrodite* and how to lead her crew. However much Sostratos might have wanted to deny that, he couldn't.

Menedemos jumped to his feet. He paused just long enough to ease himself over the akatos' side. Then, still naked, he shouted the sailors awake. They yawned and grunted and rubbed their eyes, much less enthusiastic about facing the new day than he was.

He laughed at them. "We're heading toward the finest wine in the world, and you whipworthy catamites complain? I thought I'd signed up a crew of real men." His scorn lashed them to their feet and into action. Sostratos wondered how they would have acted had *he* exhorted them like that. Actually, he didn't wonder. He knew. They would have flung him into the Aegean. Had they been feeling kindly, they might have fished him out again afterwards.

He had his own morning duties to attend to. He gave the peafowl barley and water for their breakfast. The birds ate with good appetite. He'd seen they ate better in harbor than while the *Aphrodite* moved across the open sea. That was nothing remarkable. A lot of people went off their feed on the open sea, too.

"How many men are we missing, Diokles?" Menedemos asked.

"Not a one, captain, if you can believe it." The keleustes shook his head in amazement. "I wonder about these fellows, I truly do. You're hardly a man at all if you can't go out and make a night of it."

"They want the Khian, too," Menedemos said. "Even a sailor can afford it when he buys it where they make it."

Sostratos said, "The dealers won't be so generous as the tavernkeepers will. They'll be selling their best, not the cheap stuff you get in taverns, and they'll squeeze us till our eyes pop."

Menedemos grinned at him. "That's why you're along. You're not supposed to let them squeeze us."

"Ha," Sostratos said. "Ha, ha." He brought out the syllables just like that, as if they were dialogue in a comedy. "I can't keep them from squeezing us, and you'd better know it. With a little luck, I can keep them from squeezing us quite so much."

"All right." Menedemos dipped his head. He seemed in a good mood this morning, likely because the *Aphrodite* wouldn't have to sit in the harbor while Diokles hunted down men who gave more thought to roistering than to how they earned the money to roister. He pointed to Sostratos. "Grab yourself some bread and oil and wine. I want to get out into the open sea as soon as I can."

"All right." Sostratos drummed his fingers on the gunwale. "We'll have to lay in some more supplies when we got to Khios. We're using them faster than I thought we would."

"Take care of it." Menedemos was already eating, and spoke with his mouth full. Sostratos tried to resent his cousin's peremptory tone, but couldn't quite. He was the toikharkhos; taking care of such things was his job. As he came back to the poop, Menedemos added, "The sooner I can get out of this port, the better I'll like it."

"Those Macedonians?" Sostratos asked.

"Sure enough," Menedemos agreed. "I didn't like the way they asked questions—like they were demigods looking down their noses at ordinary mortals." He dipped a piece of bread into olive oil and took a big bite. As he swallowed, his lip curled. "Demigods would speak better Greek, though."

"Khios won't be any better when it comes to that," Sostratos predicted. "It bends the knee to Antigonos, too."

"Well, yes, but it's not sitting over Kos, the way Samos is," his cousin answered. "The officers up there won't be so…eager to squeeze everything we know out of us. I can hope they won't, anyhow."

"It makes sense," Sostratos said. "You have a pretty good sense of the way the politics work."

"For which I thank you." Menedemos sounded as if he meant it. Then he added, "I may not know everything that's happened everywhere since before the Trojan War, but I do all right."

"I don't pretend to know everything that's happened everywhere since before the Trojan War," Sostratos spluttered. Only after he was done spluttering did he realize Menedemos had been hoping he would. He shut up with a snap. That also amused his cousin, which only annoyed him more.

"Come on!" Menedemos called to his men. "Let's cast off and get going. Like I told you, we're two days away from the best wine in the world." That got the men working. It got the *Aphrodite* away from the harbor ahead of many of the little fishing boats that sailed out of Kos. And it got the akatos through the narrow channel between the island and the mainland of Asia in fine fashion.

Sostratos hadn't really thought about just how narrow the channel was. "If you had stone-throwers on both sides of it," he remarked to Menedemos, "you could make this passage very hard and dangerous."

"I daresay you're right," Menedemos answered. "It may happen one of these days, too, though I hope none of Antigonos' generals is as sneaky as you are."

Half her oars manned, the *Aphrodite* fought her way north. The broad stretch of sea between Samos and Ikaria on the one hand and Khios on the other was one of the roughest parts of the Aegean: neither the mainland nor any islands shielded the water from the wind blowing out of the north. The merchant galley pitched choppily as wave after wave slammed into her bow.

The motion gave Sostratos a headache. A couple of sailors reacted more strongly than that, leaning out over the gunwale to puke into the Aegean. Maybe they'd taken on too much wine the night before. Maybe they just had weak stomachs, as some men did.

As some men did, Menedemos had a quotation from Homer for everything:

"'*The assembly was stirred like great waves of the sea, The open sea by Ikaria, which the east wind and the south wind Stir up from Father Zeus' clouds.*'"

"What about the north wind?" Sostratos asked. "That's the one troubling us now."

His cousin shrugged. "You can't expect the poet to be perfect all the time. Isn't it marvel enough that he's so good so much of the time?"

"I suppose so," Sostratos said. "But it's not good to lean on him the way an old man like Xenophanes leans on a stick. That keeps you from thinking for yourself."

"If Homer's already said it as well as it can be said, what's the point to trying to say it better?" Menedemos asked.

"If you're quoting him for the sake of poetry, that's one thing," Sostratos said. "If you're quoting him to settle what's right and wrong, the way too many people do, that's something else."

"Well, maybe," Menedemos said, with the air of a man making a great concession. *At least he's not sneering at using philosophers' ideas to judge what's right and wrong, the way he sometimes does,* Sostratos thought. *That is something.*

He soon discovered why Menedemos showed no interest in twitting him: his cousin's thought turned in a different direction. Setting a hand on Diokles' shoulder, Menedemos said, "It's two days to Khios no matter what we do. Shall we start putting them through their paces?"

"Not a bad notion," the keleustes replied. "The more work we get in, the better the odds it'll pay off when we really need it."

"With luck, we won't need it at all," Sostratos said. Both Diokles and Menedemos looked at him. He felt he had to add, "Of course, we'd better not take the chance."

His cousin and the oarmaster relaxed. "Enough trouble comes all by itself, even when you don't borrow any," Menedemos said. He raised his voice: "All rowers to the oars. We're going to practice fighting pirates—or whatever else we happen to run into on the western seas."

Sostratos had wondered if the men would grumble at having to work harder than they would have done if they'd rowed straight for Khios. A few of them did, but it was grumbling for the sake of grumbling, not real anger. And so, on the rough sea north of Samos and Ikaria, the akatos practiced darting to the right and to the left, spinning in her own length, and suddenly bringing inboard all the oars now on one side of the ship, now on the other. They worked on that last maneuver over and over again.

"This is our best chance against a trireme, isn't it?" Sostratos said.

THE MIKE RESNICK MEMORIAL AWARD FOR SHORT FICTION

An annual award for the best unpublished short story by a new author sponsored by Galaxy's Edge magazine and Dragon Con.

FINAL JUDGES:
Nancy Kress
Sheree Renee Thomas
Jody Lynn Nye
Lois McMaster Bujold
William B. Fawcett

Please visit www.ResnickAward.com for more information

2021 compitition closes April 30, 2021

www.ingramcontent.com/pod-product-compliance
Lightning Source LLC
Chambersburg PA
CBHW082227140626
46556CB00020B/3376